# NOT ANOTHER SET PIECE

*A Wedding Date Romance*

## Nikki Kwiatkowski

Cover designed by Karis Drake

This book is a work of fiction. Names, characters, places, and incidents either are products of the author's imagination or are used fictitiously. Any resemblance to actual persons, living or dead, events, or locales is entirely coincidental.

Nikki Kwiatkowski
Visit my website at www.NikkiKAuthor.com

Printed in the United States of America

First Printing: July 2019

ISBN-13 978-1-7332165-0-0

*To Chris,*
*For your continued support and taking care of all the tedious little things along the way. I could never do this without you.*

*To my parents, Angie and Raymond,*
*Thank you for always going above and beyond as mom and dad.*

*With Loving Memory, To Kevin,*
*Your belief in me keeps me telling stories.* ♥

# CONTENTS

# set piece noun

*sports* : a carefully planned sequence of movements performed by the members of a team (as in soccer)

//A *set piece* can be used on either a direct or indirect type of [free] kick, providing one of the few times during the game that a team can execute something that it may have spent hours practicing.

— Doug Roberson

Set Piece [Def. 4]. (n.d.). In *Merriam-Webster Online*, Retrieved June 7, 2019, from www.merriam-webster.com/diction-ary/set%20piece.

# CHAPTER 1

It had been nearly a week, or maybe two or three, since Piper checked her mail. Perhaps she should have waited even longer. She only checked it to clean it out. She knew when the bills came in and when she needed to pay what amount by. Considering some of the things she found in the box, it was nothing more than a waste of trees.

The silky cream envelope with gold lettering that stared at her from the kitchen counter proved just what a sad life trees lived. She didn't need to open it to know what it was. Hoping she could have avoided the whole situation, she felt sick to her stomach.

It was bad enough to be invited to the wedding of your ex-fiancé. It was even worse when he was marrying the girl he had an affair with. Just to put the icing on the cake, it was completely devastating when that girl was your younger first cousin.

Now Piper knew why her mother had been calling non-stop over the days. She was too consumed with work and kept delaying a return of the call.

Taking a deep breath, she waited, the only noise besides her racing heartbeat being that of the ringing from the speaker.

"I know you're not that damn busy," the screeching voice of her mother playfully answered.

"You obviously don't know what it's like being Blythe Carrington's assistant," Piper huffed.

It was a demanding job working for the CEO of the woman's magazine *Rogue Times*. Blythe founded the magazine seven years prior and the last two were leaps and bounds greater than expected. It gave Piper very little time for a personal life most days, but the pay was incredible and working with someone as big as Blythe Carrington was a dream for almost anyone. Plus, with the way Piper's life had gone within the last year or so, she welcomed the distraction.

"I guess the only reason you're calling back is because you've finally checked your mail?"

Piper was silent for a minute.

"It's completely ridiculous. Samantha is making more of a showing than a royal wedding," Emma Carter spat. "I mean, what normal people can just give up that much time? Then if I don't, I've got that snot of a sister to deal with."

Piper was more confused than anything, and quickly began tearing open the envelope.

"I can hear you opening it now. Really, sweetheart? You should check your mail more often," her mother scolded.

"What," Piper shrieked. "A destination wedding? A week? And Maine of all places?"

"That family always was one to show off. Ever since my sister married into oil, I suppose she thinks her poop doesn't stink as much as the rest of ours. I suppose Samantha chose Maine because of some nostalgic childhood crap. She only lived there for five years," Emma huffed.

"Mom, I can't go to that."

"Look, I know things with you and Jared didn't end well..."

Piper rolled her eyes at her mother's wording. "Walking in on him and Samantha in bed together is a little more than not ending well."

"It's been a year."

"I know. I've moved past it, honestly. I just can't take that much time off from work right now. Hell, I wouldn't even be able to take that much time off for my own wedding," Piper laughed. It wasn't funny, not even a little bit, because it was true. "In fact, I'm going to have to make this call shorter than I'd like. It's already late and I still need to make some revisions to Blythe's schedule for tomorrow. Crap!" Piper slammed her hand to her head suddenly remembering something. "I have to call the bakery and place her breakfast order before they close."

"You order her breakfast?"

She knew her mother was going to start harping on a waste of college education. "Please, don't start, not tonight."

Thankfully her mother spared her. Her job wasn't ideal for a master's in journalism, but it paid more than working at a paper like she had once hoped, and it gave her the experience. Maybe not the right experience.

\* \* \*

"Are you feeling okay," Haven asked as soon as Piper got into her tiny office.

She had overslept. Her wavy hair looked like rats had styled it. Though she usually was pristine with her suits, she noticed that the one she wore just looked frumpy and out of place. Worst of all, she was nearly ten minutes late because the bakery messed up on Blythe's coffee order. Thankfully, Blythe was too consumed on a call to notice when Piper placed her breakfast on her desk and scurried away.

"It's just one of those days. How's your article coming along," Piper quickly asked, wanting to change the subject away from herself.

Haven eyed Piper suspiciously, fully knowing that something was up. Piper seemed jittery and in another world. Generally she was calm and focused, not today.

Haven pulled the spare chair up to Piper's desk and put her elbows on the desk with her face firmly planted into her hands.

"What?"

"You're a hot mess today," she announced bluntly.

After a deep breath, "I just...I got hit with some stuff. It's no big deal."

"You are something else. Seriously, I think that you could walk in here knowing that you have days to live, and you'd try to play it down."

"You do realize you just went from not a big deal to my life ending?"

Haven laughed and her coal curls bounced like miniature slinky toys. Piper envied how bold Haven could be. Her natural hair was blonder than Piper's but she wanted something completely opposite and insisted that black was it. Piper, on the other hand, dreaded a simple trim every six weeks.

"So between no big deal and death, where does this rank?"

Piper hesitated, but finally managed. "I've been invited to a wedding."

"Seriously? Piper. Seriously?"

"Oh," she began, breathing in deeply. "It gets a lot better."

She tried to give Haven the short of it. Ex. Cousin. A week long. She found that what could have taken less than sixty seconds ended up being a fifteen minute conversation that she clearly didn't have time for; however, Haven was her best friend. It was a little pathetic when she thought about it. Work had consumed her for so long that her best, and really only friend, was someone that she worked with.

"Pick two flavors," Haven insisted.

"Excuse me?"

"Ice cream."

"I can't," Piper whined. "Not tonight. I have so much to do and my head is just—"

"I'm coming over. We're hanging out. I'll pick up an extra-large pepperoni from the creepy place you love. Now, two flavors." Haven sat back and crossed both her arms and legs in defiance.

"Fine! Umm...Neapolitan and—"

"You are so boring," Haven laughed. She stood to leave before Piper could even finish.

Piper knew exactly what that meant. Haven would end up bringing more ice cream than her freezer would allow. It was probably for the best. Now if she had to go to the wedding she could not only be single and desperate looking, she could look like she was about to find out if her future child belonged to Ben or Jerry.

* * *

"I can't eat another piece," Piper insisted.

"Roberto asked me for my number again. If you don't eat this, next time it's going to be one from a street vendor and you'll probably end up with diarrhea in the morning."

Piper had to admit, having Haven around helped ease everything since the whole Jared thing. That still didn't mean that she could eat any more pizza.

Haven excitedly clapped her hands. "So, what are we going to do?"

"We?"

"Yes, we! You really only have one option."

"Yeah," Piper scoffed. "Not go."

It didn't matter what she said, the wheels in Haven's brain were already turning. "So, you have to look awesome, which means you'll probably want to think about the gym after all that," she pointed out. She waved a finger up and down between the half eaten piece that Piper was forcing herself to ingest and the empty box. "But you know what you really have to do?"

"I can't take that much time off," Piper mumbled through a stuffed face.

"You haven't taken a day off since you've worked for Blythe that includes when you had food poisoning!"

"If I take a day off, I'm not wasting it on self-torture."

"How long until the wedding week or whatever they call this thing," Haven asked, once again ignoring Piper's comment.

"A month?"

"What," Haven shrieked. "Your cousin is crazy!"

"Well," Piper began, drawing the word out. "I really don't recall when I last checked my mail. I'm sure it's been quite some time when I think about it. I also didn't get a save the date, so I think they're just inviting me because I'm family and all."

"How tacky. Get them something monogrammed so they can't return it," she evilly cackled. "Now, on to the important part." She suddenly turned serious. "You can't show up alone."

"I'm not showing up, period," Piper wailed.

"Since you don't have a boyfriend, and you're not even close to dating, that isn't an option. Even if you did start seeing someone, inviting them for a week of wedding festivities is pretty much as bad as saying 'I love you' the first time you have sex."

"Are you listening to anything I'm saying," Piper growled.

"Of course! You're just not making any sense."

Haven began pacing, becoming more difficult to understand as she shoveled mint chocolate chip in her mouth.

"We can put you on a dating site, just for the sole purpose of spending time together for one week?"

"No."

"Escort service?"

"No," Piper screeched. "I'm not going with someone I've never met. My whole family is going to be there. That's embarrassing enough."

The conversation concluded, but Piper knew that Haven wasn't even close to letting the issue go.

Sadly, what she said didn't seem too horrible. She was twenty-nine and single, unless you counted being married to your job. While that didn't bother her, she knew the pity she'd receive as soon as she showed up at her cousin's fiasco they dubbed a wedding. She was one step away from a cat or two, if only her apartment allowed them.

Eventually Piper excused herself to shower. The last thing she needed was waking up late the next day and not having time for a shower.

Haven insisted that she needed to add a few things to her latest article; however, she didn't bother bringing her own laptop. Piper found her friend to be sketchy. She was a journalist after all, and occasionally she did go above and beyond to get her information.

"You're not friends with your ex or cousin on Facebook," she hollered through the bathroom door.

"Are you insane? Jesus, Haven. Let me shower in peace."

Haven was the most unusual person she knew. The way she thought and the things she said often bordered on manic. Piper couldn't imagine why the hell Haven would be asking about social media when she was supposed to be writing her article, until she remembered whose computer Haven was using.

"What are you doing," Piper screamed, tearing through the bedroom in only a towel.

"Damn woman, put on some clothes will you," Haven laughed.

"No, no, no. Get off my Facebook." Piper tried to grab for the laptop with one hand while holding the towel with the other. All she managed to do was keep the towel in place.

"I've come up with an idea." The glimmer in Haven's eyes said it all. Piper knew it was something insane.

"I don't like your ideas. What are you doing? Please don't tell me you posted or–"

"I would never violate your privacy like that!"

Piper cocked a brow at the comment. Haven clearly didn't know the meaning of privacy.

"Don't give me that look. I've come up with an amazing solution and all you have to do is give me permission."

"No."

"You didn't even listen to what I was going to say," Haven gasped, pretending to be offended.

"Haven, please let this go. I can't suffer through one of your crazy ideas along with trying to get out of this wedding."

"Okay, so, thankfully Jared doesn't have major privacy settings," she began, once again ignoring Piper. "I went through a few tagged photos. He actually had a gathering with a bunch of his groomsmen. Most of them are married, dating, or just really freaking ugly."

"Why are you telling me this," Piper asked hesitantly. Water trickled down her legs and sent shivers along her skin. She really wanted to dry off and get into her pajamas, but she wasn't about to leave Haven alone with her computer a second longer.

"You said that you knew most of his friends from over the years, right?"

"I am not lowering myself to asking one of his groomsmen!"

"Well, I don't know about this particular one. He made a comment about how he couldn't make it to the Vegas thing, but he'd see them all in a few weeks for the big day. His privacy is so strict that all I can see is a profile picture, and it doesn't even have his face, but his backside..." Haven looked deeper into the computer as though the content would magically change. "His about me section has him listed as single."

"Stop it. You're crazy. You've had too much wine," Piper insisted.

"Look, I'm just going to shoot him a message–"

Piper found herself screaming at the top of her lungs in protest.

"Done."

"You suck! What the hell is wrong with you?!"

"Look…" Haven's voice was calm and mellow. She stood and brought her hands to Piper's cold and damp shoulders, as if she were trying to ground her, to keep her from combusting and floating away in bits. "Please don't be mad."

"I told you no on everything. Do you know how embarrassing that's going to be? Propositioning one of his friends as a date?"

"First of all. I didn't do that. Secondly, I just sent a short message with your number."

"You what," Piper hissed.

"If he doesn't get in touch with you, and you should have to see him in a few weeks, just tell him the truth. The absolute truth being that your crazy friend enjoys fucking around on your social media. However, if it all works out like it did in my head, how awesome would it be showing up with one of his friends," Haven smirked, fully knowing that Piper couldn't stay upset with her.

Piper stormed away to finish drying off and get dressed. Maybe Haven had a point. She really didn't want to think about the worst possibility. Despite everything, one thing she tried to retain was her optimism.

"Oh, I didn't ask you who it was," Piper shouted over her shoulder while brushing her hair. In the back of her mind she knew it didn't matter. Why would one of Jared's friends escort his ex?

"Umm, T.J.?"

"I have no idea who you messaged my number to, but Jared never had a T.J. as a friend," Piper nervously laughed, now wondering just who received her number.

She returned to find her friend now digging into a pint of cookie dough. Haven had to have the highest metabolism known to man. If someone could bottle it up and sell it, they'd be richer than Jeff Bezos.

"Yes," she mumbled. "With periods. T, period, J, period."

"I don't care how he spells it, I don't know a–"

"T.J. Deer. Not like dear, like my dear, but like the animal."

That was the moment that Piper forgot the meaning of optimism, but became painfully aware as to the meaning of mortification.

# CHAPTER 2

"You look like you've just seen a ghost," Haven began. It wasn't until that moment that she came to a realization. "Oh, I take it you know T.J."

"His name isn't T.J." Piper found it hard to speak. She wanted to crawl in a hole and never see sunlight again.

Haven sprawled herself over the couch and placed her head into her hands giving that inquisitive look. "Who is he then?"

Piper gave her the easier answer which was, "One of Jared's friends from high school."

"Oh..." Haven was disheartened. She had expected something better, but the more she watched her friend unravel, the more she knew that there most definitely was a better story. "You know you can't fool me, right?"

Piper sank into her most comfortable piece of furniture, a chair that had seen better days, and buried her head in her hands, reminding herself to breathe. "Tristan Reed."

The name sounded familiar to Haven. She tossed it around for a minute. She was certain that she had heard it before, but the bells weren't going off yet.

"Tristan fucking Reed!"

If her friend had not been on the verge of tears, Haven wanted to point out that his middle name could not be as such, but she decided that the particular moment didn't call for humor.

"Come on, Haven. Tristan Reed. One of the best soccer players in the country!"

"Oh...Shit."

*Ding. Ding. Ding.*

"I had no idea." Haven actually felt really bad. "You never told me you knew any famous people."

"I don't really know him. I've met him a handful of times. Oh, god. This is so embarrassing. It's like some weird fangirl move."

"Wait, are you sure, the name–"

"His last name is a semordnilap."

"Come again," Haven asked through a mouthful of ice cream.

"It's like a palindrome. It's a word both forward and backward, but not the same word. Just...never mind. Either way, I'm most certain that's who you messaged," Piper groaned.

Tristan Reed had played in one World Cup for the United States, and he probably would have done another one or two, had he not announced the previous year that he was retiring before his thirtieth birthday. Retiring was putting it mildly. He got injured and there was speculation that rather than try to make a comeback and fall short, the best option would have been to retire. Piper knew that when it came to sports, people always came out of retirement. Tristan

Reed was no exception. Soccer was his life. Soccer and girls.

"It's cool. Maybe he doesn't have the messenger thing, maybe he didn't see it," Haven began, trying to deescalate the panic attack her friend was dangerously close to having. If she was being honest, she should have left by now, but given what she had just done, it seemed like a dick move.

The smallest buzz from Piper's phone startled the both of them.

Haven's eyes grew three times their size and an open smile spread so far across her face that Piper could see bits of chocolate in the crevices of her back teeth.

They both darted for the phone, but Haven was just a bit faster, not caring what she knocked over in the process.

"Holy shit," she wailed. "Who's the fucking *bestest* ever?!"

She waved the phone in Piper's face. It was far too rapid for Piper to see anything more than white and a splotch of color that no doubt contained text. She quickly yanked the phone from Haven, and her heart nearly stopped at the text from a number clearly not listed in her phone; however, the identity was certain.

**Tristan: Piper Carter. To what do I owe the pleasure?**

*Breathe.*

Piper couldn't believe it. Given, Haven had messaged him on his private account, not his fan page, but Tristan Reed had actually read the message and bothered with taking the effort to texting her. How did he even have time for that? Oddly, the way he worded the text made it seem like he actually remembered her.

"Well, get to the point," Haven shouted after Piper had read the text to herself about ten times.

**Piper: Hi.**

"Hi? Seriously," Haven shouted over Piper's shoulder. "I go through all this for you to send that shit?"

"I don't know what to say," Piper squealed. "I haven't seen him in well over a year and...You messaged Tristan Reed!"

**Tristan: Hi? You do know you sent me your number, right?**

"I'm going home before I kill you," Haven announced. She then waved a finger in Piper's face with her next words. "I swear to god, if you blow–"

"No. I can't. I can't ask him to be my date. I just can't," Piper began repeating.

"If he didn't want to talk to you, he would have ignored the message from Facebook."

For a second, Piper felt a flutter when she allowed Haven's words to sink in. She dismissed it. Tristan lived in a completely different universe. He was just

26

being nice by texting her. He might be a demon on the field, but Piper remembered the countless articles from time to time about his volunteer work. This was just that side of him.

**Piper: I heard about your injury and I wanted to see how you were doing.**

**Tristan: That was over eight months ago.**

Thank goodness Haven had left. There was no doubt that she'd be strangling Piper with that message.

Piper threw her phone on the sofa and began shutting off the lights in the kitchen, preparing for bed. She heard it buzz again and bit her lip in anticipation. It would be best to just leave it for the night. Maybe sleep would help her figure out a reasonable response as to why she messaged him in the first place.

**Tristan: Shoot it straight. Why did you get in touch with me?**

"Great, just fucking great," Piper grumbled to herself.

**Piper: I was watching the game and thought of you.**

"Shit! No! Don't send, don't send," she screamed at the phone. For once she missed her crappy older phone that required her to tap the screen several times before sending a message. She knew she shouldn't have picked the phone up. The pizza and ice cream had clouded her judgement.

**Tristan: Oh yeah? Who's playing?**

**Piper: I'll talk to you later.**

There. End of conversation. She most definitely would not talk to him again after embarrassing herself twice.

The buzz in her hand should have been something on his part to conclude the conversation. As much as she wanted to believe that and not look at it, curiosity always had a way of winning.

**Tristan: Does this have to do with Jared's wedding?**

Piper knew she wouldn't be getting eight hours of sleep tonight. It would be so easy if her phone was in Haven's hands right now. The mentioning of the wedding sent a whole new bubbling of emotions through her. There was no way that out of the blue she could ask someone like Tristan to be her date. Sure, she knew him better than someone from a dating site, but other than pity, he had no reason to accept.

She wasn't good with being bold. She wasn't good with lying.

She began chewing the nail on her thumb, an old habit she had broken years ago, or so she thought.

**Piper: If I'm being honest, my friend messaged you from my Facebook.**

**Tristan: Honest is good. Why did your friend message me?**

**Piper: She's a fan.**

**Tristan: A fan who gave me your number?**

**Piper: It's a long story.**

**Tristan: It's only 8 here, so I have time.**

The fact that Tristan was messaging her and engaging in conversation made Piper forget that she was three hours ahead of California's time.

Continuing the conversation on the topic of the wedding was treading into dangerous territory, but there was the tiny glimmer of hope, optimism, that maybe Haven might not be as delusional as Piper thought with her absurd plans.

**Piper: Are you going?**

**Tristan: I'm a groomsman, so I guess I should.**

**Tristan: Although a whole week for a wedding is a bit much.**

**Piper: Are you going alone?**

She held her breath as she sent it. While she didn't completely put it out there, Tristan would definitely be able to read between the lines. When his one word text finally came through, she could no longer force away her pounding heartbeat or her sweaty hands that nearly dropped the phone.

**Tristan: Yes.**

Tristan could have said more, but more wasn't required. He'd be lying if he said he wasn't a little curious as to where the conversation was going.

He was surprised that she was still awake. He assumed she still lived in New York. It had been a while since he visited. The last time he hung out with some of the guys, when Jared was still with Piper, all Jared did was complain about her job. Apparently Piper was one of those serious people who liked to follow a schedule. For some reason, Tristan couldn't imagine that staying up until almost midnight, texting a guy she barely knew, would be part of her schedule.

He waited for another text to come in, but after thirty minutes assumed that she had fallen asleep. It mildly annoyed him that she would ask something like that and then leave it.

* * *

Piper still hovered over the message the next morning. As much as she wanted to, she couldn't. He seemed nice enough, but she was too nervous to do it.

"You're a chicken. No, you're worse than that," Haven scolded her as she filled up her third cup of coffee in the break room.

"He said yes, with a period."

"Okay? He uses punctuation?"

Piper shook her head as she guzzled down the warm liquid of life. "A period ends it. He could have asked why I was asking, or he could have–"

"Wow," Haven laughed. She ripped her phone from her back pocket. "You're analyzing a one word text. I need to look this guy up."

If you asked any guy who Tristan Reed was, they'd be able to tell you his position, stats, teams, they'd probably even be able to tell you every tattoo that was embedded into his skin. Haven, however, didn't know the difference between a touchdown and a home run. It was so bad that the two times she was asked to do an article about a sports related topic, she walked out of the room. She only barely knew of athletes who had dated famous actresses or models. Perhaps if Piper could think of one of the countless women over the years, Tristan's image would register to Haven.

"Tristan Reed...shirtless."

"You did not just type that in," Piper yelled, spewing coffee in the process.

"Now I know why he makes you nervous."

Piper couldn't imagine the pictures that were probably coming up on Haven's screen. "He doesn't make me nervous."

Her words were lost as soon as Haven shoved the screen in her face. The image: Tristan on a soccer field, shirtless and covered in sweat. It was the type of image women probably pleasured themselves to.

Piper could admit that Tristan was more than just attractive. Overall, he had the perfect body. He was tall, several inches taller than Jared, which would put him around 6'4" or so. She didn't want to stare too much at the picture, but even the few times she saw him in the past, she got a glimpse of what his muscles looked like. They weren't overdone like football players or bodybuilders, but they were quite prominent. He could easily lift her and–

"You're blushing!"

Piper turned from the screen, forcing her thoughts as far away from Tristan as possible.

Haven didn't stop though. She went on and on about how hot Tristan's tattoos were. He had a full sleeve on his left arm and script between his shoulder blades but the sexiest of all was a flaming phoenix on his right ribcage.

If, for one second, Piper had entertained the idea to continue texting Tristan, that image was enough to make her think differently. She needed a date to the wedding. She didn't need someone that she had just pictured pinning her against a wall.

# CHAPTER 3

A couple more days passed with Haven constantly mentioning Tristan every chance she got. Piper had been able to refrain from texting him anymore, although there were several times she tapped on their conversation and debated.

One thing Piper did decide was to go to the wedding. With or without a date, she was going. The whole freaking week. She had a restless night or two thinking about it, but in the end, she thought it would look worse if she didn't attend. She didn't want people thinking she was too emotional or bitter about the situation. She especially wanted to show her aunt and Samantha that she wasn't the wreck they liked to imagine.

Jared and Samantha had warped their story to exclude the whole cheating aspect. He made it look like Piper worked too much and he wanted to settle down and start a family. Bullshit.

"Who the hell does a week-long wedding," Blythe snorted. "When I got married to my fourth husband...no...my third husband," she began, but paused to think and start over. "Yes, fourth. When I got married to my fourth husband, I came back to the office after the ceremony."

Piper didn't want to point it out, but maybe that was why number four was no longer in the picture either.

"Can you find one hell of a temp and still work in between?"

Piper knew that the only way she was going to get time off was if she answered yes to both of those. Piper was pretty sure that what her boss was asking completely defeated the point in her taking time off, but she honestly didn't mind. At least she'd be present and have a good excuse, an excuse that was perfect for fueling Jared's story.

* * *

"When can we arrange a shopping date," Haven murmured through a disgustingly full mouth.

Even lunch became a daily challenge. Thankfully, Haven had a moment to run to the deli nearby for a sandwich. Piper had yet to take a bite of hers. She had a mountain of work to do, not to mention she needed to get as much done as possible in preparation for her *vacation*.

"I heard there's a nude beach upstate. Maybe we could go this weekend?"

"Mhmm," Piper acknowledged.

Haven polished off the last bit of her sandwich. She wasn't even sure if Piper knew that she was in the room. Piper always worked hard, going above and beyond, but Haven hated how she had become since her breakup with Jared. It's like she didn't know anything outside of work. Haven had even tried to set her up on a few dates, all of which she blew off.

She knew exactly what Piper was going to do that week. She'd attend the necessary events and then bury herself in her room, working, whether it be for Blythe or her side job of writing freelance pieces that she kept quiet about.

Piper was too busy on her computer to notice Haven slip the phone from the side of her desk.

Tristan was surprised when he saw the incoming call. After that one night of texting, he didn't expect to hear much more from Piper. He really didn't expect for her to actually call.

"Hello?"

"What else is tattooed other than what I'm looking at online?"

Tristan pulled the phone down just to make sure it was Piper. It was.

"I'm sorry," he began. Piper had completely shut down after basically asking him if he was seeing anyone, and now, never speaking to her on the phone, these were her first words. "Are you drunk?"

He felt like a jerk for asking, but the little he knew about Piper that was the only plausible thing he could come up with.

"God, I wish. Actually, I'm Haven."

Tristan automatically assumed this must be the friend Piper had mentioned. At first he thought she had second-guessed herself about sending him the initial message and decided to lie about a friend.

"What the hell are you doing with my phone," a voice rang out in the background.

"I'm helping you out. You just get back to kissing Blythe's ass."

Tristan shook his head at what he was hearing through the phone. He knew Blythe Carrington's name well. He often appeared in stories that her magazine printed. He also knew that she was a ruthless businesswoman and he was surprised Piper made it as long as she did as her assistant.

"Here's the thing," Haven began, now directing her words toward Tristan. "My girl can't show up to that ridiculous wedding alone, not after what your bestie did to her."

Tristan was a little confused. He and Jared were far from best friends, and to his knowledge, Jared and Piper had an amicable parting.

"She doesn't want a real date, she just needs someone to pretend for a week. You got me?"

"Not even a little," Tristan laughed, trying to keep up with the spunky voice coming through.

"Please tell me you didn't call *him*?!"

Though she was far off, her words were crystal clear. With the way she said that to her friend, Tristan knew they had talked about him. It only made him wonder why she stopped texting him in the first place.

"Unless you want me to call the escort service," Haven spat.

"Excuse me," Tristan shrieked.

"Not you, sorry. We were going to go in that direction–"

"No, we weren't," Piper's voice rang out.

"So, what do you say," Haven asked.

"I'm not even sure what the question is."

"Both of you are going to this thing, can you pretend to be her boyfriend for the week?"

For a moment he had thought that Piper might ask him to be her actual date to the wedding, but he couldn't imagine why. This, however, had to be a joke.

"Are you serious? Why?"

"She can't show up alone after what those scumbags did to her," Haven sighed. Her voice suddenly turned serious.

"What are you talking about?"

"Come on. He didn't break up with Piper and happen to meet her cousin, who, coincidentally was a temporary roommate of Piper's. Your dick friend was cheating on her for months."

"Fuck you," a voice cried out before the slamming of a door.

"I guess I shouldn't have told you that," Haven admitted. "Shit, she's pissed now. I don't think ice cream will fix this."

"She left," Tristan asked.

"Yeah. Look, I know I'm stepping–"

"It'll be fine."

There was a moment of silence on both ends.

"Are you saying what I think you're saying," Haven

37

hesitated.

Tristan began to pace the room. What the hell was he saying? The words just slipped out before he had the chance to think. If he agreed, it would be one of the stranger things he had done. He also knew that Jared would be pissed, but if he really had done what this chick was telling him, then he deserved to be a little pissed, he deserved to swallow a taste of his own medicine, friend or not.

Tristan had dated some horrible women over the years, but no matter how bad they were, none of them deserved to be cheated on. Piper was in a completely different league than the women he was used to. She had an innocent beauty about her and she was incredibly talented and hardworking, even if he did think that talent was wasted as Blythe's assistant. Either way, if Jared was lucky enough to have a girl like Piper, why the hell would he do something as stupid as cheating?

"Yeah."

"Holy crap. I'm going to hang up before you change your mind," Haven squealed.

✳ ✳ ✳

Tristan sank to the couch trying to wrap his head around the conversation he just had with this Haven person. Did he really just agree to pretend to be his friend's ex-girlfriend's new boyfriend?

# CHAPTER 4

**Tristan: So, I'm one step up from an escort service?**

He had waited until he knew she'd be off work, and it was now well into the night in New York.

**Piper: Ignore everything she said. Everything.**

**Tristan: So you're already breaking up with me?**

**Piper: It's going to be so awkward seeing you now.**

**Tristan: Why?**

**Piper: Because you think I'm desperate and can't find a date.**

**Tristan: I don't think that at all. I thought as of a few hours ago, you already had a date.**

Piper thought about how to respond. Her stomach did a few flips at the thought that Tristan was willing to go along with the charade. That was a dangerous feeling.

Before she could address his text, she found herself laughing at the notification that flashed across her screen. *T.J. Deer has requested to be your friend.*

Piper hit confirm instantly. She was just about finished with her text when another request popped up that sent her phone straight to the floor. Thankfully, she had been lounging on the couch and the impact did no damage, but that would have been the least of her worries.

**Piper: Are you insane?**

**Tristan: You can't have a boyfriend, even a fake one, if your status has you as single.**

Piper couldn't reply to the request or the most recent text. What Tristan said was true. No one would believe that she just magically had a boyfriend all of a sudden upon showing up to the wedding. Technically there was no harm. It was just Facebook. Knowing most of her friends and family, they'd scroll right past it once they saw her name.

**Tristan: You know you want to. Live dangerously.**

**Piper: Haha! You did not just say that! You call that dangerous?**

**Tristan: For you, probably. For me, no. Dangerous would be letting that friend of yours pick a spot for my next tattoo.**

Finding that she was unable to stop smiling from the message, Piper hit confirm on the notification.

\* \* \*

"What did you do," Emma's voice shouted through the phone.

Piper knew she shouldn't have answered the call. "Mom, I'm getting ready for work. I really don't have time–"

"You're not doing that. You're going to talk to me, especially after the earful I got from that wonderful aunt of yours."

The woman her mother was referring to was Aunt Margaret, Samantha's mother. All the money in the world couldn't make her less of a bitch.

"I don't care what she called about." Piper put the phone on speaker so that she could put in her earrings.

"I get that you're busy and you work, but that was low. I am your mother–"

"What did that old witch tell you?"

"That you're in a relationship!"

Piper didn't know how she would know that. She wasn't friends with Margaret or Samantha.

"She said that Jared told Samantha about it last night," her mother continued, answering her thoughts as to how Margaret found out. "She said he's some thug who just happens to be Jared's best man."

Piper loved how her aunt had this beautiful way of taking something so small and blowing it to kingdom come. There wasn't a rational person in the world who would classify Tristan as a thug, but then again, Aunt Margaret was so far off the chart of rationality.

Knowing that she had to say something, "He's not the best man, just a groomsman."

"So you're really seeing someone?" Emma's booming voice turned quieter now.

For a second, Piper thought about telling her mother that it was fake, but quickly realized that her mother would think she's the insane one. It would be easier and require less explaining if she just went with it like it was the truth.

"You not answering clears that up," her mother announced, interrupting Piper's thoughts.

"I don't see why it's a big deal. Aunt Margaret needs to–"

"She needs to check into a facility, that's what she needs. She had the gall to tell me that you were deliberately trying to ruin the wedding by upstaging that twat of a child of hers."

"What?"

"Is he someone famous," Emma sighed.

Piper had forgotten about that. When she texted Tristan, she forgot who he was other than a nice and funny person behind a screen.

The wedding was still nearly three weeks away, at least the initial shock of it all would be old news by then.

* * *

The next two weeks went by faster than Piper had hoped. In that time, she had managed to find a suitable temp for Blythe. Heaven forbid she live a week with having to fetch her own coffee. Piper had miraculously made time for a few shopping trips with Haven. She even allowed Haven to pick out a dress that she insisted said, "What the hell was Jared thinking?" However, Piper wasn't exactly sure if, or when, she'd wear it.

There was one more thing that happened in those two weeks and Piper was on the fence as to how she felt about it. Tristan had text her. A lot. They were all normal conversations, but she suddenly found herself smiling more.

* * *

"Is she ugly," Elijah asked as he watched his friend pack a second suitcase. "Seriously, you're worse than a girl with all that shit."

"I don't know what the fuck you're supposed to pack for something like this," Tristan huffed. "And no, she's definitely not ugly."

"So you'd sleep with her?"

"Shouldn't you be practicing," Tristan asked, quickly dismissing the question.

If he was being honest with himself, he had always known Piper was beautiful. He didn't know how Jared had gotten someone like her, and after what her friend told him, he still couldn't believe Jared had screwed it up the way he did.

"Speaking of practice, when are you coming out of this retirement bullshit?"

"Do you think I need swim trunks for anything," Tristan asked, again changing the subject.

"Sure, why not. Look, I don't get it."

"You don't get a lot of things," Tristan chuckled.

"You're pretending to be the boyfriend of someone you're just friends with, right?" Tristan nodded. "Isn't the whole point of a wedding trying to score with all the bridesmaids and single chicks? I mean, come on, dude. As soon as Tristan Reed walks through that door, half the panties in there are going to melt. You're a fool if you don't take advantage of that."

Tristan grabbed his cologne and threw it into the bag he was checking. "Unlike you, I can keep it in my pants for a week."

"Holy shit," Elijah gasped. Soon after, he fell to the bed in a frenzy of giggles. Yes, Elijah Jacobs, one of the best midfielders around, giggles.

"Are you done?"

"First of all," Elijah managed, trying to catch his breath. "I don't think you even know how many girls you've been with. Secondly, for you to say that with such confidence, it only means one thing?"

"Oh yeah, what?"

"You like this *friend*."

Tristan threw a pair of socks at Elijah, who only busted into another giggle fit.

The truth was, he did like Piper, but strictly as a friend. They only sent message through a screen. He never pointed that out, but from what she said about her job, he assumed a text here and there was easier than trying to have a conversation. Sometimes she responded immediately, but if she was overwhelmed, it would be a couple hours before she even realized she owned a phone. It worked. She was a female he could talk to without all the emotional and girly shit getting in the way.

Occasionally she would make comments that sent his pulse racing if he allowed himself to take them out of context, but he was always able to bring his thoughts back to the present.

"Face it Reed, you wouldn't play fake boyfriend to any woman. Something about this one struck you, and if you're set on *keeping it in your pants* all weekend, you are so fucked," Elijah concluded, shaking his head with pity, all while still drying his eyes from laughing.

# CHAPTER 5

"I cannot believe you! Why didn't you tell me this sooner," Haven shrieked.

Piper was busy leaving notes for the temp that Haven insisted she would help out; however, she made it clear that Piper owed her in the future. Piper had even demanded that Haven join her at the office to get everything perfectly in order. Haven pointed out that it was Sunday, yet here they were, having this discussion in Piper's office.

"It just slipped my mind."

"I don't understand how you could do that. You. You have to have everything perfect and planned and you let him take care of everything?"

Haven was referring to the travel arrangements and accommodations.

A week or so prior, Piper had a difficult and demanding day. After talking with Tristan, he made it clear that she didn't need to add more to her daily activities. Apparently he had *people* that could book the flights and rooms for the wedding. Unfortunately, when Piper agreed to it, she was already on a much unneeded third glass of wine. By the time she realized her mistake the next morning, Tristan told her that it was all taken care of.

She allowed Jared to plan a trip once and it was then that she vowed that no one but herself would ever be in charge of that task. The fact that she put that in Tristan's hands frightened her a bit. While she knew him, she didn't really *know* him.

"He's flying in tonight?"

"Yeah," Piper acknowledged as she threw out a pack of half eaten crackers from her desk.

"Are you meeting up?"

"No. He gets in late and I need to finish packing a few things and get some sleep." Piper pretended to be disinterested in the topic of Tristan, but the thought of seeing him in person did something to her. It was a strange and unfamiliar feeling.

"What time is your flight tomorrow," Haven pressed on. Her voice wasn't as cheery now that she knew that Piper didn't have a romantic evening ahead.

"He told me to be at the airport by 9:30."

"That's not what I asked," Haven grumbled. When Piper didn't respond and continued to tidy up, she lost herself in her own thoughts. "Wait, do you even know when your flight is?"

There it was. Piper hadn't really even thought about that. She didn't know what time, what airline, nothing. She picked up her phone immediately, but before she could accomplish the smallest task, Haven interrupted.

"You trusted him," Haven pointed out.

"Stop it," Piper insisted. After Jared, she didn't trust the intentions of any men, even for the smallest of things.

"You're blushing!"

"Stop! I've been so busy I didn't realize that I never asked for specifics," she lied. She couldn't believe that she allowed Tristan to handle everything and not even question it.

"Well, what did he say," Haven cooed as soon as the phone made a noise.

Piper's expression crossed between horror and confusion. She tossed her phone at Haven and continued working on a post-it.

"Wow, he's something else," Haven cackled when she saw the message.

**Tristan: I'll have a car for you at 8:45. He'll have you at the airport by 9:30.**

"How should we respond to that," Haven pensively asked.

"We are not responding. I have to finish this and then you can come help me go back through my suitcase and checklist."

Haven groaned. It was a wasted Sunday. The only reason she decided to spend the day with Piper was because she knew that her friend's nerves were all over the place.

"I'm not going through that damn list one more time," Haven screamed from Piper's kitchen.

She rifled through a drawer trying to find the corkscrew. It was absurd that she had made it this long around Piper without a glass of wine.

With all the rambling, it became clear that Piper wasn't just nervous about seeing her ex, her insane circus that was her family, or even the wedding at all. Haven noticed how edgy Piper became with even the smallest mentioning of Tristan.

"I still can't believe he's doing this for you," Haven casually pointed out as she handed a jittery Piper one of the wine glasses.

"Yeah," was all Piper said in response.

Haven pressed on. "When was the last time you saw him?"

Piper twirled the wine in her glass and gave it some thought. She didn't want to say right away and allow an overly curious Haven to know that she remembered the day that well. "Unless you count on television, I guess well over a year ago, before Jared and I broke up."

Haven coughed on her wine. "Wait. You watch his games?"

"I don't watch *his* games, but yes, I watch soccer occasionally," Piper admitted. She watched teams other than just Tristan's when he still played. "By the way, he hasn't played in eight months. I watched soccer long before that, but you'd never know because you're allergic to sports," Piper teased.

Haven ignored the comment. "I'm going to be blunt here."

"When are you not," Piper scoffed.

"Would you hook up with him?"

Piper quickly chugged the glass of wine. "I'm not like that," she answered, heading back to the kitchen for a refill.

"Trust me," Haven groaned. "I know. I don't think you've had sex since you and Jared broke up."

Haven was free-spirited compared to Piper, and there were times that Piper wished she had a little more of that. Haven didn't sleep around too much, but she didn't think you needed a commitment or relationship to have sex. Piper's mindset hadn't gotten to that point.

Once the conversation turned from Tristan and the wedding, and once Piper had another glass of wine, she was able to relax. Eventually Haven left, much earlier than usual; however, Piper couldn't be more thankful. She threw herself into bed and didn't wake up a single time interrupted by her thoughts.

* * *

The morning was strange enough.

When Tristan said he'd have a car for her, Piper assumed an Uber or maybe even a taxi. She became a little hesitant when she saw the sleek black car through her apartment lobby windows. It was even stranger when the chauffeur exited and automatically knew who she was. Maybe that wasn't too strange. She was the only one standing there with a couple suitcases. He could easily assume that she was Piper Carter.

He made small talk with her on the drive to the airport. Apparently he was from an agency that Tristan often used when he was in New York. It wasn't like Tristan had gone out of his way finding a driver for her; however, a taxi would have been just as suitable and cost a lot less. Piper then remembered that Tristan wasn't just an ordinary guy with an ordinary career.

He was waiting for her as soon as the car drove up, and that's when the nerves began to get the best of her. Though she and Tristan had been messaging quite a bit over the last few weeks, nothing could prepare her for what it would be like when she finally saw him in person.

"I told you he'd have you here by 9:30," were the first words he said upon opening her door.

Piper stepped out, hesitant to even make eye contact. She didn't anticipate the man before her to have an effect on her, but he most definitely did. To say his body was perfect would be an understatement. The shirtless picture Haven had found quickly flashed through Piper's mind as soon as she laid eyes on him.

She attempted not to read into the way he was looking at her, but the way the morning sun flickered in his light brown eyes set on hers made her weak. In games, on the field, his expressions were demonic; whereas in interviews, he held the look of boredom. He often expressed his dislike of the media, especially when it came to his personal life. The look on his face now was nothing like the other two. Goosebumps ran through Piper and she fumbled for words, breaking the daze he put her in.

"What time is the flight? I'm sure security is a mess by now," she mumbled, attempting to grab one of her small bags from the back seat.

Tristan cut in between her and the car and pulled it out before she could, while the driver got her rather large one from the trunk.

"10:15."

Piper froze with the time he mentioned.

"Don't look so surprised. I told you I was taking care of this so you wouldn't stress out," Tristan chuckled.

"I have to check that bag. We have to get through security. Where are our tickets? What gate are we at? Where are your bags? The plane will be boarding in less than half an hour," Piper rambled, not taking a breath between a single word.

Tristan firmly placed his hands on her shoulders before she could dart inside and cause pandemonium. His touch did nothing to calm her. If anything, she thought she might jump out of her skin at the heat from his palms sinking beneath her t-shirt.

"Is this you not stressed?"

"We take off in forty-five minutes! I knew I should have handled this on my own," she cried out, attempting to yank her bag from him.

Tristan turned to a man behind him that Piper hadn't noticed yet. "Can you take care of these as well," he asked the airport employee, motioning to Piper's bags.

"Yes, Mr. Reed," he acknowledged as Tristan handed him a few bills.

"Come on," he playfully insisted. "Let's get going before you have a nervous breakdown."

✳ ✳ ✳

Piper didn't understand what was going on. This wasn't how an airport worked. You didn't hand your bags to someone with a name tag and hope they got where they needed to be. You also didn't bypass security. A normal person like her also didn't fly in first class.

"My son is a huge fan," the flight attendant giggled before Tristan could sit down.

He had given Piper the window seat and she was already making herself comfortable.

"Would you mind," the woman asked, now directing both her question and a cell phone to Piper.

Piper grinded her teeth with a hint of annoyance. "It's no problem," she said as nicely as possible.

She took the phone and just as she was about to snap the picture, the woman threw her arms around Tristan, a smile flooding her face. The little sprinkle of jealousy Piper thought that she felt quickly faded into frustration. Suddenly the escort idea wasn't looking too bad.

"Sorry about that," Tristan apologized once the woman was satisfied and went about what she was being paid to do.

"Whatever," Piper grumbled.

Tristan knew Piper flew, despite the way she grabbed on to the armrests during liftoff. A part of him wanted to hold her hand to calm her, but so far they had barely said more than a few words to each other. He found it difficult to make conversation, remembering that all their prior exchanges were just words on a screen.

Once they were in the air, Piper rummaged through her large bag below the seat in front of her and withdrew her laptop. She robotically began working. She paid Tristan little attention; he was consumed with a movie or something on his phone.

"Here you are," the flight attendant announced as she held out two sodas along with a couple miniature bottles of rum.

Piper glanced to Tristan, a look of confusion and irritation.

He shook his head, an unbelievably gorgeous smile gracing his face. "I thought you could relax."

"It's not even noon," Piper began. After looking back to her computer screen, "It's not even 11!"

"I'm aware of the time." He took all of the beverages and mixed the alcohol in both of the sodas before handing one to Piper.

Reluctantly, she closed her computer and put it aside. She rarely drank anything other than a few glasses of wine with Haven, but she had to admit, the drink was smooth and desperately needed.

"What are you watching," she asked, noticing that Tristan took out one of his earbuds.

He tilted the screen to her and she couldn't help but choke on her drink a little. "Seriously," she laughed. "You're watching *Monk*? I thought you'd be catching up on something a lot newer."

"He reminds me of you a little," Tristan pointed out with a teasing grin.

"Just so you know, I'm not above eating something I've dropped on the floor." Piper cringed the moment she admitted that. Tristan probably had a chef regulating his dietary needs and she just told him that she'd eat food from the floor.

"That actually surprises me," he laughed, knowing he was about to hit a nerve. "I meant that you're very set in your ways, even a little obsessive-compulsive."

"That's not true."

He was curious as to why she acted so differently from her texts. "You've been freaking out since I've met you."

"Yeah, because of all this, because of you," Piper blurted out.

"Because of me?"

"I don't mean you, I mean..." She became flustered after realizing how her words could be taken. If she was being honest with herself, Tristan was one of the most gorgeous men she had ever encountered and being in his presence could be tempting, if either of them had been looking for that, which she absolutely was not for the foreseeable future. "Going overboard, flaunting your money, that doesn't impress me. Thank you for handling the accommodations, but this is just too much," she concluded, once she could get past the thought of how attractive he was.

Tristan was hoping for a different response from her. "Who ever said I was trying to impress you?" He was certain that her cheeks reddened at the comment. She didn't respond, only looked away from embarrassment. "I knew you'd have a shitty week with all this, so I thought I'd try to make you more comfortable."

Piper felt bad after hearing that. She shouldn't have snapped at him. He was being generous with the entire situation. The thought of the week to come made her remember something.

Silence ensued. Piper gulped down the remaining liquid and Tristan watched her go to her bag. She withdrew a folder and proudly pulled out a typed piece of paper. He tried glancing at it without being obvious, but couldn't make out what it was. There were typed sentences that were numbered off, followed by blank lines. Piper began writing something in one of the blanks.

"Here," she proudly announced, handing the paper to Tristan.

"What's this," he asked, although he could read the title perfectly. *Rules.*

"It's what I need you to follow," she replied, as if it were perfectly normal and understandable.

"You've got to be shitting me!"

He skimmed over the madness that she presented him, noting the extremely insane ones that she thought to include.

*#3. Don't mention what Haven told you about how the relationship really ended.*

He didn't understand that one at all. People deserved to know how slimy Jared and Samantha were, even if Jared was an old friend.

*#5. Public displays of affection are needed, but limited to an occasional touch or brief handholding.*

Upon reading that, something stirred within him. After his conversation with Elijah, he had thought of the fact that they were playing a couple, and it might require them to act as such. Actually, that wasn't entirely true. Even through text, the strange woman next to him had done something. While he could control himself perfectly when he was awake, he hadn't been able to control what happened in his sleep, and a few of the dreams were a little unnerving to him.

Then he read a few lines down. All the thoughts of anything happening with Piper flew out the window.

*#8. No sleeping with the bridesmaids, or any of the guests present for the wedding. Be discreet about anyone else.*

Tristan glared at her. "Seriously, number eight?"

"I'm not stupid. I know you have needs, but that would be unbearable if you slept with one of Samantha's friends," Piper groaned.

"You think I can't go a week without having sex?"

Piper's stomach clenched at the mentioning of sex. "I don't know what you are and aren't capable of. It's just a rule."

Tristan was beyond irritated. He didn't need her giving him rules as to who he could and couldn't sleep with. "Yeah, well your rules are fucking stupid," he spat. "Just so you know, if I'm being honest, the thought never crossed my mind."

A flutter ran through Piper with those words. Tristan was without a doubt a guy who could walk into any room and have any woman, single or not. She also knew that there would be women at the wedding that would be throwing themselves at him. He had to have given that thought.

The attendant suddenly appeared, asking if they needed anything else. The flight from New York to Maine was a quick one, but they still had about thirty minutes or better.

Tristan quickly scanned to the end of the list to see the last thing Piper scribbled.

*#22. No more big gestures.*

"Yeah," he then acknowledged, as he crumbled the paper. "Could you take care of this for me?"

From the corner of his eye, he could see Piper fuming and it gave him a sick pleasure at pushing her buttons right now.

"Anything else," she cooed. She was clearly being flirtatious with him.

"Can I get another drink, the same, for this one over here?"

The flight attendant's smile faded when she remembered the female seated next to Tristan. She did as he requested and moved on.

"I didn't need another one," Piper huffed.

"Trust me, you did."

# CHAPTER 6

"I don't understand," the man behind the rental counter repeated. "You specifically requested this car. It would be nearly impossible to get someone else to rent this."

"Fine, whatever. I'll pay for it. I just need another car," Tristan insisted in a low voice, hoping that Piper wouldn't realize what was going on. "Do you have a Honda or something? Something boring and basic?"

The man gave him an odd look and Tristan realized how absurd he sounded. "You want a Honda in place of an Aston Martin DB11?"

The question was rhetorical, but Tristan answered anyway. "Yes. What else do you have?"

"Nothing. If I did I would let you pay for both, but I honestly have nothing. There are other rental agencies–"

Tristan cut him off. "Just give me the damn keys."

\* \* \*

"Are you kidding me," Piper screeched. She dropped one of her bags on the cement and turned to

Tristan once she saw the lights flash on the car, unlocking the doors.

"This was before your stupid rules, which by the way, I don't plan on following." He began loading their large bags into the trunk first.

"Clearly," she screamed, flailing her arms around.

Once the trunk was filled, and a carry-on bag and her overly large purse containing her computer remained, Tristan tried wedging them into the interior.

The car apparently could hold four people, but it didn't look comfortable at all.

The resort was still about forty-five minutes away, and they'd make it there some time after lunch. Piper had received a text during the flight that she only recently read, alerting her that her parents and sister had already arrived.

"Why T.J.," Piper found herself asking after a few minutes of silence. She knew that Tristan was having a rush driving such a nice car, so much so that he nearly forgot she was with him.

"Huh?" Before Piper could elaborate, he laughed at remembering. "It's not like I'm trying to hide. My middle name has stayed out of the media. You can even look on Wikipedia; it's not there. It gives me a little bit of normalcy. I can still have my friends and family without all the fans. I'm actually surprised you didn't just go to my fan page to contact me."

"First of all," Piper began, needing to reiterate. "Haven messaged you. She was going through Jared's Facebook. Why she thought bringing one of his friends as a date would be a good idea–"

His laughter interrupted her. "Actually, it's pretty brilliant, considering."

"What's that supposed to mean?"

Tristan turned quiet. It was one of those things that Piper didn't want him mentioning to others, but she hadn't yet talked to him about what Haven let slip. "If things ended the way I'm led to believe, showing up with one of his groomsmen is a pretty nice punch in the face."

"We're not talking about that," she insisted. She didn't want to point out that Tristan was also the hottest of all of Jared's friends.

"You'll talk to me about it eventually." The smirk on his face was nothing short of raw confidence.

Piper quickly changed the subject back. "So, what is it then?" After Tristan shot her a brief and confusing look, she made herself clearer. "The J in T.J., what does it stand for?"

His right hand went to the back of his neck and he rubbed it uncomfortably. "Promise you won't laugh?"

"Is it something like Jane?"

Though he found humor in that, as a guy he had to at least pretend to be insulted. "No! I don't have a girly name like that. It's Jude."

"Oh." Piper was expecting something brutal or bizarre, but Jude was actually a nice name. Then she had to overthink and wonder why he'd tell her not to laugh. It took every bit of a matter of seconds before it came to her. "Wait..."

"Yeah," he sighed, knowing that she got it.

"Your parents named you after The Beatles song?!"

He only chuckled and shook his head in confirmation.

"That is so adorable," she squealed.

He was a little taken aback. Adorable would not have been a word that he would have used to describe it, but the fact that she did, for whatever reason, turned him on a little.

"Are you a fan?"

"Partially. While I think they got more hype than they deserved, I'd be lying if I said I couldn't name a whole slew of songs that I love."

"Go," he insisted, now curious.

She twisted her lips, appearing to be deep in thought. Since leaving the airport, she had changed. Tristan scanned up and down her body and just from the way she was sitting now, he could see how relaxed she was. He could also see a lot of other things that had to be left to the imagination. He forced himself to stop glancing in her direction.

"Okay," she announced. "These are in no particular order, because I don't have that one that just stands out as my favorite. Okay?"

He tried to keep from smiling like a schoolboy with a crush, but she was making it difficult. "Noted," was all he said in response.

"I'll go with, 'Paperback Writer', 'I Want to Hold Your Hand', and 'I've Just Seen a Face'." She took a deep breath at the end, as if she had just made the hardest decision in her life.

Tristan thought for a moment, surprised that she didn't list bigger and more popular ones. After repeating them to himself, however, they fit her perfectly.

The conversation remained light, but Tristan quickly realized that the closer they got to the resort, all the tension and stress began to creep its way back into the beautiful and carefree girl he only got a few moments with. He wanted to know why she turned into that person, what could be so bad about this week, aside from the obvious, that would make her so nervous and anxious.

* * *

"Yes, Mr. Reed. We have your two rooms. You requested side-by-side?"

Tristan froze. He had hired someone to book everything. He absolutely did not say that the rooms needed to be near each other.

"Actually, we're here with a wedding party. Is there any way I can get the rooms moved to that part of the resort," he asked in a hush tone. It was going to be the rental agency all over again. The only difference was that Piper was right next to him. Right. Next. To. Him. Hearing everything.

"I'm sorry," the clerk began. "You booked two of our most exclusive suites–"

"No, no, no," Tristan began. He attempted to make a face at the clerk, but the man was not understanding. "There must be some mistake. I booked normal rooms for normal people and–"

"Oh, good lord, Tristan! Save it," Piper interjected.

Tristan turned to face her, trying to hide his amusement that she caught on so quickly. He thought for a brief second that she might be really irritated, but despite everything, her eyes came across as playful, as if she knew what to expect with him.

Piper was well aware that there was no misunderstanding about the rooms. Tristan had pointed out earlier that he wanted to make everything easier on her. She didn't want to tell him, but the fact that their suites were on a complete opposite side of the resort compared to most of the wedding party, that was a huge advantage. She would be able to lock herself in her room and work, avoiding almost everyone.

"What's the plan now," Tristan asked after helping Piper with her bags.

"I didn't tell my family I'm here yet. Hopefully I can catch up on some work first," she admitted.

Tristan thought about telling her how ridiculous that sounded, but decided against it. He had heard long ago from Jared about how demanding her job was; he didn't need to point that out. Instead, "Do I need to be there when you meet them?"

Piper thought for a moment. Her mother didn't seem to care much about the *relationship* now. The initial shock and hearing it from Margaret was what upset her. Piper didn't know how her father felt. "I haven't seen them in a while. I should probably go alone first."

"Sounds good. Just text me whenever. I'm going to go see if I can find a gym." His words were casual, void of any emotion.

Piper had to wonder if he was disappointed that she didn't want him with her when she met her family. She shook her head at the idea. It was a pretend relationship for the purpose of the wedding. Tristan was only being nice. He was probably happy that he could get time to himself.

# CHAPTER 7

Shortly after 4pm, Piper found herself in a bar at the resort. Her stomach was screwed up six ways from Sunday. She still hadn't met with her parents, despite getting a text informing her of a dinner as part of the kickoff of wedding festivities. It was a circus. A fucking circus.

"I hate to tell you, but you are the most depressing person I've seen all day," the bartender announced.

"That's how you greet your customers?"

"I still have a job," he laughed. "What can I get for you?"

"I don't really drink," Piper began.

"You do realize that you're in a bar?"

She fumbled for words. "No. I drink. I mean, I don't drink all the time. I will ingest alcohol. I'm just not...I don't know much about alcohol other than wine, and maybe rum and coke." She found herself smiling as she mentioned the last bit.

"Tell me why you're drinking and I can come up with a drink."

Piper liked him. He was cute, and she liked how blunt he was being. Unfortunately, Piper could easily tell that she wasn't his type. No girl was.

"Is that your superpower?"

"Try me," he playfully insisted.

Piper didn't throw her business around to strangers. Hell, her hairdresser didn't even know what she did for a living. Something about the situation, however, made her not care. "Well, I'm here for a wedding..."

"Okay, I see. Happy times..."

Piper arched a brow at how far off that comment was. "The groom is my ex-fiancé, and the bride-to-be, my cousin. Oh, also, he was sleeping with her while we were still together."

The bartender went silent. His eyes popped out and his jaw hung in shock. He shook his head before, "Oh, sweetheart. If you weren't a drinker before, you will be after that."

Piper found herself blabbering everything. "To add to it, my pretend boyfriend that's here with me is a groomsman."

"The name is Spencer," he informed her as he began mixing some bizarre concoction. When Piper didn't say anything, "I have a feeling I'll be seeing you a lot. I figured you should at least know my name."

Piper wasn't sure about the blue drink he placed in front of her. It smelled divine, but she knew it had hard liquor in it, and she wasn't big on some of those tastes, especially tequila.

Spencer eventually went to a couple on another end of the bar, leaving Piper to sip her drink alone. The alcohol helped her nerves, thankfully she didn't taste tequila, and she couldn't help but laugh to her-self. She had to have the relaxing effects of alcohol to get through dealing with her entire family. Then she remembered the drive from earlier.

Tristan had that same effect. He made her laugh, made it easier to breathe, put her at ease. The only difference, Tristan was more dangerous than any drink.

**Piper: I need you.**

Tristan's pulse raced upon reading the unexpected text. He couldn't refrain from the thoughts that lingered in the back of his mind. He was quickly able to dismiss any further naughty ideas after another text came in.

**Piper: I'm at the bar.**

"Shit," Tristan hissed to himself.

The drinks on the plane didn't affect her, but there was no telling what all she might be getting into at the bar.

To his surprise, when he found her, she was still very much sober. He figured she was still on her first drink.

"Everything okay," he asked. He hated that it sounded like he was out of breath from rushing to meet her.

She turned so that he could see her whole face. "I changed my mind. I want you to come with me to visit with my parents before the dinner tonight."

He found it incredibly sexy how she was saying what she wanted. Judging from how uncomfortable she was, it had to be something that she didn't do very often.

"Okay."

She looked shocked. "Okay? That's it?"

"What kind of pretend boyfriend would I be if I didn't meet your parents before the rest of whoever all those people are," he laughed. She wasn't laughing though. He noticed how her eyes crinkled at his words and he wondered if there was one in particular that did it for her. *Pretend.*

\* \* \*

Oddly enough, Tristan found her parents and sister to be fairly bearable. He expected a lot of questions, but none of them really seemed to care about the extent or details of the relationship. He caught her sister occasionally whispering to Piper, which usually ended with giggles and blushing. He knew Lucy was making comments about him and he loved seeing that it did something to Piper.

"I guess we better herd in like cattle for that dinner," Nolan huffed, glancing at his watch.

"I don't know how mom got him to come," Lucy whispered to Piper. "If you think mom didn't want to be here, you don't want to know what he was like."

"I'm pretty sure no one here actually wants to be here," Piper laughed.

"I just can't wait until he meets Aunt Margaret," Lucy announced so that Tristan could hear.

"Aunt Maggie?"

Both girls' faces dropped and they shook their heads.

"How did you," Piper began, shocked that he knew that would drive her insane.

He chuckled. "You keep calling her Margaret, so I figured she'd be one of those." When both girls gave him a confused and suspicious look, "We had a public relations woman that was the same way. She insisted that she be called Elizabeth, so I called her Liz and Lizzy just to piss her off." He lowered his voice to only Piper and Lucy. For some reason he intended to make a halfway good impression on Piper's parents. That consisted of toning down his language in their presence. "In the locker room she was known as Elizabitch. Horrible and evil woman." He slightly chuckled as a memory of the stuck-up hag that he didn't miss entered his thoughts. She just loved to tell him how he was a lost cause when it came to presenting himself to the general population. He shook it from his mind and drifted back to Margaret. "I'm sure your aunt will love me," he concluded, rising from his seat with both Piper and Lucy. He playfully winked at Piper after the comment, which sent little flutters throughout her stomach.

Emma and Nolan walked ahead of the girls. Tristan remembered that Piper hadn't seen her family in quite some time, so he hung back, giving her and Lucy some privacy. Unfortunately Lucy had a rather loud and high-pitched voice.

"He's freaking hot," she squealed. "Don't get me wrong, I looked him up online. Did you know there's a picture of him on the field without a shirt?"

"Yes," Piper hissed. "Just shut up." She pulled Lucy closer to her in hopes that her words would become even quieter.

"What about the sex? I bet it's amazing!"

Tristan quickly got out his phone and scanned through the news, pretending that he was not able to hear what they were going on about. He slowed his steps a little, but a part of him stayed close enough behind so that he could hear her answer.

When she didn't answer, Lucy pressed on. "Tell me something! A guy that looks like that has to be incredible when–"

"Yes, okay. The sex is mind-blowing, best I've ever had. Now shut the fuck up," she spat, shoving her sister forward toward their parents.

Lucy turned and teasingly stuck out her tongue, then caught up with her parents.

"The best you've ever had," Tristan whispered in Piper's ear.

She was taken aback by his closeness and nearly tripped over her own feet. "You heard all that?"

"She's something else."

"I just told her what she wanted to hear," Piper admitted, although a part of her wondered how many women would back up her words.

There were a million things that Tristan could say in response. All of them would heat her skin to boiling; however, he decided against it. He still had a hard time reading her. He knew she wasn't impressed with money. She probably wouldn't be impressed with him bragging about his skills in the bedroom.

Just before they entered the reserved dining room, Tristan reached for Piper's hand. Their eyes met, and both had to wonder if the other felt the buzzing electricity from their skin touching. Tristan saw that it did something to Piper when her cheeks turned to roses. What he couldn't understand was what it was doing to him; oddly, he became acutely aware of the beating in his chest.

# CHAPTER 8

"We're both so glad that you all could make it for our celebration in a place very dear to my heart that I will always call home," Samantha giggled as she nuzzled into Jared.

Lucy mumbled something about Jamaica instead of the frigid North Pole that Piper barely caught. Maine wasn't all that cold as of now; although it definitely didn't scream destination wedding.

"We have tons of activities set up for all of you. You should have received an email earlier last week, but if you didn't, we have some printed ones here," Samantha announced.

Piper didn't get an email. When she shot her little sister a look, Lucy only shook her head and stuck her finger in her mouth like she was about to vomit.

As if reading her mind, "Oh, it gets good. There's a hike, a dinner cruise, couple's massage sessions."

"You're kidding," Piper snorted.

Tristan had leaned in closer than needed and she could feel his breath on her with every word. Just his presence alone made her calmer. She hated how he did that. It was too much for pretend.

Once the narcissistic speeches concluded, the band started up and guests began to disperse to the bar that was set up, as well as the food table. In total there were only about forty to fifty people. Mostly the groomsmen, bridesmaids, and close family, which still led to a rather large number. All others would be arriving Thursday, two days before the wedding.

"What the hell is this? You'd think this is the fucking wedding," Nolan huffed shortly after the band started.

Piper excused herself and made her way to the food table. She was very aware that she missed every meal of the day so far. When she got to the table, she was only further disappointed. She'd look like a pig if she made a plate to suffice her appetite. There was no real food. There were tons of finger foods and a lot of healthy options, but nothing greasy or filling.

"Yeah, this blows." Piper didn't realize Tristan was present until that moment.

"If this is how it's going to be all week, I'll starve," Piper sighed.

Tristan pulled her away. "Come with me to get a drink."

Piper reluctantly went, although all she wanted was tea. They stood in line behind two very giggly girls who probably didn't need another drink. Piper immediately got the impression that they were two of the bridesmaids.

"That was just low of her, like disgusting. She's just jealous of Samantha and Jared," the brunette ranted, tossing her hair in the process.

"I can't believe she's so stupid to think he'd be into her. I mean, he's dated models! I just don't get it." The other girl then thought for a moment and gasped like an idea had fallen from the sky into her peanut of a brain. "I bet if you flirted with him, you two would so hook up."

It was obvious to Piper that the two girls were talking about her. She tried to tell herself that it didn't bother her, but it still hurt. She did nothing wrong to Jared and Samantha. She didn't say one tiny thing about the breakup to anyone, aside from Haven and her family. The fact that everyone thought she was this evil and vindictive person was insane.

She couldn't take listening to the two idiots in line; in fact, she couldn't take any of it. It was a bad idea to ever subject herself to this.

Piper was halfway down a hall leading from the dining room when she felt a strong grip on her wrist yanking her backwards. When she was spun around, she nearly collided into Tristan's chest.

"Why won't you say anything," he spat.

He was angry. She couldn't fathom why he'd be angry, and at her of all people.

"What are you talking about?"

"Those bimbos! Why don't you set shit straight?"

Piper shook her head. He didn't get it. "Samantha always comes out on top. She's this delicate little flower that can do no wrong. If I say anything, I'm still looked at as a crappy person. If I say how they really got together, people will only think I'm trying to get revenge. It's their word against mine, and honestly, it's just not worth it."

Tristan released her and suddenly she felt cold. She was losing her mind. Simple touches like that shouldn't have the effect they were, especially after a single day.

"Everything they said was wrong," he insisted.

Piper laughed. She knew he was trying to cheer her up. "Don't be ridiculous. You and I both know that if you weren't a nice guy and doing me a favor, which by the way you're doing for no benefit to yourself, you'd totally hook up with one of them. And that's fine, really, they're both beautiful."

"Clearly you don't know me," he growled, anger flaring in his eyes. "Just because that asshole cheated on you doesn't mean you shouldn't think more of yourself. You're brilliant and absolutely gorgeous, and if you can't see that, then I feel really sorry for you."

Piper couldn't feel any worse. She had never been like that. Ever. She wanted to scream at the fact that somewhere along the way she had lost her confidence and became so self-conscious. The most gut-wrenching part about it, a guy she barely knew was making her see that.

Tristan snapped Piper from her thoughts. "Now, do you want to go back to your room and cry your heart out over something so worthless, or do you want to get back in there and play this game."

Tristan nudged Piper playfully as they made their way back. "No one has ever labeled me as a nice guy."

That wasn't true. While most of the articles out there were only concerned with who was last seen hanging on Tristan's arm, which since his accident had been very few, if any, Piper was well aware of his charity work with children and animals.

"Considering how you play…"

She was teasing, but Tristan went with it. "Continue."

"I'm just saying. If you were still playing, you'd be giving Sergio Ramos quite a run with the cards."

Tristan laughed, really laughed. "First of all, I don't have that many. Secondly, I'm not a defender."

"Could have fooled me."

He loved the fire that blossomed in Piper. He wanted to see more of that, but upon reaching their table, he was forced to watch as a wave washed all that away.

Samantha and Jared, along with an older woman, Aunt Margaret, were going about from table to table greeting their guests. Margaret was easily identifiable as she dressed the part of a wealthy snob perfectly. Not a hair out of place and dripping in head to toe designer everything. Her whole ensemble cost more than a normal person's rent.

The three were just about to move on when Tristan and Piper approached.

"Oh, Piper," Margaret cooed, Piper's name dripping in disdain. "And this must be the boyfriend."

Silence followed for a moment. Piper watched as Tristan and Jared made eye contact. In that second, they didn't look like friends. Piper only became further confused when Tristan pulled her closer into him, in a more protective way than needed.

"Umm...Tristan this is–"

He interrupted her and held his hand out to the woman. "Aunt Maggie?"

Lucy snickered at the look that came across Margaret's face.

"Margaret," she corrected. She didn't take his hand, only eyed him up and down, her eyes cringing as they scanned over the tattoos.

Samantha cut in before her mother could say something potentially embarrassing. "How are your accommodations? We had rooms blocked out for the groomsmen and bridesmaids, but I didn't see that you had checked in." Her words were only directed to Tristan. Since Piper wasn't a bridesmaid, only an obligatory familial invite, she was on her own when it came to accommodations.

"We're actually in a different part of the resort." The smirk on Tristan's face told Piper just how much he was going to enjoy this.

"What different part," Jared asked with a look of concern and skepticism.

"We're in a suite near the ocean."

Both Samantha and Margaret gasped. Even Piper's parents appeared to be shocked. Piper had to wonder how much those rooms cost if it was such a big deal to be staying there.

"Only the best for this one. She deserves it," Tristan concluded, pulling Piper in and giving her a quick kiss on the top of her head.

"Aww! You guys are too cute," Lucy chimed in.

Nolan, who rarely laughed, chuckled once the three excused themselves to speak with another table. "Maggie. I love it. I'm going to start calling the old hag Maggie," he announced, throwing back a swallow of beer.

"You do know that woman is my sister," Emma said, appearing to be offended.

"That's not what you were calling her on the trip up here."

Lucy buried herself in her phone while Emma and Nolan playfully argued about Aunt Margaret.

Shortly before eight, Piper remembered that she still hadn't eaten. She was eager to get back to her room and hopefully find a pizza delivery nearby. She kept checking the time on her phone, wondering when people would be dispersing. It was still early and she figured they'd party for a couple more hours, but that didn't interest her in the least.

Tristan had excused himself to go mingle with some of the groomsmen. Piper expected that and was thankful that he wasn't attached to her the entire time; however, every time she looked up to find him, she found his eyes locked on hers. They had no expression, which was even more unnerving.

Just as Piper began to say her goodbyes to her family, Tristan pulled her away.

"Dance with me."

Piper looked around. No one was really dancing. The band was playing, but for the most part people were just mingling. She then noted the calculating look in his eyes.

"Okay, fine. I wanted to push your aunt's buttons," he finally admitted.

Piper became skeptical. "And your solution is to dance?"

"She's easy to read, all of them are. If they're not the center of attention for two seconds–"

"You're evil," Piper laughed.

Tristan neglected to tell her the conversation he overheard with her aunt and another woman. It would only do more damage than good. Margaret had gone on and on about how she knew Piper would end up with someone like him, someone jobless with no future. Either Margaret knew nothing of sports, or she knew exactly who he was and was trying to make it seem deplorable. The little he did know about Margaret, he was going with the latter.

Piper reluctantly agreed. Tristan was accustomed to attention, but she wasn't. The only thing that made it even remotely better was the fact that she could dance to most music and wouldn't end up making a complete fool of herself.

"I think you'll like the choice of song," Tristan told her when they neared the area that should have been used for dancing.

"You talked to the band? How did you know I'd say yes? Can you even dance?" Questions bubbled out of Piper's mouth.

"Just relax and have fun," he said, now placing her in front of him.

Piper could have died from laughter when the song started. Tristan was absolutely unbelievable. She tried to focus when he spun her around, but the giggles wouldn't stop.

"It was the only one of the three that they knew," he confessed. "A bit ironic too."

"And why is that?"

"Wasn't there some rule about occasional hand-holding," he teased, pulling her in for one of the two slower parts. If he was honest with himself, that was one boundary that he was both hesitant and curious about crossing.

"You've met your quota for the day," she quietly told him, unable to make eye contact.

Even though a few others had now joined in on the floor, Piper could feel most eyes watching them, but those did nothing to her. Tristan's were the only ones that made her uncomfortable and nervous.

"Do you trust me," Tristan asked before the song finished.

It was an odd question, one that Piper couldn't understand why he'd ask. It was also a very difficult question to answer, at least for her. Trust was a big word. The way he said it, with the sinister grim on his face told her that he had some calculated reason for doing so.

"Yeah," a voice unrecognizable to her own answered. She was shocked that it was so easy to say that.

A smile spread across Tristan's face just as the song was ending. Piper attempted to break from their embrace but Tristan pulled her closer.

His hand slid up her neck until it cupped her face, and that's when Piper realized what was about to happen.

His lips met hers, soft and hesitant at first. Only when he felt the tension ease from her body did he push further. It was intended to be a kiss just for show, but once he had her, he needed more. He needed to taste her. When he tried to part her lips open, she was compliant and willing, but she didn't allow him to take full control. She was giving just as much as she was taking and it drove him wild. When a moan vibrated from deep within her into him, he nearly came undone. A kiss shouldn't be having the effect that it was, and with the way his body was reacting, if it didn't stop soon, he'd have to drag her to the closest room he could find.

Breathless, he pulled away, hoping like hell that what she did to him wasn't too visible.

Whatever Piper felt during the kiss slowly faded with the ever-changing expressions on Tristan's face. At first he looked like he wanted her in every way possible, which then turned to confusion, and now his eyes bordered on horrified.

They were shaken from their bubble by the rest of the world. Neither knew if the applause was for the dance or the kiss. Piper's cheeks flushed with embarrassment.

"Get it, Reed," a groomsman shouted, raising his beer in the air.

At that comment, any moment between them that they may have had was lost.

"I think now would be a good time to call it a night," Tristan nervously laughed.

Several more remarks were made to Tristan as they left. Piper couldn't look at her family, but the dings on her phone that she neglected to silence let her know that her sister already had a comment.

Only when they met the cool night air did Piper feel her skin drop a few degrees. She knew why Tristan asked that question now, and she was glad that she had trusted him. Though the kiss was planned and nothing more than a gimmick, it was still amazing and left her on a high that she didn't want to come down from.

Tristan didn't know what to say. He intended to kiss her, but he never thought that it would turn into what it had. It wasn't *just* a kiss. He couldn't remember the last time he experienced a kiss like that.

"You really know how to put on a show," Piper told him, her voice cutting through his thoughts.

Her words were crushing, but he tried to hide the expression coming to his face. She was basically telling him that the kiss did nothing for her, that the kiss was just as much pretend as their relationship.

"Anyway, I should probably head back. I have some work I need to take care of," Piper continued when Tristan didn't respond.

"Do you want me to walk you back?" He felt like an idiot once he said it.

Piper nervously ran her fingers through her long blonde hair and avoided looking in Tristan's direction. "I think I can manage," she finally said.

There was a part in Piper that longed to be carefree and not bother about the consequences that followed, and tonight, that part was screaming to get out. If he walked her back, the entire time she'd be going back and forth deciding whether or not to invite him inside. Saying goodbye now was easier.

# CHAPTER 9

"Hey, sweetheart," Elijah answered.

"Now is not the time," Tristan huffed. He paced along the darkened shore, void of anyone else. "I messed up."

"Dude, I told you! If you're going to pierce your nipples I have to be there," Elijah joked.

"I kissed her," Tristan blurted out. Silence followed on the other end. "Eli?"

"That's what you called about?" His voice was exhausted and annoyed. "We're not in middle school. You kissed a girl. Big deal. Now if you have a threesome with a couple bridesmaids..."

"No. I kissed her...and...I don't know..."

"Hey, man. Are you okay," he asked, voicing real concern.

"I can't explain it," Tristan sighed, kicking at a rock. "I felt something."

"So, why are you telling me this instead of her?"

"Because the kiss wasn't real," he admitted.

"Dude, I am so confused here!"

"I kissed her just for appearances. I don't think it meant anything to her."

"You want my advice," Elijah asked, but before Tristan could respond, "Forget about it. Don't make shit complicated. Get through this week and then get your ass back to training. You and I both know that you've still got something left in you."

Elijah was right. It would be best if Tristan kept it strictly professional with Piper. He was doing her a favor and in the end they'd go their separate ways.

* * *

"Your temp screwed up Blythe's coffee. Twice! In one day," Haven shouted as soon as she accepted the call.

"Well, hello to you too."

"Why are you calling? Shouldn't you be doing whatever people do for whatever kind of wedding this is?"

"I needed to talk to someone."

"So you call someone from work," Haven teased. She knew they'd stay friends regardless where their jobs took them, but she always liked to pick on Piper about working so much that she couldn't even bother looking for friends elsewhere.

"Something happened."

"Okay. You've piqued my interest," Haven sang out.

Piper didn't want to throw it out there so bluntly, and she knew that Haven would want details. So she paced her room and started from the beginning.

The end result was Haven laughing so hard that Piper thought she might have to call an ambulance for her.

"That is," she began, only to stop to laugh again. "Oh, god," she sniffled.

"Are you done," Piper growled.

"That is the dorkiest shit ever. I'll never be able to listen to that song again," she coughed. "But damn, I bet Samantha and Jared nearly pissed themselves."

"I don't care about them." It was the honest truth. "What do I do now? We didn't really talk about it and just went our separate ways."

"You're sure that it was just for show," Haven asked, now becoming serious.

"Yes. He looked horrified after it happened. I don't know, maybe he wasn't expecting me to basically jam my tongue down his throat," Piper groaned as she landed on the bed.

"Then don't make things awkward. Don't be all clingy and try to find out if it meant anything to him. If it did, I doubt you'd be alone right now," Haven cautiously mentioned, knowing she didn't use the best choice of words.

Haven was right. Piper wasn't looking for feelings and a real relationship, and getting involved with someone like Tristan Reed was nothing more than a disaster waiting to happen.

After taking a long walk and attempting to clear his head from the entire day, Tristan was finally able to focus. The truth was, he did plan on playing again, soon. While he had options, his life was in California, plain and simple, but in one night a little voice told him that maybe it didn't have to be.

It was a little before ten when he returned to his suite, there he noticed a man leaving Piper's door. He couldn't control it; his heart skipped a beat. It wasn't until the man passed by him that he got a good look at what appeared to be nothing more than a teenager, a teenager wearing a shirt with a long Italian name and a giant pizza slice.

Tristan laughed to himself, but his stomach took note of what he had just seen and was very aware that he had only eaten a meager breakfast before meeting Piper earlier that day.

Tristan didn't want to go ice cold on Piper because of the kiss and what it did or didn't mean. After quickly changing into a t-shirt and shorts he decided to text her.

**Tristan: I'm still starving. Have you eaten?**

He walked up and down in every direction awaiting her reply. At least he hoped she would reply.

**Piper: Funny you mention that! I actually just got my pizza.**

**Tristan: That sounds like heaven right about now. Where from? Any good?**

**Piper: I haven't tried it yet. Trying to find a show. I don't think they deliver past ten. Sorry.**

Tristan typed and deleted what seemed like a million responses. Finally he gave up. For once he really didn't know what to say.

**Piper: I did go a little overboard.**

He was surprised that she didn't let the conversation die. And quickly fired off a reply, now curious as to what she ordered.

**Piper: Large pepperoni. Wings. Cheesy bread. Cookie pizza.**

Tristan laughed so hard that he was certain she could hear him through the walls. He honestly didn't know how she even attempted to eat like that and have the body that she had. His mind flashed back to one time when he and some of the guys were watching a game and she came in exhausted from work and yanked away a bag of their Cheetos, moments later coming from her room to throw the empty bag away.

**Piper: I'll share if you don't mind watching *The Golden Girls*?**

Tristan didn't want to appear too eager. While a part of him wanted to rip out his stomach knowing that pizza was so close, another part simply wanted to spend time with her. After only a day, he genuinely liked her as a person. Even when she was stressed out about nothing, she was still nice to talk to and be around. It was something that he never would have noticed in the past. He didn't want the rest of his week with her to be ruined just because of a mistake on his part.

\* \* \*

"Okay, it's not so bad," Tristan admitted, falling back into the couch.

Everything was eaten. Everything. They were both wired from the two large bottles of soda that Piper neglected to mention in her text.

"I'm actually into Sophia," he continued.

Piper shot him a look, and Tristan quickly realized how bad that comment came out.

"I just mean that she's my favorite. I do have an age limit," he joked.

"I've forced you to watch enough. Want to do an episode of *Monk*," Piper found herself asking.

Being around Tristan was easy. She didn't have to pretend to be someone that she wasn't. Even though it was after midnight, and she knew she'd see him tomorrow, she hated for the night to end.

"Actually, I should probably get some rest. I wanted to hit the gym pretty early." That was only partially true. He could have watched another hour or two of television with her, but he saw the sleepy look in her eyes as she gradually came down from her sugar high.

Piper walked Tristan to her door and he gave her a brief hug. When he pulled away, she was certain that there was something more in his eyes. She was certain that he glanced down at her lips. More than anything, she was certain that the kiss earlier had to have been more than just for show to those around them. She was also certain that she was sleep deprived and possibly looking for a raindrop in a desert. What she saw was probably nothing more than a mirage.

Piper sank into the door as soon as it closed. Her head was a mess. If she thought about the day as a whole, it was perfect. Every imperfect thing made it perfect. Worst of all, just being around and talking to Tristan was...perfect.

After going through her nightly routine, Piper plugged in her phone and climbed into bed. When the screen lit up, she was very much aware of the texts she had purposefully neglected to read.

**Mom: Do you want to send me to an early grave?**

**Mom: As soon as you left, Margaret told me what a 'harlot' you've become. Do people still use that word?**

**Mom: You're not responding. If you're having sex, please use protection.**

**Mom: Your father is hung up on calling your aunt Maggie.**

Piper couldn't help but laugh. She didn't expect for most of the texts to be from her mother. It wasn't until she went back to her main message feed that she saw a single text from her sister.

**Lucy: I'm not stupid. We need to talk. 9am? Mimosas at the bar?**

"Just fucking great," Piper sighed, throwing her phone back on the nightstand and turning off the light.

# CHAPTER 10

Piper was still accustomed to her work schedule. Despite whatever time she went to sleep, she was always able to wake in the morning by 6:00. She was a little lazy this particular morning, but found that she was able to dress in some athletic gear and make time for herself.

Normally Blythe kept her so busy that she had little time to work out. Actually, working for Blythe was practically the equivalent. She remembered that Tristan had talked about a gym in the resort. He had wanted to wake up early for that purpose. He'd no doubt probably already be there. As tempting as it was to head to the gym, Piper thought that it also might be a little creepy, plus, she rarely got to go running outdoors anymore.

Though the sun was already well into the morning sky, the air was still very cool. It was perfect running weather. Every step she took calmed her. Running near the shore had such a soothing effect, as if each wave washed away all her worries, freeing her.

When she didn't think she could go any longer, she reached for her phone, attached to her waist and glanced at the time. It was now after 8. She had slowly been making her way back toward the resort, but knew that by the time she got to her room, she'd have less than forty minutes to shower, fix herself up for the day, and hydrate before meeting her sister.

Just as the elevator doors were about to close, in stepped one of the last people Piper wanted to see. Jared.

He looked just about as horrified and uncomfortable as she did.

"Hey," he said, reaching for the same button that she had already lit up.

Piper began to panic, but tried her best to hide it. He shouldn't be in this part of the resort. Why was he here? Why hadn't he selected a different floor?

He casually broke the silence. "I thought you didn't like to run?"

That was incorrect, but Piper wasn't about to harp on the fact that he never listened to a word she ever said. "I never had time before," was her only response.

"Seems like a lot has changed with you in the last year or so."

Piper tried not to make eye contact, but she could feel his eyes dragging over her body. She wasn't dressed sexy, but her loose fitting tank top clung to her damp skin, revealing a black and blue sports bra beneath the thin material.

"What are your plans today? Are you coming on the hike with Tristan," he asked. Piper took notice to the bitter way that he said Tristan's name.

"I need to shower and meet my sister. I assumed the hike was for the wedding party, like just bridesmaids and groomsmen. I actually have–"

He cut her off. "To work."

Piper turned to him, an evil smirk plastered to his face like he knew her so well.

"I think your parents are even going," he continued to blabber. Piper watched the elevator finally get to her floor, and they both exited. "Your aunt was talking to her last night after..." Jared allowed his words to drift off, suddenly remembering why he had come to see Tristan.

Piper neared her door and froze. She couldn't go into her room. It would send red flags in all directions if she went into a different room, a room that wasn't with Tristan.

"Do you have your key card on you," Jared casually asked.

Piper pretended to search her pants. Of course she had her card. *Her* card, to *her* room. She didn't have one accessing Tristan's room.

Jared shook his head and proceeded to knock on Tristan's door. Piper held her breath, trying to think quickly. She needed to meet with her sister, but maybe she could postpone that. In any case, she couldn't go into her room. She thought of an excuse so that she could go downstairs and return once Jared was in Tristan's room; however, before she came up with anything, a shirtless Tristan, in nothing more than the shorts he slept in, answered the door. So much for waking up early to workout.

"Hey, man," he greeted. His eyes became more awake as soon as he saw Piper with him.

Piper could tell that Tristan was confused by the situation, and for once Jared's rambling paid off.

"I was coming up to see you and ran into Piper coming back from a run," he announced as he entered, which answered a few questions for Tristan.

Piper entered as well, unsure what to do.

Jared looked at her annoyed after a moment of pleasantries. "I thought you needed to shower and meet your sister," he said after looking at the time on his phone.

Piper looked to Tristan for help, but he only gave her a shrug and pointed to the bathroom. It wouldn't be so bad. She could take a shower, throw on her gross clothes and quickly step back to her room as soon as Jared left. He couldn't be staying too long if there were events he needed to get to.

"What's up," Tristan asked as soon as the door to the bathroom locked and the water started.

Jared paced around the room until he was at the large window overlooking the cliffs and the water below. "Last night, that was pretty low," he began.

"Oh yeah?"

Jared could sense the lack of seriousness in Tristan. "Did you really have to make a scene with her?"

"We just danced and got caught up in the moment. I didn't think anything of it."

"That's the problem, you never think," Jared growled. "I mean come on, dating her?"

Tristan became a little agitated. "What's wrong with that?"

"Whatever happened to bros before–"

"Let me stop you right there," Tristan interrupted. "She's nothing close to any words that you're about to say." He shook his head.

"Look, I just came to tell you that I don't appreciate what's going on between the two of you–"

"Then it's a good thing that neither of us need your approval," Tristan interrupted, but realized how harsh he came across. "Look, you've both moved on with your lives. We're cool, yeah?" The truth was, there had always been tension in their friendship. Tristan knew Jared would never admit it, but there was jealousy there. The fact that he was acting as Piper's boyfriend couldn't be helping the situation right now.

Jared only laughed with a sinister smile. "I've known you since high school! I don't know what this is, but you and I both know that you don't plan on settling down, and if you did, she's not the kind of girl you go for. She's basic and boring."

Tristan could have punched Jared, blackening every inch of his skin. Instead, "I think you need to go. We'll see you on that hike later."

Regardless what Piper was or wasn't to Tristan, no woman needed to be talked about like that.

Shortly after Jared left the water turned off, and Tristan rifled through one of his bags and found a black t-shirt. He quickly knocked on the door, assuming that Piper was about to put on the clothes she came in with.

"Yeah?"

"Just open it a pinch. I've got you something," he told her through the door.

Once Piper did as he said and realized what his offering was, "Oh, thank you so much!"

Tristan couldn't stop from staring when she emerged from the room a moment later. He didn't know if he had ever seen a woman in his clothing, but if he had, none of them had anything on Piper. His large shirt drowned her small frame, hiding all the curves that he knew were there, but she still looked adorable. Sadly, she had put her running pants back on, concealing her legs.

"Thank you," she murmured.

Her voice forced Tristan to stop scanning her body; however, he knew she was doing the same to him, particularly focusing on the brightly elaborate phoenix tattoo on his side. That's when he realized he had not yet put a shirt on. Normally he wouldn't care, but the given situation held an air of intimacy, and for some strange reason, he felt oddly uncomfortable.

"Anyway, I'm really late to meet my sister," Piper continued, looking away. "I'm sorry about all this," she said as she motioned her hands to the entry door, bathroom door, and her shirt. "He caught me as I was coming back from my run and assumed we were staying in the same—"

Tristan interrupted her rambling. "It's fine. I think it was mentioned last night. Plus, why wouldn't you be staying in the same room as your boyfriend?" He changed the subject slightly after the mentioning of the word. "He just came by to bring up a few activities. I hope I'm not being presumptuous, but I said we'd be joining the hike later today."

Piper fully intended to work on an article or two after her chat with her sister. She wasn't about to tell him that, as it had already been established numerous times that work was more important than anything to her. No one ever figured differently.

* * *

"I didn't think you were going to show," Lucy announced when Piper breathlessly sank into one of the seats at Lucy's chosen table.

Lucy already had two mimosas on the table and she was half into hers.

"Are you sure you're old enough," Piper joked, trying to get some air. She gulped her drink to match her sister, but she really would have preferred water.

"I've been meaning to mention, most loving sisters send alcohol when their sibling turns twenty-one. You sent me a voucher to the college bookstore," Lucy grunted.

"I'm helping with your education. Plus, you're twenty-one, go buy your own alcohol."

After moments of silence and sipping, Piper knew that her sister was planning something. Her text had been very ominous.

"That was quite a performance last night. I almost believed it," Lucy finally stated.

Piper couldn't reply. She wasn't sure what her sister was getting at, so she only shot her a dumb and curious look.

"Come on, Piper. I've known you my whole life," she began, nearly polishing off her drink. "The look on your face said it all. That was the first time the two of you ever kissed." She placed her glass down and signaled to the bartender. Spencer. "I am a little disappointed. I was really hoping the sex was as awesome as you said."

"Please don't say anything," Piper caught herself blurting out.

"I'm your sister. Hell no am I saying anything. I just can't believe you had to get a fake date," she concluded.

Piper saw the sadness in Lucy's eyes. Lucy felt sorry for her. That was exactly why she went through with everything in the first place.

"So everything was that obvious," Piper asked, panic beginning to set in.

Lucy laughed just as Spencer brought two more drinks. "To me, yes. To everyone else, that was an insanely hot kiss."

"Wait," Spencer interjected. "Was this with the guy who met you here yesterday?"

"You know the bartender," Lucy asked.

Piper felt a bit overwhelmed, and took a sip to avoid answering. "Yes, to both," she managed.

"Oh my god," Spencer gasped. "That was the guy doing you a favor? He is insanely sexy. And you kissed him! This week might not be so bad for you after all."

Once Spencer left, "You confided in the bartender and not me." Lucy acted like she was hurt, but Piper knew she really wasn't. "You're so paying for the drinks."

# CHAPTER 11

Tristan reached out for Piper's hand, to help her a few steps. It was unnecessary, especially if her parents could do it, but the gesture was sweet.

"Your mind seems to be somewhere else." His voice was soft, only heard by Piper.

"I just know that I should be doing other stuff."

"Work?" He didn't realize how cold that one word came across, and before she could answer, he forced himself to continue on. "I'm sorry if I opened my mouth about us going on this. If you need to get back, I'll make up an excuse."

"No," Piper lightly laughed. "I need some air anyway. Most of my days are spent in an office. This is nice."

Farther ahead they could hear squeals and piercing words.

"Is that a bug? Do I have a bug in my hair," Samantha shrieked.

"It's the outdoors, baby. There are bugs. Just flick it away," Jared grumbled.

"That is the dumbest advice. I don't know why you wanted to do this as a group activity. You should have done this with your boys," she spat back. One of her bridesmaids rushed to her side and helped in smoothing Samantha's now ruffled hair.

You couldn't tell from the looks of it, but Jared was very much into the outdoors. Working in finance didn't always allow for it, but he loved golfing and hiking. Samantha, on the other hand, Samantha loved shopping.

Without meaning to, Piper found her attention drifting to the arguing couple rather than watching her footing. It was a minor slip, one where she could have easily caught her own balance, but instead Tristan did.

"Are you okay," he quickly asked. Nothing happened to Piper, but those were the only words he could think of with her in his arms.

"Yeah. I'm a little clumsy today," she admitted, not wanting Tristan to know that her attention was on Jared and Samantha.

Tristan released her when he felt a hand clamp on his shoulder.

"None of that," Brian, one of the groomsmen, joked.

"Hey, man." Tristan forced himself to put all his attention to Brian.

"I'm going to go on ahead," Piper mumbled, excusing herself.

"I must say," Brian began, once Piper was out of earshot. "You did well with that one, much better than the hotel heiress."

Tristan didn't respond. Brian's comment made his attention drift back to Piper and the way her jeans clung to every small curve of her body. When he looked at her, he was constantly fighting with his imagination.

Brian found himself repeating his question that Tristan had tuned out. "Are you coming golfing this afternoon? All the groomsmen are going."

If Tristan was being honest, he'd much rather find something to do with Piper. He had been a little messed up since the kiss, so much so that he overslept and missed a much needed workout. He needed to spend more time with her; however, he knew what his purpose was for being present. He was the only one that didn't go to Vegas. He'd look like a total jerk if he started bailing on the guy only festivities.

"Yeah, sure."

The guide finally reached a stopping point, and most of the party was grateful for that. The majority of the younger guys were the office types. The most exercise they got was walking to the bathroom. Samantha and her friends clearly just did not like outdoor activities. Sitting at a pool trolling social media was about as far as they got.

"Lucy, stand there, by that tree. No, face that way. I want the water in the background," Emma barked with a camera in one hand.

Lucy grumbled and threw her small backpack at Piper. She then proceeded to do just as her mother instructed, although the smile was beyond forced.

"Good lord, woman," she shrieked. "Five is enough!"

"No, just one more. I don't think–"

"Save it for Piper," Lucy playfully teased, winking in Piper's direction.

Emma turned to Piper. "Piper get over here!"

"We're not children. You don't have to take so many pictures," Piper grumbled. She still followed her mother's demands.

"Wait," Emma insisted.

Piper thought she was done after a dozen clicks from the camera. Her palms turned sweaty as soon as her mother flagged Tristan over.

Emma frowned. "You two could at least act like you want to be together."

"Just take your picture," Piper hissed.

Tristan's arm snaked around her and his hand rested on her hip. "Give her a picture. It's not a big deal," he whispered.

Something about it was a big deal to Piper. They had all been hiking for more than an hour and Tristan still smelled crisp and clean. His cologne was simple but intoxicating; Piper picked up on notes of sandalwood and bergamot. She tried her best not to fall into him any more than her body already had.

"See, now that's adorable. Something to show the grandkids," Emma giggled.

Behind her Lucy began choking on a gulp of water at her mother's comment. Emma ignored her and only focused on the image through the lens. Once she was satisfied, she moved on to find Nolan.

Piper turned to face Tristan, making a mental note that his hand still lingered, though she had moved.

"I'm so sorry about that."

Tristan could see how embarrassed she was, but he wasn't sure if it was all from her mother.

"You deserve a medal if you make it through this week," she went on.

Tristan saw Piper's eyes glance down, down to his hand he didn't realize still rested on her waist. He quickly pulled it away. "It's not that bad so far."

Actually it was bad, very bad. The bride and her minions were one thing, Jared and the groomsmen another, and he didn't even want to start thinking about Maggie and the rest of Piper's family, but all of that he could handle. What he couldn't handle was whatever had started happening to him when he was around Piper.

"Piper, can I see you a minute," Lucy hollered, jolting Piper and Tristan back to reality.

"I need to go talk to some of the guys anyway," Tristan lied.

Piper could see that Lucy wasn't too happy. She should have taken Tristan up on his earlier offer to come up with an excuse so that she could be alone in her room right now.

"What's going on," Lucy hissed, dragging Piper by her elbow farther away from the others.

"I don't know what you mean," Piper started, which only elicited a scoff from her sister.

"I saw how you reacted, even before mom made that ridiculous comment." She shook her head, sadness coming to her face. "Piper, if this is all fake, you're going to get hurt."

"I don't know what you're talking about."

"You're starting to really like him, aren't you," she blurted out. It was a simple question, no need to tip-toe around it.

"He's a nice guy. Yeah, I like him, but only as a friend. After this wedding I'll probably never see him." Piper didn't realize how difficult those words would be to say.

Tristan acted like he cared what Derek was telling him, something about mortgages. Realistically he was intrigued with the conversation happening with Piper and her sister. At first her sister looked angry as hell, but that quickly faded to sadness. They were much too far away from him to pick up on any of it; however, once it concluded, he saw that a light had faded from Piper's vibrant green eyes. If he had thought it was nothing, something that would quickly pass, he was wrong once they started the walk back. Piper became distant.

He liked the little touches before, occasionally bumping into her side, holding her hand over rocky patches, even though it wasn't needed. That all changed.

"I'm good," Piper told him, dismissing his out-stretched hand for the fourth time now.

Piper would be lying if she said her sister's words didn't get to her. First of all, yes, Tristan was beyond attractive. That alone could get him any girl. Looks aside, he was really sweet. She hadn't known him that long, so he could be harboring some demons, but his life was pretty open. The worst thing about him in the tabloids in the past was his revolving door of girls, which actually slowed once he became injured, almost to the point of extinction. The only other problem he had was his aggression on the field. He had been a hell of a player, but he was extremely belligerent and competitive. Piper saw immediately that those were two separate people. When he wasn't playing, like now, he was relaxed and had a calming presence that she envied. Knowing all that, she lied to Lucy. There was a crush there on her part.

"Is there anything on your agenda for the day," Tristan asked.

Piper couldn't contain the little flutter within, wondering if Tristan had plans for them to do something together. "No."

"Cool. Hopefully you can get some work done."

With those words, the flutter was squashed, as though he had taken a baseball bat to a delicate little butterfly. "Yeah. Hopefully."

"I'll see you later. Jared and the groomsmen are due for golf in thirty minutes and I need to change." He hated being so mechanical and withdrawn, but Piper had done so first. He was giving her what he assumed she wanted.

"Have fun," she told him and went in another direction, not toward the elevator to their rooms.

# CHAPTER 12

Tristan regretted his choice to play golf before they made it to the second hole. Golf wasn't his thing. It wasn't that he couldn't play, he could, but it bored him. No one goes to watch golf and screams and throws beer when the ball goes in. He soon found out that apparently his buddies were using this whole golf bonding trip as a means to get away from the women and drink. He drank, not excessively, and he hadn't been wasted since his 21st birthday. He didn't like the lasting effect alcohol had on his performance. One bad game from a night of a few too many shots and he was over it.

By the eighth hole, he was done.

"We're all on our own tonight," Derek shouted, downing his fifth beer. "Who wants to find a bar away from the resort?"

A couple of the others were all in for that. Tristan had one beer earlier to be social, making it last for nearly an hour. There was no way he wanted to spend an entire night with these guys. He didn't realize how much he had obviously changed in the last year or so.

"What about you," Brian asked, patting Tristan on the back. He had opted out of a third beer. He gave up on a lot of that once he welcomed his first kid into the world.

"I should check with Piper first." Tristan realized what he said after it was too late.

"Dude! Are you that whipped," Derek busted out. "She tells you what you can and can't do?"

"It'll be fine," Jared chimed in. "She's probably working anyway."

Tristan didn't want to respond to that, and silence soon filled the air. So far no one had mentioned the commonality. Jared referring to her brought awareness to the rest.

"Let me guess," Derek continued. "You two are doing that couple's massage thing?"

"Hey," Eric spoke up. He was just as buzzed as Derek, but hadn't spoken much prior to now. "My wife and I have that on our schedule too."

Derek proceeded to laugh even more. There was no missing the fact that currently he was the only single one.

"Piper would never do that." Jared spoke up once again. Tristan hated it. It was like Jared was going to constantly bring up how well he knew her. Tristan forced himself to ignore it. People said and did stupid shit under the influence of alcohol. "She hates strangers touching her, actually most people. She's pretty frigid with that. Hell, she barely felt comfortable giving my mom a hug in all the time we dated," he added.

111

That Tristan did not know. His stomach flipped a little at the thought. Was that why she put only minimal handholding in her list of rules? Maybe that's why she turned so cold during the hike. Technically he was still a stranger to her. If that was the case, he fucked up big time with the kiss.

The glint in Jared's eyes made Tristan forget those prior thoughts. His competitive side told him that this was one pissing match Jared was going to lose.

"I guess things have changed since then. She was ecstatic when I booked us a spot," he responded. The satisfaction left Jared's face and he mumbled something about getting back to the game.

*Goal.*

Tristan tried to make it through another hole, but ever since Piper was brought up, he felt a tension. It was a tension that didn't need to be there and he didn't understand why it was.

He played with his phone and finally announced that he had to cut the game short. He had calls to return. It was only partially true. The calls could have waited. In fact, maybe they should have gone unreturned. He didn't know anymore. For once he wasn't sure about anything.

\* \* \*

Piper kept looking down at her phone. Her mother had planned a family dinner away from the wedding party; however, she insisted that Tristan come. Piper hadn't asked him. Personally, she needed space from him. How was that even possible? It hadn't even been two days and she felt as though she needed space.

Each time she thought about texting him, she decided against it. Jared always reprimanded her whenever she bothered him while he was with the boys. It was easy to assume that Tristan wasn't like that, but if he was busy, her words would only go unanswered.

She desperately needed to finish her article and she was having a terrible time at doing so ever since her mother told her about dinner. The only way she'd be able to get to work is if she had no other lingering things on her to-do list.

**Piper: Sorry to interrupt. My mom arranged for a family dinner.**

There. She had done it. She groaned because she deliberately made it so that she was informing him and not necessarily inviting him. Her thoughts of getting back to work were dismissed when no sooner than she put the phone down, it alerted her to a new message.

**Tristan: Cool. I think some of the guys are going for drinks tonight.**

He didn't know why he said that, but Piper's text came across as saying that she was busy. If she said anything else, he'd clear up any confusion. If she didn't, she could assume he was busy as well.

**Piper: I guess I'll see you tomorrow then.**

If that was all she was going to give him, he had no choice but to take it.

**Tristan: I don't think I'm going. Also, I think I'd like to catch a few episodes of *The Golden Girls*.**

Piper could have thrown her phone across the room. He made it impossible not to like him. Not wanting to send her next message, she decided to go for it anyway.

**Piper: My mom did invite you as well. I just assumed you'd have wedding duties.**

**Tristan: What time?**

**Piper: 7, but the restaurant is about a ten minute drive.**

**Tristan: Are you riding with them?**

Things had changed. Piper planned on going with her family, but it sounded like Tristan was accepting the offer; therefore, she left it at a single word and waited for his response.

**Piper: Depends.**

**Tristan: I'll meet you at 6:40 then.**

\* \* \*

Piper put a little effort into getting dressed that evening, probably more than she should have. She debated about wearing the dress Haven picked out, but decided against it. If it were just her and Tristan, she might have. Being almost thirty and trying to look sexy while eating dinner with your parents was plain pathetic. Instead she settled for a loose fitted top, skinny jeans, and a pair of dressy flats.

When she opened her door to the knock, which happened to be at precisely 6:40, she felt like an over-sized vacuum sucked all the air from the room. Tristan looked incredible in nothing more than a pair of dark jeans and a black dress shirt. The sleeves were halfway rolled up so that the intricate details on his left arm were still seen.

The look on her face said it all to Tristan. She was absolutely checking him out, and it appeared that he had left her a little speechless. He could have made a joke about it, tested her comfort level, but he was too pleased with the way she was looking at him that he decided not to ruin the moment.

"I did something stupid," Tristan announced once they got in the car. Piper didn't answer him, only gave him a brief glance. "I put us in one of the reserved massage spots."

"Why would you do that?"

He ran a hand through his messy dark hair. He thought about lying. "Some of the guys mentioned it today and then Jared made a comment how you'd never do that." He paused, trying to think how to make his following words sound better than what they were, but he lost all train of thought when a beautiful laugh fell from her lips.

"So you did that just to win some competition?"

"I wouldn't have gone through with it, but since the slots are paid for by Samantha's family, they see who attends."

"I can try." It was meant to be a thought in her head, but she said it aloud.

"You don't have to. I didn't know you don't like being touched." He flicked his eyes in her direction to gauge her reaction: an eye roll and a deep breath.

"Don't believe everything Jared says. He hasn't known me for a long time," Piper sighed.

She couldn't believe Jared told Tristan that. Was it true, yes, but it was something she was working on. Last week she even high-fived one of their delivery people for dropping off early.

\* \* \*

"I'm starving," Lucy whined. "That so-called meal last night was shit."

"Lucy! Language. This is a nice place," Emma hissed.

It was a pretty good place. Most of the Italian restaurants that Piper preferred were a little too romantic for a dinner with Haven. This one didn't look overly expensive and it held more of a family oriented vibe.

"What are you smirking about," a hangry Lucy directed to Piper.

Piper smirked. "Actually, when we left, I ordered pizza."

"You asshole! Thanks for the invite!"

"Damnit, Lucy," Nolan interjected.

Lucy raised her brow and crossed her arms, glaring at her father attempting to scold an adult for her language when his was no better.

Nolan ignored her and quickly tried to cover his mistake. "So, Tristan. Looks like you've come a long way with that leg."

"I've worked really hard."

Piper saw the proud gleam in his eyes. Soccer was his world. She didn't know how he lived without it.

"Thinking of playing again?"

"Yes, sir. Nothing has been set in stone, but I'd like to give it a few more years if I can." As soon as he said those words he swore that he saw a flash of disappointment come across Piper's face. "I'm aware that my age is a big factor against that, but I'm hoping that if given a chance, they'll see that I'm still in my prime," he continued.

Tristan and Nolan continued to talk about sports while Piper, Lucy, and Emma had their own conversation. Piper listened to Lucy rant on about her last year of college, but found that her focus wasn't fully on their conversation. From time to time she would look to Tristan only to find his eyes on her, and each time she felt a heat rush over her. It was a feeling that was very new and different.

Emma interrupted the story she was telling, something about Aunt Margaret and her neighbor's cat. "Sweetie, you'll have all night with him. I'd appreciate if you could listen to this story."

Piper froze.

"What are you talking about," Lucy asked through a mouthful of pasta.

"Your sister has barely heard a word of this because she's too busy making bedroom eyes," Emma teased.

Piper looked down at her plate, unable to make eye contact with anyone. Both her father and Tristan heard that comment.

A strange feeling stirred in Tristan as soon as Piper reacted to her mother's words. Her embarrassment was cute, but more than that, he had to wonder if there was even the slightest amount of truth to what Emma said. Thankfully Lucy eased the tension.

"First of all, eww! That is gross coming from you," Lucy squealed, pushing her plate aside. "Secondly, mom. Don't ever say that again. No one says that."

"Really?" Emma appeared to be genuinely shocked. "What do you say then?"

Piper cringed and shot her sister a mortified look. *Don't you dare say it.* The devilish smirk on Lucy's face said it all.

Very nonchalantly, "They're called fuck me eyes."

"Lucy, what the hell is wrong with you," Nolan boomed from the other side of the table.

Lucy was having a full on giggle fit and much to Piper's horror, Tristan found it all very amusing as well. Piper quickly excused herself to the restroom.

"Mother, get out," Piper groaned into the mirror.

"Don't act so humiliated," Emma laughed. "I was just joking with you. Although I really didn't know about the new phrasing that your sister pointed out."

Piper wasn't sure why she didn't do it sooner.

"We're not together," she admitted. When the up-beat and happy look on her mother's face turned to concern and confusion, Piper poured the whole truth out.

"Wow," her mother finally spoke. "You sure know how to make a mess of things."

"So, can you tone it down with grandbaby comments or whatever the hell that was back there?"

Emma didn't answer at first. Piper hated that. It meant her mother was deep in thought about what she had just told her.

"I hate that you felt like you needed a date. Sure those assholes would have said something about you being alone, so what? I raised you to be stronger than that." Piper felt like someone kicked her in the stomach. "I know that Jared cheating on you crushed your self-esteem, but if you let those insecurities linger, you're going to miss out on so much."

Piper thought she might cry at her mother's words. Sometimes the truth sucked.

Attempting to lighten the conversation, "Whatever arrangement the two of you have, you were definitely giving him fuck me eyes." Emma shook her head. "No, I hate that terminology. I'll stick with the old way."

Piper's oncoming tears faded into light laughter as she sank into the sink. Her mortification from the dinner had subsided, and something bigger took center stage.

After Jared left, she quickly realized that she wasn't genuinely in love with him. Marrying him would have been a mistake. Aside from all that, she couldn't help from feeling humiliation at being cheated on for so long and not realizing. She was ready to get past that. She couldn't let one bad relationship affect her self-worth, and that's exactly what she had been doing. Haven had pointed it out before, but something about right now made it stick.

# CHAPTER 13

"Stop apologizing," Tristan insisted as they walked into the resort.

"They're not usually that embarrassing." Tristan raised a questioning brow and Piper corrected herself. "Okay, yeah, they are."

"I'm pretty sure it was worse for me. After that your dad kept giving me this deathly glare."

"You didn't have to take care of the check because of that," Piper grumbled.

"I did that because I wanted to show my appreciation for being invited."

It drove Piper crazy how Tristan always seemed to say or do just the right thing to pull her in. Telling herself that this was only one week, only pretend, that by Monday he'd be in California and she'd be in New York, was becoming a struggle.

She pushed those thoughts aside when Tristan proceeded past the elevators to their rooms.

Seeing the confusion on her face, "Do you have a minute?"

Though skeptical, Piper followed. Just the little Tristan knew of her in less than two days, he could tell that she had a small comfort zone. If she wasn't with him or her family, she was in her room on her computer.

"The resort has a conservatory," Piper gasped, confirming Tristan's speculation that she didn't venture much. She then noticed the sign on the glass door that showed the hours. "Maybe tomorrow?"

Tristan shook his head. He wouldn't tell her that it was his intention to come after hours, knowing no one else would be around. He was still uncertain with Piper, uncertain of her thoughts and feelings, and definitely uncertain of his. Although gradually, what he wanted with her was becoming clearer by the moment, and it scared him.

Tristan pulled a card out. Piper only got a glance but it wasn't a typical hotel card.

"I may have talked to a guy," he admitted, holding the door open.

The awe and wonder in her face when she stepped through caused his chest to tighten. He could see that he had done the right thing by arranging this.

Piper moved along the paths, her eyes brightening with each new flower that she encountered. Tristan found himself unable to appreciate any of the plants. Her presence had captured him completely. The faint lights from above imitated that of moonlight dancing across her body. As the waves of her dark gold hair danced over her shoulders and along her back, the lights made every strand sparkle.

Tristan felt that there was a lot of ambiguity between the two of them. He hadn't been one to talk about feelings, and Piper gave off the impression of being closed off in the romance department. Taking her to the conservatory, when it would only be the two of them, was another impulsive decision. He had been making more of those than usual lately.

"This is so beautiful," she breathed.

He brought himself closer to her, but not close enough to scare her off. After her mother's comment, he saw how she was hesitant with every look and every choice of wording. "I thought it would be something you'd like."

"You do know, pulling strings to do this kind of falls under the 'no big gestures' category," Piper played.

"Honestly, those rules were ridiculous. I'm sure by the end of the week they'll all be broken."

Piper gave him a look that was lacking in emotion. He wondered if she was thinking about her list. He didn't want to bring it up, but there was absolutely one rule he would not break. If he did, it would break her in the process.

"Just so you know, my family knows the truth now," Piper blurted out, as she sniffed at a rose.

"Since when," Tristan asked. He was shocked. It didn't appear that way at dinner.

"Tonight." Piper thought for a moment. "Well, my sister knew after…" She let her words drift off. Thinking about the kiss only further screwed with her confusion over her feelings for Tristan.

"How did your sister know," he pressed on once he saw that she had a difficult time looking at him.

"Just…It's nothing," Piper said.

She moved down the path, distancing herself from Tristan, trying her best to keep their time together as casual as possible. Before she could collect herself, she felt a tug on her elbow that lightly spun her around until she was facing Tristan.

His light brown eyes twinkled with little specs of gold from the faint lights above. It was near impossible for her to look anywhere else.

There was a mischievous grin plastered on his face. "Piper, how did your sister just know?"

"Fine," Piper exclaimed, throwing her hands up. "She knew when you kissed me."

Tristan was a little confused. The kiss was awesome, perfect, bordering on the hint of something more. Seeing how uncomfortable Piper became mentioning the kiss, he let it go. He didn't want to know anymore.

"If we're just around my parents, you don't have to pretend anymore," Piper stated.

Tristan didn't know how to respond to that. That comment came across loud and clear that friendship was all she wanted from him. He was confident when it came to the opposite sex, but Piper had a way shaking his confidence.

He tried to lighten the conversation as they continued through the trees and hanging vines. It was then that he uncovered something he wasn't expecting. All this time that he thought Piper was working, she wasn't working solely for Blythe. Piper confided that the last few months she had been dabbling in freelance articles. She insisted that while working at

*Rogue Times* was a great opportunity, she needed just a bit more to add to her résumé, and the slight bit of extra income wasn't bad either. She was working on an article now about ocean pollution. Though she appeared embarrassed about her work, Tristan did get her to promise to allow him to read it once it was done.

"You sounded really excited about playing again," Piper mentioned. She paused and stood in the middle of the path, facing Tristan.

"It's something that's in the works," he told her, treading lightly with how much he divulged.

"I'm sure your teammates miss you."

Tristan rubbed the back of his neck, growing uncomfortable. "If Los Angeles still needs me." That wasn't the truth, not even close. Earlier that day he had done something else, one of the most impulsive and reckless things to date, but he knew if he told her, she'd freak out.

"Whatever," she laughed, playfully pushing at his arm. "They'd be stupid not to take you back. You're one of the best."

People said that all the time, but he had never allowed it to mean anything until now. Hearing her say it filled him with a pride that made him want to be the best. To be the best for her. That was part of the effect that she was having.

Piper's eyes widened when Tristan took a step toward her. His cologne mingled with the floral scents in the air. His eyes raked over her entire body, but darted from her eyes to her lips more than once. Another step and their bodies were almost touching. He reached for her face, her name a whisper on his tongue.

Piper waited in anticipation for their lips to connect, but before his hand could even grace her cheek, they were drastically interrupted.

Sprinklers shot out in all directions, quickly coating them from head to toe in icy liquid, and ruining any moment that may have happened between them.

Water droplets streamed down Piper's face, blurring her vision. She felt Tristan's hand clasp around hers and pull her beneath a small tree so that the water from above failed to reach them.

The darkness. The glimmers from above. The water cascading down their skin. His warmth on her. It was the most romantic moment she could think of, but the look in his eyes had faded.

"The door is that way," he informed her, motioning behind him. "The pavement might be a little slippery."

Piper gritted her teeth and nodded.

The elevator ride was silent. Tristan walked her to her door, but told her that he needed to go back downstairs to return the card. He informed her that their session was at nine the next morning, but if she didn't want to go through with it to text him first thing. Then he left, without so much as a hug goodnight, leaving her mildly annoyed and frustrated.

"You're going to be so pissed," Tristan began, once he stripped from his damp clothes.

"Well, when you start a conversation like that…"

"I might have a spot next season," Tristan blurted out. He sank to his bed, staring up at the blank ceiling and waited for Elijah to calm down.

"Dude! That's awesome! Who all knows," Elijah screamed on the other end, causing Tristan to momentarily pull the phone from his year.

"Just you for the most part. I have a meeting in a couple days."

Elijah paused and turned serious. "Why don't you sound more excited?" He heard Tristan sigh one time too many. "Shit, you did something stupid. You did something without thinking it through. Man! What the hell did you do," Elijah began rambling.

"I might be playing for New York."

Silence.

Dead silence.

Tristan pulled the phone from his ear and held it out, bracing himself, and it didn't take long.

"Are you fucking kidding me?! What the hell is going on?! Holy shit! It's the girl! Is this because of a piece of ass?!"

"Stop," Tristan growled. "It's not like that." He sat up, his whole body tense and on edge.

"Then why not come back to play for L.A.?"

"I know how crazy this sounds. That's why I didn't let myself think it through and I just went for it. I don't know what's going to happen with Piper–"

"Nothing! Because it's fake! Another stupid decision on your part," Elijah interrupted.

"I like her," Tristan quickly admitted. "I know there isn't a chance in hell that we'd have a shot if we're on opposite sides of the country."

"Do you know how psycho that sounds? You've known her for what, 48 hours," Elijah continued to chastise. "Just so you know, that's the title of a crime show, not some romance bullshit, and if you're serious about what you're telling me, you sound like the first. Stop being such a lovesick puppy and get your head where it belongs. Newsflash, it isn't New York. I'm sure the sex is great but there are a ton of–"

"We haven't even had sex." Tristan hated that he felt the need to clear it up and wished he could have taken the words back as soon as they flew from his mouth.

"Are you on drugs," Elijah honestly asked, to which Tristan only laughed. "I don't even know you right now."

Tristan expected Elijah's reaction. He was going to play for some team, why not New York? It would be a change. Realistically the only thing keeping him in California was soccer, and currently that was up in the air. If, at the end of the week, things with Piper were still nothing more than him helping her get through the wedding, then he wouldn't even tell her about his choice of team. She could find out in the media just like everyone else. Then an idea hit him.

**Tristan: How's the ocean article coming?**

The notification startled Piper. It also made her well aware that it was now after eleven. She definitely didn't expect for Tristan to be texting her so late.

**Piper: How do you know you didn't wake me?**

**Tristan: Because I know you.**

Again with the butterflies. It was a simple text but it continued to fuel her crush on Tristan.

**Piper: Fine. I'm almost done.**

**Tristan: Why don't you try writing an article for *Rogue Times*?**

**Piper: I doubt Blythe would publish anything from me.**

**Tristan: You'll never know until you try.**

**Piper: And write about what?**

*Rogue Times* catered to all women, and some men. There were the articles about fashion and beauty, even celebrity gossip, but there were also articles about politics and world issues.

Piper was stunned when she read the incoming text.

**Tristan: Me.**

# CHAPTER 14

Piper found sleep difficult after Tristan texted her. He had already gone above and beyond with helping her this week. Trusting her to do an article on his return completely floored her. She must have been on her computer until 2:00 coming up with something fitting. He actually gave her a list of rules.

*#1. Keep it professional, nothing bordering on tabloid.*

*#2. Don't mention any teams.*

She had to admit, his rules were a lot easier than hers, and so far she was off to a great start. After five hours of sleep, she felt ready to take on the day.

Tristan fully expected a text the next morning alerting him to a cancellation on Piper's part, but no. Instead she text him that she was going for a run and would meet him outside the spa a few minutes before their scheduled time.

\* \* \*

"I can't believe you're doing a massage," Haven squealed.

Piper was a little early for her meeting with Tristan and took a seat on one of the benches outside the doors to the spa. She had a few minutes and wanted to chat with Haven.

"You're secretly freaking out and doing breathing exercises aren't you," Haven joked.

"Actually, no. I'm a little anxious but in a good way," Piper admitted.

The hour long session included a thirty minute massage and then a thirty minute relaxation soak.

"Tell me you're at least wearing a sexy two piece," Haven mischievously asked.

"Nope. Fully covered one piece."

Haven grumbled her disappointment on the other end.

Tristan saw Piper talking on the phone and decided to hang back a minute, allowing her to finish her conversation. He didn't intend to eavesdrop, but when he heard his name mentioned, that idea faded.

"He's nice, that's all," Piper giggled. "I don't do flings."

"Right, relationship or nothing."

Piper twirled her hair, for a brief moment thinking what it would be like to be in an actual relationship with Tristan. She had to quickly dismiss it. It wasn't happening. "A relationship isn't something I'm looking for in the near future. He's nice. A friend. That's all. Just drop it."

"Wow. That sounded like a mess. You haven't convinced me or yourself."

Piper hated how annoyed she was by that. The times that she had been around Tristan, things felt real, and every time she allowed herself to fall a little more. She had to scold herself for being so ridiculous.

"I'm serious. I don't want a relationship, and if I did, it wouldn't be with him," Piper insisted.

Haven laughed on the other end. "You're so far gone it's not even funny. Look I have an edit to do real quick. Enjoy getting fondled."

"Uncalled for," Piper hissed, acting like she was angry.

"Love you too," Haven concluded, leaving Piper to continue waiting.

Tristan debated when he should announce his presence. Glancing down at his phone he saw that their session wasn't for another twelve minutes. He didn't want to spend that time anywhere near her after hearing that.

He took a walk around the resort, suddenly feeling sick. New York hadn't given him the green light, but he knew they were very interested the moment he contacted them personally. He had made worse decisions in his life, but never because of a girl.

Something about Piper was special and it killed him to think that he wasn't relationship material for her. Actually, she didn't exactly say it like that. Maybe she didn't want a relationship because she put her job to the forefront of her life. That didn't make sense either. She had that job for the entire two years that she and Jared were together.

Tristan didn't allow himself to get worked up over it. He just needed to put it in the back of his mind. It was only Wednesday. He still had several more days of pretending to be in a relationship with someone who clearly didn't want one. Perfect.

"I almost thought you were going to chicken out," Piper nervously laughed when Tristan approached.

He tried to act normal, like he hadn't overheard her very blunt conversation moments ago. "Are you sure you're not going to have a meltdown," he asked, trying to forget his disappointment.

"Very funny, I'm fine. You're kind of the one who looks a little nervous," she teased.

He let the conversation die and held the door open for Piper to step through. He was mildly nervous, but it had nothing to do with the massage.

The room they were taken to was beautiful, filled with tropical botanical elements and clean scents. Two massage tables, a little more than an arm's length away from each other, were in the center of it all.

"Don't laugh, but I searched last night about how this is supposed to work," Piper confessed.

Tristan found it a little humorous and couldn't hold it in. "You take off as much as you feel comfortable with and you get on the table. Pretty straightforward."

"Yeah, yeah. Smartass," Piper mumbled, taking her time removing her flats.

Tristan took no time at all and soon was only in a pair of swim shorts. Piper waited until he was on his table with his lower half covered by one of the drapes. He turned to her suspiciously.

"Any day now," he chuckled.

"Okay, well," she stammered. "Turn around."

"Seriously," he scoffed, now resting on an elbow watching her every movement. "You're wearing a swimsuit under that," he pointed out, motioning his finger up and down her body. "I can see the little bow that's tied at the back of your neck."

Piper shot him a narrowed look and turned so that her back was facing him. Hesitantly, she pulled her t-shirt dress up and over her head and scurried onto the table, quickly covering herself up to her waist.

Tristan did get a small glimpse, a black one piece. The back was completely open, showing off her creamy skin. Much to his displeasure, he wasn't able to see any of the front.

"I take it you don't go swimming?"

"I brought a bathing suit, didn't I," Piper shot back.

"I've seen your luggage, you probably took all precautions, even bringing snow boots?"

"I did not bring–"

Piper was interrupted by his outburst of laughter and hated that she didn't see sooner that he was just picking on her.

Tristan clammed up once the massage began. He fully expected two females. He didn't expect the muscular blonde with a British accent that had his hands all over Piper's body. If it couldn't get worse than that, he thought he might lose it when he heard what those hands were doing to her.

The sounds that fell from her lips whenever he hit a spot that was good for her did something to Tristan. Her moans and groans from how good he made her body feel pierced through Tristan's ears. It wasn't until then that he knew without a doubt he wanted to elicit the same from her.

"You seem so tense," Piper's masseur pointed out.

"It's been a stressful week," Piper responded.

Ten minutes later, Piper was having a decent conversation with Jacob. Personally, Tristan didn't care much about the woman working on him. She wasn't bad at her job, but she wasn't very memorable either. Her hands were cold and off-putting, doing nothing for him. No, that wasn't true. They were warm, but they were just hands. They weren't Piper's and, from the conversation that continued to linger in his head from earlier, they never would be.

"Oh, god. Right there. That feels awesome."

Tristan had to wonder how long they had been laying there and when it would finally end. He was thankful that by laying on his stomach, his reaction to Piper's enjoyment was easily hidden.

When thirty minutes finally came around, it couldn't have been soon enough. Once the two left the room, Piper sat up and tied the strings around her neck back into a bow, suddenly forgetting how shy she was around Tristan only half an hour ago.

Tristan didn't want to make it obvious how badly he was checking out every inch of her body, but knew he might not get the opportunity again. She was dainty and petite, with skin so pure and untouched, void of any intentional markings, unlike his. Her suit concealed just enough, allowing his imagination to run wild. At first he was hoping for something insanely low-cut, in hopes that one of her breasts might find a way of slipping out. What she gave him instead only heightened his desire for more, knowing that she wasn't putting her entire body on display with scraps of fabric.

"We can skip the hot tub if you want," he found himself suggesting.

"Are you kidding," Piper squealed. "After that? You can, but I'm dying for a nice warm soak." She rose and headed through the door that led to a small and private oasis.

Tristan debated. Going would only be self-torture. He didn't realize how intimate this would end up being for him. All he wanted at the time was to shut Jared up. He really needed to work on his competitiveness.

After a few minutes of silence, the sole sounds coming from the water bubbling around them, Piper opened her eyes, only to find Tristan's intense gaze on her.

"You look uncomfortable and tense. I thought massages were supposed to relax you," she pointed out, flicking a splash of water at Tristan.

"I have a lot on my mind," he replied rather coldly.

Piper watched him carefully. He appeared strangely frustrated and she couldn't understand. She cautiously considered how to progress the conversation, believing that something was indeed bothering him.

"Thank you for setting this up. I didn't think it would feel so good."

A chill ran through Tristan at her choice of words. She had no idea how good he wanted to make her feel. He hated how he suddenly had little control over where his thoughts were beginning to travel. "It didn't bother you?"

"What?"

"Him touching you," he growled.

Piper's eyes narrowed as soon as he asked. "No, he was great."

Tristan's eyes immediately left hers and every muscle in his body tensed up.

Afraid she had said or done something wrong, Piper continued on. "It's not that bad. I just always had an issue with people I didn't know very well hugging me," she pointed out.

When Tristan gave no response she left it alone and allowed her eyes to close and her head to fall back, enjoying the effervescence circling around her.

"What about me," he ventured.

Piper could feel her face redden and she quickly brought her head up, now wide-eyed. "What about you," she asked back, unsure how to respond.

"Are you uncomfortable with me touching you?" Since knowing Piper, he didn't know if he had ever been so blunt.

Piper met his eyes searching for something that would indicate that he was teasing, just playing around, but found nothing. He was dead serious with the question and she didn't know what he was getting at. Hell, she had allowed him to kiss her, even kissing him back. He couldn't possibly be serious.

"No, Tristan," she whispered, turning away.

In her moment of vulnerability, Tristan found that he was unable to help himself. He reached for her hand and before she could react differently, he pulled her through the water into him. He held her in his arms protectively, finally feeling the warmth of her skin against his.

"Are you sure," he continued, gauging her level of comfort.

Words were unable to escape Piper's mouth. Her head was clouded by the beating of her heart that was racing from her skin into Tristan's, the heat enveloping them coming from more than just the water.

Piper scanned over Tristan's body, drinking in every muscle, ever scar, every tattoo, until she reached his eyes, firmly locked on hers, the light brown turning darker by the second.

Tristan allowed his fingers to lightly and hesitantly graze over Piper's back, all the while watching the lust wash over her eyes. His body took on a mind of its own and he saw the panic crash through Piper's eyes once she felt the hardened pulsing beneath her.

"Tristan," she stammered. "I..."

He quickly, yet gently, threw her body from his and rose from the water, grabbing his towel and turning his back to her as he dried off.

"Sorry about that," he mumbled.

Before Piper could respond, he shot off some excuse about needing to cut his time short, leaving her alone, both confused and aroused.

# CHAPTER 15

Being rejected like that was one thing. Little did Piper know how much worse her day would get.

She couldn't believe that she was being subjected to lunch with her aunt. Her mother and sister were there as well, but that didn't help at all. Her aunt hated her, plain and simple. It hadn't been all her life. Her aunt was always a bitch, but ever since Samantha and Jared got together, she had it in for Piper more than usual.

Piper sat picking at her salad and ham sandwich on the second floor outdoor balcony café. It was one of the several restaurants located in the resort. At the moment, Margaret was complaining about how they should have waited for a table inside. She didn't like the breeze. Piper welcomed it, finding that it soothed the heat that still lingered from Tristan.

"You'll understand when one of your daughters get married," Aunt Margaret concluded.

Piper had tuned her out. She had no idea what the conversation had been about, but the look on her mother's face seeped in annoyance.

"I know, right," Lucy began with a mouthful of food. "Thank goodness same-sex marriage is legal now, otherwise I'd be fucked."

Margaret coughed on a tomato and Emma attempted to kick her daughter beneath the table. Piper only shook her head and rolled her eyes at her sister attempting to get a rise out of their aunt.

Lucy winked at Piper, and Piper knew that her sister wasn't even close to done. "It's cool, though. I still have a year of the college thing. Call me a feminist but I'd like to be able to make it on my own, with an education, not just a man."

If Margaret's lips could get any tighter, they'd be sucked into her whole face.

Though Margaret tried to act as though her life was perfect, the truth was that her pride and joy didn't finish college. Samantha, a little older than Lucy, started college late, after not taking high school seriously. How the hell she managed to get into NYU astounded everyone. Actually, not really. Money worked wonders.

Piper was nice, too nice, and despite what she thought about her family, she was always ready to help out. When her mother mentioned the idea of Samantha staying with Piper for a month until her apartment was ready, Piper was reluctant, but agreed. A month ended up being three, and then one night Piper walked into the end of her relationship with Jared. Needless to say, Samantha barely made it through her first year before calling it quits.

The comment from Lucy about college was enough to start a world war, yet everyone remained civil and quickly changed the subject.

\* \* \*

After the massage and hot tub incident with Piper, the only way Tristan could manage not to combust in his own skin was to run. If he did it long enough, it would weaken all the carnal thoughts that kept racing through his mind.

The blaring music in his ears did nothing to erase Piper. He had to wonder if he made a mistake. Maybe he should have gone for it in that moment. Then he remembered the conversation. The tabloids made sure to point out that he was not relationship material, obviously Piper knew that. Hearing those words from her call was devastating. Then he saw the look of horror in her face once his penis betrayed him, reacting more to her closeness than his own mind.

After two hours, the steps became harder, as they should have. He had done more than just a casual jog. He wanted his body exhausted, to be drained of life, to not feel.

When he finally had enough, when his face and chest were drenched in sweat, he headed back. As he trudged across one of the plazas, he heard the rushed tapping of heels closing in.

"Tristan Reed," a girl giggled.

When he turned, he immediately recognized the two women. They were the same two from the first night, some of Samantha's bridesmaids.

He nodded in acknowledgement. He didn't want to have anything to do with them after recalling the conversation they had about Piper.

"I'm Bridget, and this is Erin," the brunette introduced.

The blonde, Erin, proceeded with a small and innocent wave.

"Hi," was all Tristan gave them. He wanted to shower and pass out. He didn't have time for whatever this was.

\* \* \*

"Are you kidding me," Lucy gasped, nudging Piper and pointing over the balcony.

Piper felt sick and dizzy when she looked over and into the plaza. There stood a shirtless Tristan with two of Samantha's friends. She cringed when the dark haired one ran her hand over Tristan's bicep. It shouldn't have, but jealousy crept through her veins like the most poisonous venom.

Emma and Aunt Margaret took notice and directed their attention over the railing.

"Oh, that's Erin and Bridget. They're such sweet girls," Margaret announced.

Lucy shared a look with Piper. They were both well aware of girls like that. Piper shook her head and sank back in her chair, trying to ignore the situation below.

"You'd think he could at least put a shirt on," Margaret huffed.

For once, Piper agreed. She hated seeing the way those two were drooling all over him. She especially hated the one that actually touched him. If she could have broken all her fingers, she would have.

"I'm going to say something," Lucy whispered through gritted teeth.

"It's not worth it. Let it go," Piper insisted.

* * *

"We have a few girl things but we're free after 8. Maybe you could come out for drinks with us," Bridget asked in an overly seductive voice.

Tristan wasn't an idiot. He knew exactly what *drinks* meant for someone like Bridget. Both the women before him were attractive and looked exactly like every other girl he had known, except one. The dyed hair, low-cut tops with fake cleavage spilling out, and insanely short skirts just wasn't doing it for him right now.

"I have plans with my girlfriend," Tristan responded, perhaps a little coldly.

Their eyes widened in disbelief. Tristan genuinely couldn't believe that they thought they could lure him in so easily. Before either had a chance to respond, they were interrupted by shouting from the café balcony.

"Skank alert! Skank alert! Your results came back, you've tested positive for parvo!"

Tristan turned to see Piper pulling Lucy back to her seat. While a part of him found humor in the situation, another part felt dread. He wondered how much Piper had seen and what she thought. He shook that. She was a woman; he knew exactly what she thought, and he hated that she would for a second think that he was entertained by the idea of either of the two females in front of him. "What a bitch," Bridget huffed underneath her breath.

* * *

"Damnit, Lucy," Emma hissed. "What the hell is wrong with you?"

Lucy shrugged like she had done nothing wrong. She had caught the attention of some of the other diners, who were quick to look over the balcony.

Piper glanced in Margaret's direction. She was seething from Lucy's outburst. If her eyes could set Lucy ablaze, they were dangerously close to just that.

"I swear," Emma sighed, pretending to be more disappointed than she actually was. "They had to have given me a different child when I left the hospital."

Once they were finished eating, Emma and Margaret went their separate ways, but Lucy hung back for a moment with Piper. Eventually she insisted that they go to the bar. Piper wasn't fond of drinking in the middle of the day, especially when she had writing to do; however, she was aware that Lucy had recently turned twenty-one and wanted to live it up, so she reluctantly agreed.

"Water, seriously," Lucy grumbled. "I can finally go to a bar with you and you get water."

Despite not at all being in the mood for laughter, Piper chuckled at the comment. "Someone has to make sure you can stumble back to your room."

"I'd like to stumble into Derek's room," Lucy admitted with a playful wink. Before Piper could lecture her, "Yeah, yeah. I'm aware that he's nine years older, and he's one of the wilder ones. So what?"

"Here you go, darling," Spencer interrupted with their drinks. Rather than leaving them, he rested his elbows on the bar and continued making small talk. He and Lucy hit it off instantly, like they had been friends their whole life.

\* \* \*

The cold shower after the run helped ease some of Tristan's frustrations, although it would only be a matter of time before they scurried back in full force. He threw himself on his bed, completely exhausted.

He reached for his phone, expecting some kind of message from Piper, but had nothing. He considered texting her, feeling the need to clear up what she saw with Bridget and Erin, but he wasn't sure how to go about mentioning that.

Then a thought hit him. He remembered one of the worst games of his life, back in the beginning of his career, the night before he drank a little more than he should have. He was dehydrated, fatigued, and played like shit. He fully expected one hell of a lecture from his coach. He didn't receive that. His coach's disappointment was far worse than any lecture. Though he didn't give Tristan life altering words of wisdom, what he did say stuck.

*If you're not willing to put all your effort into the game, your whole head and heart, then you might as well not even play.*

That was the last time Tristan ever drank the day before a game.

Considering how that advice could relate to Piper as well, he picked up his phone.

* * *

"You did not," Spencer gasped after hearing Lucy's story from lunch.

"You don't even know the half of it. Those two are the quintessential mean girls," Lucy continued, sipping on her second concoction now.

Piper's phone made a ding and they both sent her a look. Piper glanced down to see Tristan's name fading from the screen.

"Oh my god, it's him," Lucy screeched as soon as she saw the look on Piper's face. "What did he say?"

Piper wasn't sure if Lucy was excited or angry. The alcohol had already started impairing her sister's range of emotions.

**Tristan: Dinner tonight?**

Piper held the screen so that Lucy and Spencer could see it.

"What the hell is that supposed to mean," Spencer scoffed. "That's a crappy way of asking you on a date."

"It wouldn't be a date," Piper insisted. "Just dinner."

Lucy made a noise that sent remnants of her drink flying from her mouth. "He deliberately worded it like that so that he could gauge your reaction. If you ask him if it's a date, he'll know that the idea crossed your mind. If you don't say anything, he'll be left to wonder."

"Yeah, but then we still don't know if it's a date," Spencer chimed in.

Piper allowed them to debate on it, tuning them out as her thumb hovered over the screen. Her pulse raced knowing that Tristan wanted to spend time with her tonight and not anyone else. Not wanting to be too eager or to assume anything, she kept her response short. She wasn't sure what she was doing, as it had been some time since she was in a situation as such.

**Piper: Sure.**

**Tristan: Reservations at 7. Don't wear jeans.**

Two sets of eyes were focused on Piper. She rolled her own and held up the phone.

"That sounds like a real date," Spencer immediately told her.

"Not really. It just means they're going somewhere nice," Lucy huffed.

The conversation soon changed and Piper couldn't have been more thankful. Once Lucy was finished with her drink, she began to leave, telling Piper to pay because she was still a broke college kid.

"She's something else," Spencer commented, waiting on the credit card to process.

"You'd never know we're actually related," Piper chuckled.

"Now that she's gone," Spencer leaned in and whispered. "Text your friend to meet you here for a drink before dinner."

Piper eyed him with a great deal of skepticism.

"Look, if I know one thing from working at a bar," he began. "Actually, no. I know so much about human behavior after this job."

"Spencer," Piper sighed, sensing that he was getting off topic.

"Sorry. Look, he made you a little jealous with dumb and dumber right?" Though she didn't want to admit it, Piper nodded. "Return the favor. I promise you that in the process, you'll know loud and clear if it's a date."

It was juvenile. Spencer even acknowledged that. It was also something Piper never would have done, and that alone made her want to do it even more.

# CHAPTER 16

Tristan hadn't thought things through, as usual, when he sent Piper that text. He shouldn't have messaged her at all. He should have knocked on her door and asked her out in person.

He had put serious thought into his appearance, even adding a sport coat. He planned on putting effort in tonight. It had been a while since he had gone on an actual date. Most of his time was now spent dedicating himself to rehabilitation and training, but that was paying off. Now there was only one thing he wanted more than soccer. Piper.

As soon as he walked in the resort's bar, he felt like he was drowning in the depths of the Mariana Trench. To say that Piper took his breath away was putting it mildly. She always looked beautiful, but tonight she was insanely gorgeous, so much so that he could feel the nerves working their way into his throat, and he rarely got nervous.

Piper looked up from her glass of water and met Tristan's gaze across the room. His face held little expression, like he was deep in thought. She gave him a small smile and glanced away, feeling his presence gradually coming closer.

She debated about her choice of wardrobe for nearly an hour, very unlike her. Though she was self-conscious about the dress Haven had picked out on their shopping excursion, she went with it. It was a one-sleeved black number, form fitting at the top and flaring off at the waist. It was a little tighter and shorter than Piper would have liked. Balancing the asymmetrical style, on the side without the cap-sleeve, snaked a line of dark teal roses.

"Hey," Tristan managed, once he reached the table. Such a simple word had become difficult.

"Hi."

Tristan tried to ease the awkwardness by getting them a drink. When the waitress left to get their order, he decided to ask Piper about her article and that's when her face lit up. He dreaded whenever there was an article about him, but from the sound of it, Piper was doing a good job so far. He knew it would go a long way for her if she decided to break away as Blythe's assistant.

"Are you sure you don't have wedding duties or something," Piper asked in between sips of white wine.

Tristan honestly didn't care if he did. He was positive that where he was right now was where he was supposed to be. "Not that I can think of." He was hesitant to bring up events from earlier, but they had become so comfortable now that he decided to go for it. He didn't want Piper thinking for a minute that he was interested in any of Samantha's friends. "Your sister had quite the outburst."

Her laughter at the comment was one of the most seductive sounds she could have made. "We were at lunch with my mother and Aunt Margaret, so you can imagine how that went." She intentionally skirted around mentioning Bridget and Erin; however, was shocked when Tristan was the one to bring them up.

"I'm thankful she spoke out when she did," he began, taking a sip of his beer. "I was exhausted from my run and they just didn't get the hint." He watched for any type of reaction on Piper's part and was only satisfied once he saw the relief come across her face. He hated that those girls ever walked up to him.

"Excuse me," the waitress hesitantly interrupted. "This is for you," she whispered to Piper, setting another glass of wine before her.

"I didn't–"

"It's from the gentleman at the bar," she told her in a very low voice.

Tristan heard her words loud and clear. He and Piper both looked in the direction that the waitress nodded. A man around their age held up a glass of something amber and winked at Piper.

A strange feeling shot through Tristan like a bolt of lightning. He could not believe the audacity. What guy buys a woman a drink when she's clearly on a date with someone else? He tried to remain calm, tearing his eyes from the man and back to Piper.

Piper wasn't sure she could go through with it. Spencer's so-called plan was the most immature thing she had ever done. She wasn't good with playing games; she wasn't even good with flirting. After taking a moment, pretending to check the man out, she brought her attention back to Tristan, acting as though she was flattered.

"Do you know him," Tristan asked through gritted teeth.

"No, but I should probably thank him."

Tristan didn't know if she was being serious right now. On her behalf he gave a nod and two finger wave to the man at the bar. "There."

"What was that?"

"I told him for you," he huffed.

His tension came through with every word, and Piper hated what she was about to do. "I'll be right back." She could feel her hands shaking as she quickly rose before Tristan could say anything else.

She made her way to the man at the bar, daring not to look back at Tristan. Along the way she made eye contact with Spencer, who gave her a very subtle thumbs up.

Piper held out her hand to the man once she reached the bar, making sure she kept her back to Tristan. She was horrible at acting; her facial expressions would give her away.

"Nate," he told her.

"I take it you're a friend of Spencer's," she asked, a bit embarrassed by the situation.

"It's a little more than that," he admitted, attempting to look as though he was flirting with her.

"Oh, wow," Piper began, a little shocked.

"Usually between the two of us, I'm the one getting hit on by both men and women. He thought I'd be perfect for this little ruse," he told her. The situation was awkward for him as well, but he generally went along with Spencer's strange ideas. "So I'm going to write a number down on this napkin," he told her as he reached over the counter for a pen. After seeing the look on Tristan's face, Nate had absolutely no intention of writing down his own number. "Whatever you do, make sure Zeus over there doesn't call it. It's the number to a local Chinese place. Sorry," he laughed. "It's the only number I have memorized. No idea why."

"Zeus," Piper questioned.

"Yeah. If I don't get out of here soon, it looks like your boy is going to start throwing lightning bolts in my direction."

Piper still couldn't turn around. Tristan always appeared so calm. Could he really be jealous? A sick part of her definitely wanted that to be the case.

When Nate handed her the napkin he stepped in to whisper in her ear. "Whether you believe me or not, it's absolutely a date."

Piper's heart raced at his words. She gave herself a moment, trying to collect her sanity, after he left. She hadn't been on a date in quite some time. Being around Tristan was easy. They were either faking it for the purpose of the wedding or hanging out as friends. Something shifted in her now. She had considered that it might be a date and that he might be into her. What she didn't consider was how she'd act if that thought was confirmed.

When she returned to their table, she shoved the napkin in her purse, knowing that Tristan was very much aware as to what it was. She proceeded to gulping down her wine.

"Well..."

"He was nice," was all Piper managed to say.

"Are you into him," Tristan pressed on, watching her every movement.

"I just met him," Piper pointed out.

"Physically," Tristan continued.

Piper nervously laughed. "That's a little shallow."

"So be shallow."

Tristan's carefree attitude was gone. When he cracked his knuckles and didn't remove his gaze for a second, Piper knew he was absolutely serious. He wanted to know what about that guy Piper found attractive. Piper considered dismissing the topic altogether, but Tristan could be quite persistent.

"Fine," she began, tearing her eyes from his. "Well..." She thought. To be honest, while Nate looked nothing like Tristan, they did share similar and vague traits. Tristan was going to hate what she was about to say. "He has a nice body, clearly works out. I'm generally more attracted to darker hair tones, so he has that going for him. Oh, and he had a tattoo, a ship, on his forearm. Incredibly sexy."

Tristan sat back, crossing his arms so that the sleeve of his jacket came up a little. Piper saw what he was doing. She had intentionally described the characteristics that both he and Nate shared. Tristan could have pointed that out; the door was wide open, but he chose not to.

"We should probably get going, reservations and all," he announced calmly, but his body language suggested something entirely different.

✳ ✳ ✳

"It should be under Reed," he told the hostess when she asked about his reservation. Apparently that was the only way to get into the place, despite the fact that there were several available tables throughout.

"Oh, yes. I see you had a few extra specifics," the woman giggled, eyeing Tristan up and down.

There was a stab of jealousy there, but Piper was very much aware that Tristan wasn't attempting to entertain the woman at all. It was difficult reminding herself that Tristan was a famous athlete that women threw themselves at. To her, he was just Tristan, a sweet, funny, and kind person.

Piper swallowed hard and had to repeat to herself to breathe once the hostess led them to their table. It was a secluded corner booth, away from most of the other patrons, very private, and with far more candles in the area than those near the other tables.

As soon as Piper sat down, Tristan could tell that it wasn't what she was expecting. She looked more nervous and uncertain than she had the entire week. Technically, finding this place and taking her would have fallen under the 'no big gestures' category; it was then that he was thankful that the menu didn't include the prices. There was no doubt that Piper would make a big deal about it.

Before the waitress took their orders, two glasses of wine were placed on the table. Piper eyed Tristan suspiciously, but said nothing, wondering if the specifics referred to earlier included a secluded table, extra candles, and now a wine that looked more expensive than the average bottle. She had to give it to him, it was insanely good wine.

"This is really nice," she admitted, once she had decided on the steak dinner of her choosing.

"I didn't tell you earlier, but you look beautiful. You always do, but..." He let his words trail off.

He wasn't good with that kind of shit. Generally women were easy for him, but Piper was different. He couldn't just tell her that she was hot and suddenly she'd throw her panties at him. Piper was the kind of girl that wanted to be wooed, and that had definitely never been his thing.

"So, brunch and that dinner cruise tomorrow," Piper began, not sure if it was a statement or a question.

"Unfortunately, yes." He reacted quickly when he saw her uncertainty. He didn't want her thinking that the unfortunate part would be attending with her. "I'm not a fan of boats." He loved hearing Piper laugh; it gave him the strangest warming sensation. "I mean come on, *Titanic*?"

"I doubt there are any icebergs off the coast of Maine," she assured him.

He was glad that the tension had gone away, and Piper was able to relax. Sadly for him, listening to her eat was nearly as bad as listening to her massage from earlier. The damn food was even doing it for her.

"I'm kind of wondering why you're even here," Piper said in between bites.

Tristan found her question odd. "What do you mean?"

"I don't think you've enjoyed yourself since you've been here," she pointed out.

He debated being bold, remembering how she froze when he complimented her, but also knowing that if he didn't go for it, someone else would. "I'm enjoying myself now, with you."

Tristan tried his best not to laugh when her fork slipped from her hand and clanked on her plate. Redness crept to her cheeks and while she looked nervous, he was sure that she enjoyed it.

"I mean, you left golf early," she stammered, hating what Tristan's few words were doing to her.

"I left golf early because all they wanted to do was get drunk," he pointed out. "Also, I think there's a little tension with Jared." He didn't mean to admit it, but it slipped out.

"I'm sorry. I really hope that you doing this favor for me doesn't ruin your friendship with him."

Tristan hated everything about that sentence. He and Jared had been insanely close in high school, but that was more than a decade ago. They had both changed in that time and their high school bond wouldn't be enough to keep them together forever. If he truly thought about it, he didn't even understand why Jared would ask him to be a groomsman.

What bothered him most of all about her statement was the idea that she still thought he was doing her a favor. Did he have to tattoo it on his forehead that she was currently on a date with him? He hadn't specifically referred to the evening at any point as being such, but didn't girls always jump to conclusions with those things? His insides twisted at the thought that Piper didn't think this was something more.

# CHAPTER 17

"That food was amazing. Thank you so much," Piper said for the millionth time as they exited the elevator.

They continued on toward their respective rooms. Tristan couldn't believe the nerves that were kicking in. He never had issues with girls, but Piper was something else entirely.

He grabbed her wrist delicately when she reached into her purse for the card to her room. Their eyes met and Piper saw a change in Tristan, his light golden brown eyes growing darker with each passing moment.

"Give me the napkin." His voice was deep and raspy.

Piper's eyes widened in confusion. She opened her mouth to speak, but Tristan proceeded to cutting her off.

"I know he gave you his number," he growled, taking a step closer, towering over Piper. "Give it to me."

She wasn't accustomed to someone being so assertive and demanding. She debated for a moment. Surely Tristan wouldn't call the number. If so, she'd have to brush it off that obviously Nate wasn't all that interested and gave her a fake number.

He released her wrist and waited. Piper pulled the napkin from her purse and handed it over. Tristan didn't even look at the name or number written on it. Once he had it in his possession, he tore it to shreds, allowing them to fall at their feet.

Piper didn't know how she felt about that. A part of her found it a little aggressive, but another part found that it turned her on. She took a step back and her body collided into the wall that separated their two rooms.

"That was a little unnecessary," she stated.

Tristan took a step forward. If he could play in front of thousands of people, he could do this. "You don't need his number. You have mine."

"How do you know what I need," Piper asked before she thought about her choice of words.

Her heart pounded in her chest when he took one more step, their bodies now separated by only a breath. Heat rose throughout every part of her, and she pressed her hands to the wall, hoping to steady herself. Tristan's right hand came up to the wall beside her head. She expected him to whisper a smartass or cocky comment in her ear, but that never happened.

He lowered his face to hers. "If I kiss you right now, I won't be able to stop." The way his words came out sounded like it was the most painful thing in the world for him to admit.

He waited for a response from Piper, but got nothing. Lust flashed through her eyes and selfishly, he took that as a green light. His lips crashed into hers with a hungry passion that needed to be fed. It didn't take Piper long to respond; she wanted it too much. Tristan pushed himself into her, plastering her body to the wall. Her taste on his tongue was better than he could remember. The best part, now they both knew it wasn't pretend, wasn't for show.

Tristan pulled his lips from hers and softly sank them into her neck. He wanted every inch of her body. Piper let out a breathy moan when he lightly tugged at her skin.

"You don't know how bad you screwed me up today," he groaned into her ear.

"What," was all Piper could respond. His breath sent sensations throughout her body that left her unable to think.

"When we were getting massages. You don't know how much I wanted you. It pissed me off to no end that another man's hands were on you, giving you pleasure, making those sounds escape your lips," he admitted.

Piper looked him in the eyes. There was something feral and animalistic about him, but something far greater than lust.

Tristan pulled his card from his coat pocket and scanned it near the handle to his room. Before Piper could say anything, he had her pulled in with her back against his door.

"Tristan," she breathed, causing him to pause. "What happened in the hot tub then?" She didn't want to ruin the moment, but why hadn't he done something sooner?

He pressed their foreheads together and laughed. "I was stupid. As soon as you..." He thought for a moment, not expecting to have such an awkward conversation. Actually, a couple minutes ago he thought all talking was done for the night. "When you felt what you did to me, you looked horrified and–"

"I was surprised," Piper interrupted. "I didn't think you were attracted to me, at least not like that."

"Of course I'm fucking attracted to you," he growled, pressing himself into her so that she could feel his very obvious attraction. "I backed off because I didn't want to try anything with you if you didn't want it."

"And now?"

"I meant what I said out there, but if you don't want this, I need to know right–" Before he could finish his sentence, Piper yanked him by the collar and pulled him into her.

She deepened the kiss immediately, circling his tongue with immense force and pressure. Piper pushed Tristan's jacket at the shoulders, and it quickly fell to the floor. He stopped her once she began furiously working at the buttons on his shirt.

Tristan spun her around until her back collided into his chest, completely taking her off-guard. "Not so fast," he chuckled in her ear.

His voice was nearly enough to make her come undone. Clutching her at the waist with one hand, he slid his other farther down her body. Once he reached the hem of her dress, he slowly brought his hand up, skimming the warm skin of her inner thighs. The closer he got to his destination, the more rushed and panicked her breaths became.

He was elated once he felt how much she wanted him, felt what he had done to her body. Piper gasped at the first touch of his finger against her wetness. His other hand rose to massage her breasts through her dress as his finger began to dip deeper inside of her.

"Oh, god," she moaned, throwing her head back and falling into Tristan.

He had perfect access to her neck and trailed his tongue along her skin until he hit a spot that did it for her. He sucked softly at first, trying to be gentle with her, but when he inserted a second finger into her and she bucked hard against him, a savage part of him got a little rough. Piper yelped, but insisted for him not to stop, though she was sure that she'd already regret it in the morning.

"I want to feel you fall apart in my arms," he breathed in her ear, quickening his pace between her legs.

Every spot that Tristan touched sent sparks radiating throughout her body; she was about to give him exactly what he asked for. If he wasn't holding her up, she would be slowly melting to the floor by now.

He worked slowly, just enough to put Piper on the verge of that wonderful sensation she desperately craved. Little by little, Tristan's fingers went deeper inside of her. Piper rocked back and forth into him. She needed him to pick up the pace and stop teasing. She needed him to send her over the edge.

"More," Piper hoarsely breathed. She gripped at his arm that was holding her, caressing her chest, and latched on to it for dear life. "It feels so good," she managed through quick and short breaths.

Moments later, Tristan felt her whole body clench up and a second more, every part of her was trembling against him with his name piercing through the walls. He allowed her to come off her high before turning her and taking her in his mouth.

Her fingers reached for the remaining buttons on his shirt, just as he rapidly pulled at the zipper on her dress, all the while walking them closer to the bed.

Once the back of Piper's knees hit the bed, Tristan gave her the extra push and she collapsed into the plush linens. She tried to slip her arm out of the side with one sleeve while Tristan impatiently yanked at the bottom. After that was removed, Piper sat up, undoing the strapless bra that was far too tight.

Tristan took a step back, pulling off his shirt and reaching for his belt. She looked absolutely beautiful before him. Her body was so simple, so real, untouched by surgery or fake sun. If he wasn't on the verge of exploding just from the sight of her nearly naked body, he could have admired her for much longer. Only when he was down to his boxers did he think to rummage through his suitcase for a condom.

Piper's brows clenched in a questioning way, when he climbed on top of her.

"So you did expect to screw around this week," she playfully pointed out, although the idea of him with another woman made her sick.

Tristan laughed. "I told you that I could make it a week. I also told you I wouldn't *screw around* with anyone here for the wedding. I was hoping that didn't mean you as well."

Piper had to force herself to breathe, knowing that this wasn't just a passionate night where they lost control. At least that's not what it sounded like when he said that. It sounded like he had considered the possibility long before now.

Tristan continued speaking while slowly removing her panties. "I enjoyed our chats, even if they were only through text. I'd be lying if I said that I never thought about this, that I didn't want this."

It killed Piper to hear that. In a few days he'd be back in California and she would be slaving away for the insane Blythe Carrington. Saying what he just said confused her. It confused more than her mind. It confused her heart.

Just as Tristan began slipping on the condom, he saw something flash over Piper's face. It would be devastating if he had to stop now, but it would be worse if they partook in something that she wasn't entirely comfortable with.

"If you don't want to do this–"

"I do," Piper confirmed, raking her dainty nails down his chest.

Tristan wished it would have been harder. He actually didn't mind marks being left behind. He groaned slightly at the touch, making sure that she was aware as to how much he loved it.

Slowly, he pulled her into him and adjusted himself so that he was hovering over her. A savage part of him wanted to dive all in, to break every part of her, but seeing her splayed beneath him, her golden locks painted across the grey sheets, her emerald eyes looking into his with a trusting innocence, gave him pause. Instead, he softly connected their lips, allowing her to set the pace for what was to come. As he expected, the kisses soon became deep, but they weren't frantically rushed.

Piper's fingertips lightly dug into his back, silently pulling him downward. Tristan obliged and soon his arousal was skimming along the heat of hers. She moaned into his mouth as soon as they touched. As if this wasn't their first time together, Tristan knew what she needed, what she wanted.

He broke the kiss, keeping their faces only inches apart. He reached down and grabbed himself. Slowly he began massaging her entrance with his cock, gradually adding more pressure, but never fully entering her.

Her eyes darted from his to their connection below. With each passing second, they pleaded for more. Tristan couldn't take it and finally gave in all the way.

Piper let out a painful gasp followed by heavy breathing. Tristan thought about pulling out, but Piper must have sensed that and quickly began shaking her head. "Don't. It's fine. I just didn't expect you to be so..." Her voice trailed off and a deep crimson spread from her cheeks all the way across her chest.

Tristan couldn't help but laugh. He began with slow, barely there thrusts, which were torture for him. "You're so tight that it's taking every bit of my restraint not to turn into a vicious monster," he roughly breathed into her ear. "Just so you know, your nails feel really good. Don't hold back," he added.

Piper's eyes widened. The idea that Tristan was having to restrain himself for her well-being was insanely sexy.

Her body quickly adjusted to him and she began bucking her hips for more. He crushed his lips back onto hers, claiming every part of her body. Piper's nails dug into his back which only made his thrusts into her that much deeper and stronger.

Piper pulled away from the kiss, screams and a string of vulgar words erupting from her lips. When she was able to open her eyes she saw a ravenous set focused on her. Tristan's look was indescribable. There wasn't a time that Piper could ever recall a lover looking at her like that.

Tristan pressed their bodies closer together, careful not to put too much weight onto Piper. He cradled her head in his hand and allowed their cheeks to touch. It was something far more intimate than he was accustomed to, but something told him that this is what she needed, what they both needed.

Piper bit down on her lip and dug her nails into Tristan's arms to keep from exploding into a million tiny pieces once she realized what was happening.

"Relax," Tristan groaned after feeling Piper tense up, knowing that she was so close. "Enjoy it."

Unlike before, he softly kissed her neck, drawing wet circles against her pulse with his tongue, and before he knew it, he had sent Piper over the edge once again.

His name, a scream from her lips, her body, convulsing, shaking, unraveling beneath him, the grip her walls had on his cock, was too much for him to last any longer. Darkness took over and he fought to allow himself the same intense pleasure that he had just given Piper.

He couldn't see, couldn't breathe, as he came down from his climax. Sex was good, but rarely had it ever been that incredible for him.

Tristan fell off of Piper onto his back, both of them attempting to catch their breath. Piper felt Tristan's eyes locked on her, but she couldn't tear hers away from the ceiling. Rationality began to weasel itself into her thoughts, and slowly thoughts of how unbelievably amazing the sex was turned to facing the fact that she had only really been around Tristan for three days.

She didn't know what made her do it, but as soon as Tristan got up to take care of the condom, Piper immediately began throwing on her discarded clothing. It wasn't until she was almost done fiddling with the zipper on her dress that she looked up to see Tristan across the room, hovering in the doorway to the bathroom. He had put on a pair of boxers but nothing else. A t-shirt dangled from his hand as he confidently made his way toward Piper.

"I thought you might want to sleep in this," he cautiously asked, motioning to the shirt.

The situation was awkward for the both of them. Sex hadn't been part of their arrangement, and now that it had happened, there was an uncertainty as to what the next steps were.

"I actually should probably get back to my room. I have a few things to finish up on for your article," Piper began to ramble, finding it difficult to look at Tristan, especially as she saw the marks that she had etched into him.

"Does tonight have any effect on that," he asked, jokingly, but noted the way Piper's face reddened at the mentioning of it.

Much to his displeasure, he walked her toward the door, not pushing for her to stay. After what had just happened, oddly for him, he wanted to try the whole cuddling and falling asleep together thing with Piper.

"This was," Piper began as she placed her hand on the handle.

Tristan placed his hand on top of hers, as he stood behind her. He wanted to turn her so that he could see her face, but something told him better. "Don't," he insisted. "We'll talk tomorrow."

Anything that was about to come out of Piper's mouth would be something that would dismiss whatever happened between them, and Tristan didn't want to hear that. He felt her suck in a breath after he spoke. Sensing her uncertainty by his words, he decided to reassure her so that she knew what happened was something more than just one night, one moment of passion. He leaned into Piper, the smell of her hair alone caused him to want to pull her back from the door and into his bed. "Thank you for agreeing to go on a date with me." Then he released her, and she could not have left the room any faster.

* * *

Tristan stared up at the ceiling from his bed. After his run, and especially after Piper, he was exhausted; however, his mind had different plans that wouldn't allow sleep to take over.

Something was different when it came to Piper, but he couldn't place it. All he knew was that both his body and mind reacted to her unlike it had with any other woman. He was extremely frustrated that she didn't stay the night with him, which was completely new as well. Maybe he should have asked her, but the look on her face as she prepared to leave wouldn't allow him to torture his ego with definite rejection.

Without giving it too much thought, he hit the call button on his phone. It was a weeknight, already after nine in California. He expected Elijah to be at home watching Netflix, no doubt preparing for an early morning workout.

"This is unexpected," Elijah's voice came through the speaker. He sounded very awake but there was silence in the background.

"How's it going," Tristan began vaguely.

He tried to focus on Elijah's words, but found it difficult. With each passing second he thought he might explode from his thoughts of the night. He didn't expect the best advice to come from Elijah, but he had to talk to someone about it, and Elijah was the only one who knew about the situation Tristan had placed himself in. Actually, he would have preferred to talk to Piper about it, but that was clearly not going to happen.

"Now tell me why you really called," Elijah asked, completely ending his story in the middle after realizing that Tristan was far too quiet.

"Honestly, I needed someone to talk to," Tristan hesitated. "Stuff happened."

"Unless you're going to elaborate, that's a horrible story," Elijah scoffed. Clanking came from his end of the line and Tristan realized that Elijah was just now finishing his very late dinner at home. "It's about the girl, isn't it," Elijah asked before Tristan could think of how to bring it up.

"Yeah," he sighed.

"You realized you're crazy and going to play for New York isn't the sanest decision, and you're fully coming back to Los Angeles?"

"Eli…"

The pop on the other end of the line led Tristan to believe that Elijah was opening a beer. "Hit me with it. What happened?"

"We went on a date," Tristan began, not wanting to bluntly throw a more massive fact out there.

"You know there are women here that you could date," Elijah immediately responded. He didn't understand why, after a kiss and a date, Tristan was doing the most irrational thing he had ever done.

"We had sex."

Elijah was silent for a moment and then there was a burst of laughter piercing through the phone. "I knew you couldn't go all week without hitting something over there!"

"Don't," Tristan warned.

"Come on, man. I'm surprised you didn't have a drunk, desperate, bridesmaid the first night," Elijah continued.

"It's not like that," Tristan growled, slamming his fist into the damp sheets. "I could have gone without any of these women, but I couldn't go without her."

Elijah's laughter quickly came to a screeching halt. Through the excellent speakers, Tristan could hear Elijah polishing off the rest of his beer. Finally, "What the hell is wrong with you?! That's some sissy shit to say!"

Tristan smiled at the comment, knowing that while his words were true, so were Elijah's.

"Three days man! You've known her for three days," Elijah continued to shout.

Tristan refrained from pointing out the technicalities of it. He had met Piper a few brief times during her relationship with Jared, and over the course of the last month, even though it was only through text, they talked often and had gotten to know each other more. Everything didn't just happen within the last seventy-two hours. However, from the moment Tristan first saw Piper at the airport, there was an immediate attraction. Even though it had only been a few days, after spending more time with her, that physical attraction had drastically turned into something else.

"So what? She has a golden vagina or something?"

"It's more than that." Tristan wasn't sure what he meant when he said that, but it wasn't just about wanting to get laid that made him push forward.

Elijah sighed, knowing he had lost the battle. "Then why are you telling me this shit and not her."

That's the part that made Tristan cringe, and he knew he was treading dangerous territory if he told Elijah everything about the evening. He decided to face the humiliation anyway.

"She went back to her room," Tristan blurted out.

There was a light thud on the other end, followed by silence. Shortly after, there was maniacal laughter in the distance. Tristan heard the refrigerator door close and another pop from a beer bottle as Elijah tried to catch his breath from his very obvious amusement.

"Dude," Elijah managed when he picked the phone back up. "I had to get another beer on that one."

"I'm glad you're finding humor in it," Tristan huffed, growing more frustrated with the situation.

"Wait, you're serious? Really serious? She just got dressed and left?"

"Yeah..."

"Wow," Elijah began in amazement. "Normally you have to chase the women away the next morning. What did you do?"

Tristan thought for a second before realizing how stupid it was. He didn't do anything. Whatever caused Piper to leave was part of her own internal battle.

Elijah pressed on in his very useless way. "Did you do something freaky like slap her ass and call her Coach? I did that once and ended up with a black eye."

"I don't even know why I bothered calling you," Tristan grumbled. Elijah was an amazing friend but his lack of seriousness was just as great as Tristan's impulsiveness. Together they were often a bad combination when it came to decision making.

"Why did you call me?"

Tristan didn't have to think on it. "It was more than sex for me."

"Ouch," Elijah screamed. "You're ripping my heart out!" He had to joke about it, and while he didn't understand how Tristan could be falling for someone so quickly, he knew that he was. "Look, shooting you straight, talk to her, although I'd leave out the New York part. That sounds like some psycho one-night stand gone bad shit."

"For the record, I considered New York before we had sex. The sex didn't magically change anything," Tristan corrected.

"Bullshit. If the sex didn't change anything, we wouldn't be having this conversation," Elijah pointed out.

Elijah was right. Tristan had been falling for Piper since before he saw her in person a few days ago, the sex had only confirmed that there was something more going on between them, at least for him there was.

# CHAPTER 18

Upon looking in the mirror early the next morning, Piper rushed to find her phone. There was only one person she could seek advice from with something like this.

"You're technically supposed to be on vacation," Haven sang out when she answered the phone. If she were the one in Piper's shoes, she wouldn't have been up that early. Unfortunately she still had to get to work, so she most definitely was wide awake and on her second cup of coffee.

"Oh, god. I messed up. Shit, I have to be at brunch later." Piper's voice came across as rushed and panicked.

"Whoa, calm down. What did I miss," Haven asked, attempting to focus on Piper and concentrate on her mascara all at the same time.

"So much, but I need advice. How do you get rid of a hickey," Piper spat out.

Haven's mascara brush fell to the sink. "Shit!" Then Piper's words really hit her. "What the hell are you talking about? Who has a hickey?"

"I do," Piper grumbled. She stood in the mirror staring at the physical proof that last night had definitely not been a dream.

"I am so confused. You need to start from the beginning."

"I don't have time for a lengthy story," Piper squealed. "Do you know or not?"

"Calm down, I'm on Google now. By the way, you could have done the same if you hadn't freaked out. Now talk," Haven insisted as she scrolled through a ridiculous article of remedies that would not work in such a brief amount of time.

"The short of it, I went on a date with Tristan and things escalated." Piper left it as vague as she could, hoping for once that Haven wouldn't press on.

"In my experience, if you end up with bruises on your neck, something besides kissing happened," Haven speculated.

Piper sank to the toilet, suddenly needing to sit after recalling the events from the previous night. "It was amazing," she sighed.

"Holy crap! You really slept with him? I can't get you to go on a date with a guy and you slept with him after just one date? Is there really a vixen alien that has taken over your body," Haven joked.

Piper went on to tell Haven about the evening, although she kept most of the intense details to herself.

When Piper finally finished, "That was a shit move."

"What was I supposed to do? I don't want to come off as clingy. We're not in a real relationship. I don't want him thinking that I'm head over heels after one night."

"You are though, aren't you?" Haven's voice had turned very quiet and serious. When Piper didn't respond, Haven let out an exasperated breath. "I don't want to see you getting hurt–"

"I know," Piper interrupted. "I know that this time next week we'll be on opposite ends of the country and it will just be a great memory. We weren't thinking and just lost ourselves in the moment," Piper lied, hoping her words would at least convince Haven. It was too late for them to do anything for her.

Haven cleared her throat. "These ideas all sound absurd. Throw on a little concealer and wear it with pride."

Piper forced herself to laugh. "You're ridiculous, you know that?"

"Go enjoy your freak show wedding," Haven said, attempting to conclude the conversation. "Oh, and Piper," she added. "Talking never hurt anyone. If you need to clear things up, there's only one person that can help you with that."

Piper hated how right Haven was and her cheeks burned at the idea of having to talk to Tristan about what happened between them.

* * *

He wasn't sure the game that she was playing when an email with her article as an attachment came across his phone as he was getting ready to head down to brunch. He also wasn't sure on the protocol for what he was supposed to do after last night. Just as he decided to leave his room to knock on her door, another alert, a text, came through.

**Piper: Headed to brunch. I'll see you there.**

If he expected her to be like every other woman he had been with, he was completely wrong. The sex had to have been good for her. Hell, the whole evening, with the exception of the guy from the bar, had been great. He even mentioned the word *date* at the end in case there was any confusion.

By the time he got down to the small conference room where brunch for Samantha and Jared was being held, Piper was just taking her seat with her parents. She must have left her room just moments before him.

Piper made brief eye contact with Tristan when he walked in and headed toward the coffee bar. She couldn't look for long, as once their eyes met she remembered the way he looked at her the night prior and feelings started to flood through her.

Her parents greeted her, but Piper watched as Lucy's eyes grow ten times their size while she shook her head in horror. Piper saw where her sister's line of vision had gone and she quickly parted her hair in the back so that one side draped more over one particular shoulder, concealing what her concealer had obviously failed to do a good job at.

Tristan couldn't wait to get to Piper's family. He wondered how she'd react if she was forced to deal with him. He quickly poured a cup of black coffee, rolling his nose up at all the frilly add in items set nearby. Once he turned, Derek and Jared arrived deep in conversation. Their conversation broke up as soon as Derek glanced at Tristan.

"What the hell attacked you," Derek laughed.

Tristan didn't follow and looked down to see what Derek was talking about. Images of Piper combusting against his body and writhing beneath him soon flooded his mind when he saw the scratch marks cascading down his arms. He couldn't help but meet Derek's eyes with a satisfactory smirk.

"Seriously," Jared added. "It looks like you got in a fight with a mountain lion," he exaggerated.

Derek gauged the look on Tristan's face before throwing his hand in the air for a high five, which Tristan dismissed. "Come on, man," Derek huffed. "If I would have gotten that kind of action last night, I'd be standing on this table right now letting everyone know."

Jared stopped swirling the mix around in his coffee when he realized where the conversation had gone. "I always found Piper to be somewhat boring in bed," he added.

Derek stopped laughing as soon as Piper's name was mentioned, feeling the air getting quite thick between the three of them. It was a more than unnecessary comment on Jared's part; it only put

Derek in a more awkward position when Tristan responded.

"No woman is ever boring in bed," Tristan began,
sipping his coffee. "If it comes across that way, the
guy obviously doesn't know what he's doing."

"Okay, okay, we get it," Derek said, feeling the
need to step forward a bit so that he was in between
the two. "Both of you have slept with the same
woman, you're with her now," he said, directing his
words toward Tristan. "And dude," he nearly
shouted, clasping Jared on the shoulder. "You're
days away from marrying the love of your life. Let's
not ruin any friendships over nothing."

Tristan agreed and walked off, leaving the two of
them. Piper was far from nothing. Prior to finding out
about Jared cheating on her, Tristan had no hard
feelings toward him. Even after knowing that Jared
cheated, he didn't hate the guy. It was a crappy thing
to do, but it didn't seem to bother Piper anymore, and
that was the most important thing. What he couldn't
get over was why Jared would ask him to be a
groomsman, and then do nothing more than insult
his relationship with Piper. It was as though every
time he encountered Jared, Piper's name had to be
brought up, all of which with unsavory comments.

"Hey," Tristan announced as he pulled out a chair
next to Piper. He intentionally scooted it closer to her
when he sat down.

"Hi," Piper murmured. The clean smell of his body
wash easily overpowered her cup of coffee that she
tried to hide behind.

"You look nice this morning."

Piper sent a comical and skeptical look his way. "Thanks, I guess."

Tristan wasn't good with romance. At. All. He also became acutely aware how awkward last night now made things between them. He wanted to pull Piper away so they could talk, just the two of them. While Emma and Nolan continued to snack on the skimpy breakfast, Tristan couldn't ignore the glare that Lucy was shooting him from across the table. She had to know something, and from the looks of it, she wasn't happy about it.

"I got your article and consent form. I'll send it in later," Tristan told Piper, attempting to lighten the heavy aura floating over them. He watched as Piper's face twitched slightly. "It was good, really good. You made me seem a lot better than what I am," he complimented. Satisfaction hit him when a pure and genuine smile spread across her lips. Drawing his attention to her pale pink lips while at breakfast with her family wasn't the best idea and caused his insides to swirl when he thought about where he'd rather have them right now. Had she stayed the night, he doubted they would have ever made it to brunch.

"Don't act humbled," Piper laughed. "I've never seen someone as specialized with set pieces as you are."

Tristan felt the heat creeping to his face. Her words quickly setting him on fire. His maneuvers on the field took a great deal of practice and going precisely by the plan. It was a skill he was very proud of, and the fact that someone like Piper acknowledged that only fed to his ego more than he should have allowed.

"Good morning, Aunt Emma and Uncle Nolan," Samantha cheerfully exclaimed as she wrapped her arms over the two. Though she was exceedingly happy, Piper assumed it had less to do with her upcoming nuptials and more so the empty mimosa glass.

Following close behind Samantha was none other than her helicopter of a mother.

"Are you all looking forward to the dinner cruise this evening," she asked, announcing her presence.

"Like a root canal," Lucy managed through a mouthful of waffles.

"Ouch," Piper squealed upon receiving a blow to her ankle.

"Sorry," Emma began. "I thought that was your sister."

"Well it wasn't, and that hurt."

"I don't get it," Lucy interrupted. Piper shook her head for her sister to stop, but her boldness and lack of a filter knew no bounds. "Why is your rehearsal dinner on a boat? You're not getting married on a boat. Nothing about the wedding has anything to do with a freaking boat."

"Well, maybe when you get married you can do things your way. Our wedding site wasn't available for rehearsal and we thought this would be something everyone would enjoy," Samantha piped up, thankfully before her mother could.

"I'm just saying. A boat was stupid. Haven't you seen *Titanic*?"

Just like that, as if they had known each other for years, Tristan held out his hand from across the table. Fueled by caffeine, the gesture registered and Lucy met him with a high-five.

This caught Margaret's attention. "Mr. Reed, so glad to see you're still with us."

Tristan didn't know what she meant by the comment. Her eyes raked over his body, full of disgust. "What's up, Maggie?"

Piper sucked in a breath. Margaret was big on formalities. Nothing in those three words would have been to her liking.

"What is that," she asked through pursed lips.

For a moment Tristan thought that she was talking to him, but saw her eyes zeroed in on Piper. He glanced over her and saw what everyone directed their attention to.

Piper tried to flip her hair back over but gave up and pulled it all back. There was no point in trying to hide it.

"Piper," Emma hissed, shaking her head.

Tristan would be lying if he said it didn't look a little hot. It sounded animalistic and barbaric, but he liked knowing that he had left his mark on her. What he didn't like was the look her father was shooting him from across the table.

"Oh, goodness," Samantha gasped. "I can't believe you would let someone do that to you, especially at your age."

Piper had to clench her teeth at the comment. She could have been petty, could have made a comment about Jared lacking in the bedroom, could have mentioned the earthshattering orgasms that followed the evidence left on her neck, but she chose not to. No matter how awesome it was, she didn't want to lessen the night before to just sex. It was something else. Something that she didn't need to advertise just to get a hit in with Samantha.

"I hope you can cover that up a little better come Saturday," Margaret insisted.

Thankfully Jared's mother called from across the room, taking their attention to another table. Unfortunately the damage had been done.

Emma was the first to speak, albeit after a long sip of coffee. "I'm confused."

"Oh, you're not the only one," Nolan soon followed.

Tristan didn't dare meet the eyes that he could feel blazing through him. He had never been in the type of relationship where he had to meet the girl's family, especially the father. For some reason, Nolan gave him that stereotypical vibe. He was looking for him to pull out his shotgun at any moment and start cleaning it.

As though Piper could read his mind, "Stop it, dad. I'm almost thirty, not sixteen."

"I'm just confused," Emma repeated.

"They had sex," Lucy announced throwing up her hands.

Piper cringed. Her family was pretty open about most things. She remembered being in the grocery store as a child listening to her mother explain the differences between certain pads and tampons with her father when he brought the wrong kind home. This, however, truly tested her comfort level.

"I thought this was all fake, just pretend," Emma asked.

"Apparently there wasn't much pretending going on last night, and that thing on her neck sure as hell isn't fake," Nolan growled.

Piper was just about to say something to calm the escalating scrutiny when her sister once again chimed in.

"Whoa, whoa. While I have some reservations about whatever the hell is going on between the two of them," she began, as though Piper and Tristan weren't sitting at the table. "Prior to a few days ago, we all thought the relationship was real. If they were in a relationship, obviously they were screwing each other. Now we just know that they're not in a relationship, only screwing each other. And if I'm being honest," Lucy hesitated. Piper shook her head, hoping that Lucy would shut up. "Piper hasn't dated since that idiot," she said, pointing to Jared. "She needs to get laid just like everyone else, and from the looks of it, he did a good job."

"Oh, god," Piper groaned. Her sister's words did absolutely nothing to help the situation.

"What are your intentions with my daughter," Nolan asked Tristan through gritted teeth, Lucy's words suddenly causing him to go into an intense papa bear mode.

That was Piper's breaking point. "Dad, seriously? I'm not a kid. Cool it."

Before anyone could say another word, Tristan spoke. "Actually, sir, I feel like that's something I need to talk with your daughter about." With those words he clasped his hand over Piper's, giving it a reassuring squeeze.

Piper's heart raced at his words. She could feel the beating pounding throughout her whole body. Last night had changed so much for her. It tore her in two, the part that wanted to explore something with Tristan and the part that was painfully aware of all other circumstances.

# CHAPTER 19

Once the brunch concluded and everyone began dispersing for the day, free to do what they wanted, Piper headed back up to her room, alone.

Tristan, however, was able to pull Jared to the side. There was that goodness in him that wanted to make things right with everyone.

"Got a minute?"

Jared look mildly annoyed but nodded anyway.

Tristan didn't know where Jared was walking to, but fell in line with him. "I just wanted to apologize if I've offended you." The words were difficult to say, but hopefully would ease the tension.

"You just don't get it do you," Jared laughed. "You take enough of the attention just being here."

"What's that supposed to mean? Wait, you asked me to be a groomsman."

"I didn't expect you to be the center of the show," Jared scoffed.

The jealousy came through loud and clear. It started long ago, with soccer. Jared never had any intention of taking his playing to the next level; however, Tristan did, and it paid off, and Jared would always be a little bitter about that.

191

"It's cool having you here, but…"

"You invited me because it made you look good? You needed a washed up player to make you look important," Tristan asked, attempting to lessen the blow by dismissing the fact that playing or not, he was still pretty famous.

Jared snorted at the comment. "Fine, yeah. When Samantha insisted I ask you, I thought it would look awesome having a national star here." Jared quickly veered the subject into another territory. "Were you dating her when I asked?"

"Of course not. I would have told you." Tristan was being truthful with his words, which only made him feel a little guilty about posting it on Facebook prior to mentioning it to Jared, knowing that Jared got easily offended by everything.

"It makes me look bad," Jared continued.

Tristan tried his hardest to breathe. Apologizing was also something he wasn't good at. He thought it was supposed to be a little easier than this.

"You've been with actresses, models, popstars. If Piper is good enough for you, it makes me look crazy for leaving her," Jared went on.

Clearly the only way for Tristan to smooth things over was to take the horrible words that Jared was throwing at him. He was dangerously close to giving in to the rage boiling inside him as Jared continued to ramble.

"I know you man, so we're cool," Jared finally sighed after he got everything off his chest. "There's no point in throwing away more than a decade of friendship for some fling."

Jared carefully watched Tristan's reactions, but got nothing. He had no idea what Tristan might be thinking, which meant he had no idea just how serious or not Tristan and Piper were.

Tristan couldn't respond to that. For the sake of getting through the week, he let Jared have the hit.

* * *

Tristan had every intention of knocking on Piper's door. While he was pretty sure she was spending such a beautiful day locked away on a computer, he needed her more. He couldn't stop thinking about his response to her father.

Just as he reached their doors, his phone rang. He recognized one of New York's area codes and immediately answered as he slipped into his room.

"Hello, Mr. Reed. I'm Blythe Carrington with *Rogue Times* I needed to talk with you about an article sent in, and your people put me in contact with you," she began, as if reading from a script.

"I'm aware of the article. I'll send in my consent form in just a bit," he responded, neglecting pleasantries, as he began rifling through his bag for his laptop.

"While the article is a very nice piece, I did have a few questions," she said rather hesitantly.

"Shoot."

"Did Miss Carter come to you about writing this for our magazine?"

"Actually, no." Tristan powered on his laptop. "I knew she worked for you and I suggested the idea."

"Then you must know that she works as my assistant, not one of our writers," Blythe delicately stated.

"I also know that she's capable of more than filling your coffee order."

Blythe was shocked by Tristan's boldness and lost her words for a second. She changed the subject away from Piper and back on the article. "While her piece is quite nice, it lacks a little bit of the personal aspect that a good portion of our readers would find interesting."

"By personal aspect, you mean personal life? Who I'm dating? What do I look for in a woman," Tristan scoffed.

"Well..."

"Look, it's a sports piece. If you don't want to be the first to publish a story about my return to the field, rest assured a bigger magazine than yours will take it. I'm not even asking for payment here."

As soon as the issue of money was mentioned, Blythe's attitude changed greatly. Tristan wasn't stupid, he knew without a doubt how much he could get for an exclusive about him returning from retirement. It wasn't about the money. This was something nice that he could do for Piper, and she deserved that.

"Well, Mr. Reed, it's been a pleasure. I've just received your form, and as long as you're aware that you won't be compensated for this..."

"I never expected to be," Tristan quickly interrupted. "This was all for Piper."

"You two seem to be pretty good friends then." It was a statement that had an underlying question, one that Tristan was quick to dismiss.

"If you need anything else, don't hesitate to reach out," Tristan told her, concluding the conversation.

He wouldn't bring up the conversation to Piper. Hopefully Blythe Carrington would realize what an asset Piper was when it came to research and writing.

Rather than surprising Piper, or interrupting whatever she was doing by knocking on her door like he originally planned, Tristan sent a quick text.

**Tristan: Want to do something?**

Surprisingly, Piper responded immediately, and the strangest flutter rushed through his chest when she did.

**Piper: What do you have in mind?**

He laughed at the message. There were so many inappropriate things he wanted to text back, but first he needed to gauge where they stood after last night. One thing he could easily tell about Piper, especially after her sister's outburst at brunch, was that Piper was not a one-night stand type of woman. However, things had gotten intense pretty fast last night, and he had to wonder if she acted in the moment and regretted it. There was still the memory in the back of his mind where he very vividly recalled Piper's conversation with her friend on the phone.

**Tristan: I thought we could just hang out.**

He cringed as soon as he sent it, realizing how vague and juvenile it sounded. He was certain that he used to have more game with the opposite sex. Then again, Piper wasn't his usual type.

**Piper: I'll be ready in a minute.**

# CHAPTER 20

Tristan thought about telling Piper to wait once he put the Aston Martin in park; however, she had her door open before he could finish thinking it.

"What exactly are we doing," Piper asked once Tristan joined her on the sidewalk.

"I just wanted to get out. I thought you might like to check out some of the shops," he replied, not really knowing what his intention was when he asked her to spend time with him. All he really knew was exactly that, that he wanted to spend time with her, alone.

"Ah, so because I'm a female, I must love shopping," Piper teased.

"What? No, I mean, I thought...shit," Tristan stammered. "We can go back if you want."

Piper placed her hand gently on Tristan's forearm as she turned to face him. "I was joking."

"Right, but still–"

"This is awkward, right," she interrupted him. "Things are weird because of last night, aren't they?"

Tristan was hoping to hold off on the conversation for a little longer. He tried to avoid eye contact but

found it impossible to do so with the green orbs staring up at him. He couldn't read her face. He didn't
know how she wanted him to answer. He really
wasn't good with anything in the romance department. Sex, that he could handle, but whatever was
going on now was something new.

"Is it awkward for you," he asked, cowardly allowing her to set the tone.

Piper bit her lip and fell back to Tristan's side and
continued walking. "It was unexpected. I didn't intend for that to happen. You're just supposed to be
doing me a favor..." She let her words drift off. What
did he expect her to say? That she got butterflies
every time he looked at her. That her heart raced with
the slightest touch. That she craved his presence
when he wasn't there. That she desperately wanted a
repeat of the night before.

She couldn't say any of those things. Those were
all leaps and bounds beyond clingy. Even thinking
those thoughts made her feel a little psychotic after
only knowing Tristan for such a short amount of
time. Maybe it would have been different if there
wasn't a time limit, but the truth was, it was just a
wedding date situation, albeit, a very long wedding
thanks to Samantha.

"I guess I can be a little impulsive when it comes
to getting what I want, and I clearly wanted you last
night," he boldly admitted.

Piper cringed at the comment. She tried not to
overthink it, but it sounded the same no matter how

she read into it. He wanted her sexually the previous night. That's what he wanted and that's what he got.

"Then I guess we're all good," Piper hastily announced.

"Wait, what?" Tristan was confused. He told her he wanted her and she completely brushed it off.

"Last night was good," she replied, although with little emotion. "It happened. I just really want to get through this week."

Tristan was shocked that that's all she thought about their encounter. He definitely had words to describe it and none of them were anything as plain as *good*.

"Oh, wow," she quietly gasped as they started to pass by a boutique. Her footsteps slowed slightly.

"Do you want to go in," Tristan quickly asked.

He had to assume that whatever the hell just happened had come to a conclusion. He anticipated more. Did he anticipate that Piper would fall in love with him after one night of sex? No. Was he under the assumption that she might want to take the word *pretend* out of their relationship? Possibly. He didn't expect for her to brush it off the way she had. He was pretty sure that's not how those conversations were supposed to be.

"I really don't need anything."

"Sometimes it's not about what you need, it's about what you want."

Piper couldn't help but turn to face him. There was a darkness in his eyes as they met hers. She could feel her hands becoming clammy. Her stomach felt like she was on a rollercoaster, the one where you're constantly being flipped and everything is happening too fast. That's what being around Tristan was like for her.

One of them stepped forward, maybe they both did. Neither could be sure. Tristan brought his head down slightly and Piper knew it. He was about to kiss her. If he kissed her, then maybe last night did mean more than just sex.

They were both jolted out of their haze with the bell from the door behind them, the bell to the boutique.

"Oh, excuse me," a woman whispered as she made her way through Piper and Tristan, who were blocking the entrance.

Tristan tore his eyes from Piper and raked his hand over his jaw like someone had just punched him in the face. He stumbled for words but only managed, "You should at least look."

No sooner than they stepped through the eccentric glass doors, a bubbly young redhead bounded up to them like an eager puppy.

"Hi, I'm Trixie. How can I help you today?"

Though Piper tried not to be judgmental until she had a reason to judge, the name alone caused two things to run through her mind. Trixie was a good name for a puppy. It was also a good name for a stripper. The woman combined the two well. Despite working in what appeared to be an expensive and up-scale boutique, Trixie looked like a stripper clearly making puppy dog eyes at Tristan.

"We're just looking," Piper quickly responded. She didn't mean for her words to come out with such a sharp tone like they did.

The clothes were exquisite, although something as simple as a hoodie ran over a hundred dollars. Piper splurged every once in a while, but tried not to if she could help it. Call her a little boring, but she preferred to invest her money, and looking like a movie star every day of the week was not going to help her retire by fifty.

"Are you looking for anything specific," Tristan finally asked after watching Piper thumb through several racks of clothes.

"Well," she began, rolling her eyes up to the ceiling, appearing to be deep in thought. "I'm not sure what I'm wearing tonight. I was planning on wearing the dress Haven helped me pick out, but I'm doubting that now."

"What does it look like," Tristan quickly asked, walking around a rack closer to Piper.

"The one from last night."

"No."

Piper was shocked. Tristan had even complimented her in it. "Why not? What's wrong with it?"

Tristan hesitated. After their conversation on the sidewalk he thought it best to tread lightly, but if he was being honest, there was only one way to say it. "I don't think I could take seeing you in it again."

"Haven picked it out," Piper laughed. "I'm sure I didn't do it justice."

"Stop," Tristan insisted, now more serious. "I don't want you wearing it because every time I'll look at you I'll remember every second of you stripping it from your body. Then I'll remember–"

Piper immediately cut him off. His words were heavy and if he continued, her body would do more than just blush in response. "What about this," she asked, holding up the first thing she could grab.

Tristan gave a grunt and shook his head. Perhaps he should have kept those words to himself, despite how true they were. He distanced himself from Piper so that she could skim over the clothing without feeling pressured or rushed. He was also curious to see what she would pick for herself. He breathed a little easier when she gave him the faintest of smiles and excused herself to a dressing room.

Tristan waited nearby, both assuming and hoping that she'd come out to show him. At this point, it honestly didn't matter what she wore. The more time he spent around her, the more captivated he was becoming.

"I know who you are," a bubbly voice announced, taking Tristan by surprise.

"Oh, yeah?" He turned around, coming face to face with the woman they were first greeted by, Trixie.

"Well, I don't watch sports, but I still know who you are. I'm surprised to see you in our small little town," she giggled, stepping into Tristan's comfort zone.

"I'm here for a wedding."

Her eyes widened, slightly in shock. She motioned over her shoulder to the dressing rooms. "Not your own I hope?"

"No."

"How long will you be around," she asked immediately.

Tristan had to admit, he encountered some bold groupies over the years, but he couldn't believe this woman was attempting to hit on him, while he was a customer and the woman with him was yards away in a changing room.

"It all depends on my girlfriend," he replied, glancing over the redhead toward the changing rooms. He hoped that would be enough to shut down any further flirtation on her part.

As if her brain was an Etch A Sketch, she reached for his left arm, her nails softly raking over one of his tattoos. Her hands felt nothing like Piper's. "This one is so cool," she gasped. Tristan heard the fakeness in her voice. He glanced down briefly, not knowing if she was talking about the cross or the lion, and honestly not caring. He didn't want to be a jerk and pull away, but he definitely tensed, feeling uncomfortable having her hands on him. "I love your sleeve. I bet it took a long time. Was it painful?" Her words dripped with lust.

Tristan wanted to vomit. She was really laying it on thick. She didn't give two shits about soccer or tattoos. Trixie was just another woman that wanted bragging rights for sleeping with an athlete. It was sick and degrading.

He felt a blow to his gut when he looked up to see Piper standing on a platform, surrounded by a trio of mirrors. Part of her bottom lip was clenched between her teeth, and though she tried to hide it, her wide eyes were a mix of questioning and disappointment.

"Babe, wow," Tristan burst out, tearing himself away from Trixie and nervously making his way toward Piper.

Piper's right brow shot up in confusion at the term Tristan used. She was just about to address it when he met her on the platform, drawing himself impossibly close.

"I like this one," he sheepishly admitted, his uncomfortable nervousness fading.

Piper ignored the scene she had just witnessed. "I don't know, you don't think it's too simple."

The dark green design was fairly plain. It contained a high neckline and the sleeves went almost to the elbows. It flared slightly and concluded several inches above the knees. Overall it screamed elegance and innocence, which only made Tristan want Piper to show him the exact opposite behind closed doors.

Tristan's eyes drifted farther down taking in the way the material clung to her perfect breasts and petite waist. She looked so tiny and breakable as she stood before him. He could feel his body beginning to react. The thought of throwing her into the dressing room for his pleasure flashed through his mind.

"Which do you think," Piper asked, interrupting all the naughty and depraved thoughts Tristan knew he needed to keep at bay.

"Which what," he asked. Apparently his vivid imagination had drowned out some of Piper's words.

"If I do buy this, it also comes in black. Which color do you think?"

"The green," Tristan immediately answered without even thinking. "It looks good with your eyes."

Piper took a step back toward the dressing room, but not before Tristan noticed the redness creeping across her cheeks.

Tristan remained nearby. He didn't want another encounter with Trixie. The last thing he wanted was Piper thinking that he could be so easily entertained by any female's presence.

"Shit," he heard from behind Piper's door, followed by a soft groan of frustration.

"Are you okay?" He tried not to laugh.

Although she sounded to be struggling, "Yes, I'm fine." When Tristan didn't respond, she let out a heavy breath. "No. The zipper is stuck and the fabric doesn't have enough give to pull over my head."

Tristan wasn't sure what she was getting at, but assumed it meant that she was stuck. "Do you need some help?"

Piper gave a faint laugh. "Unfortunately. Could you get your friend?"

The thought didn't even cross Tristan's mind as he reached for the handle. Thankfully it was unlocked. He slipped in and shut the door behind him. Piper turned and a look of shock spread across her face.

"What are you doing in here," she gasped. "I told you to get the–"

"My friend?"

Piper glared at Tristan. "Well you did seem awfully friendly."

"Turn around," Tristan demanded, shaking his head.

Piper did as he asked and pulled her hair to one side, giving him access to the zipper. While at first she was mildly annoyed by his bold invasion, his presence in the tiny space had lit a fire in the room. She sighed knowing that he could so easily send her body into a heated mess.

Tristan placed one hand on her back while his forefinger and thumb on the other gently tugged at the zipper. He could have done it faster, but something about slowly revealing inch by inch of her skin was erotic as hell. It was a moment he wanted to savor, even if it was torturous knowing that nothing would come of it.

"You don't have anything to be jealous of," he insisted, needing to clear up whatever Piper thought she saw.

"I'm not jealous," Piper scoffed. She should have left it at that, but her nervous rambling got the best of her. "You're free to do whatever you want as long as you're discreet about it. You'd remember that if you hadn't thrown away my rules."

"Fuck your rules," Tristan spat through gritted teeth. He cringed as soon as he said the words, knowing they were a little harsh. On the other hand, here he was thinking about fooling around in a dressing room and she was giving him permission to go for someone else, like there was nothing happening between them.

"Thank you," Piper meekly told him once the zipper stopped along the lower part of her spine.

Tristan didn't bother waiting for her to turn to face him.

* * *

"What the hell are you doing," Tristan laughed as Piper hung the dress back on the rack. He hoped to lighten things a bit, knowing that it got a little heated only moments ago.

"Well," Piper sighed, rolling her eyes around like she generally did when she was thinking something through. "I gave it some thought."

Tristan wasn't following. "And?"

"Honestly, this costs twice as much as what I spent on the dress I'm wearing to the actual wedding."

With a raised brow and crossed arms, "So? Can't you wear it another time besides tonight? If so, you'll get your use out of it."

"Well, yes, but..."

Tristan grabbed the dress off the rack and started for the register with Piper attempting to catch up to his long strides.

"Wait. Stop. I don't even know if I want it," she began, trying to deter him.

He stopped dead in his tracks and turned. When Piper met his eyes, she noticed how dark they appeared to be turning. They did that often. "You want it. Stop pretending you don't and just say so."

It took Piper a second to recover and follow after him. Those words played a trick on her heart and she wasn't sure if he was only talking about the dress.

He was already handing his card to Trixie when Piper reached the counter.

"That's not necessary," Piper whispered, opening her purse.

Tristan's hand came down on top of hers causing her to freeze. She'd have to repay him later; there was no way she wanted to get into an argument about it right now, and the look he was giving her said as much.

"You two make such a cute couple," Trixie added as she handed the receipt to Tristan, sincerity lacking in her words.

Piper felt the need to clarify. "Oh, we're not–"

"Thank you," Tristan interrupted. He then proceeded to nudge Piper toward the doors.

# CHAPTER 21

They walked in silence.

Piper could see a dark cloud had fallen over Tristan. She felt like she had done something wrong, but the only thing that came to her mind was Trixie. She was just about to apologize for possibly cockblocking him when he crashed down on a nearby bench.

"What was that about?"

Piper took a seat next to him. "What do you mean?" So she did do something wrong.

"I'm pretending to be your boyfriend in front of your family. The least you could do is pretend as well."

"I'm confused. I thought you were upset that I ruined something with Trixie."

Tristan rubbed his forehead in frustration. "No. She was just another girl that wanted to screw around with an athlete. I wanted her thinking we were together."

Piper understood. That explained the 'babe' comment.

"Look, I know how cocky this is going to sound, but let me be honest. Yeah, women throw themselves at me. It happens a lot, and I'm sure you know that.

Hell, your magazine loves writing about all that shit. Anyway, after every game I could have had a dozen of them lined up, one right after another. When I was younger I gave in more than I'd like to admit." Piper didn't know why he felt the need to go off on such a rant, but it made her cringe thinking about him being with so many other women. "That back there, and those friends of Samantha's, it's the same thing. They have no substance and it would be an easy fuck, *if* I were interested. Which I'm not. You'd see that if you weren't so damn insecure with yourself."

That was a trigger. "Excuse me?! I am not insecure!" Piper was fuming at the suggestion.

"Why were you so desperate to have a date? Even to the point that you debated on an escort service?"

"That was Haven's idea," Piper insisted, but realized how immature her response sounded.

Tristan let it go and continued on. "Why haven't you dated since Jared?"

She honestly didn't have a good excuse to that. Haven had tried convincing her to do dating sites, but a part of her was a little scared getting back out there. "I don't have time," was the only answer she could give Tristan.

"Bullshit! I get that walking in on him screwing your cousin sucked, but that was him. He isn't every other guy out there. Stop thinking every guy you meet is going to end up cheating on you. They're not! If you keep thinking that, you're going to have a pretty miserable life. Alone," he concluded. He only stopped when he saw traces of tears coming to her eyes. He didn't want to argue with her, or hurt her feelings. "I'm sorry if that sounded a little harsh," he sighed. "I just wish you'd stop being so uptight and worrying about things."

"That's easy for you to say," Piper coldly began pushing away any tears. "You do whatever you want without worrying about the consequences."

Tristan felt that cut a little more than he'd like to admit. He couldn't even begin to debate that. It was the absolute truth.

* * *

"I've got a few calls to make before heading out tonight," Tristan informed Piper as they made their way to their respective doors.

"I guess I need to do all that girly stuff of getting ready," Piper laughed.

Tristan let his eyes fall down her body. Though he had seen her briefly in the dress, he couldn't wait to see her in it tonight, knowing how pristine and sophisticated she'd be compared to some of those in attendance.

As if reading his mind, "Thank you for this, but I really want to get straight with you."

"Piper," he sighed, playfully shaking his head. "This is one of those things you need to let go."

She couldn't help but welcome the warmth that rushed through her. Though she felt bad about the cost, the gesture overpowered it. She wasn't sure where they stood after last night. The little they did talk about it didn't clarify much. Despite that, she felt like a hug was acceptable.

When her body softly stepped into Tristan's, a wave of emotions passed through them. Everything about the embrace felt right. Both could feel the other. Tristan felt Piper's heavy and uneven breathing and she felt the pounding of his chest against her cheek. Though they wouldn't say it, both became increasingly aware as to what was happening. There was something more. There had to be.

* * *

After going through a few emails and checking in with a frantic Haven, Piper finally decided to start getting ready. Lucy had informed Piper earlier that she'd be coming over to get ready together, so about thirty minutes prior, Piper hopped in the shower.

Before long, she found herself standing under the steady hot stream, allowing the water to cascade down her body, embracing the heat sinking into her skin, yet knowing that the water had nothing on the fire Tristan put in her. Even now, just the simple thought of Tristan caused a need in her to grow.

Memories of last night flickered in her thoughts. His breath on her neck. His face hovering above her. His touch. She'd give anything to feel his skin on hers. Hesitantly she began massaging over her breasts, her nipples already hard with thoughts of Tristan, wishing instead that it was his tongue sending the pleasurable sensations through her body.

She allowed her hand to drift farther down her body. A soft moan came out once her fingers reached the same spot Tristan had touched the night prior. Falling against the cool granite wall, she gently began massaging her clit. Needing more, she inserted one finger into her wetness, soon followed by a second. It felt good, giving her a small piece of the stimulation she craved. Her eyes closed and her head fell back. Images of Tristan flooded her mind as she furiously worked to find her release.

She would have given anything to have him in the shower with her, to have her face plastered against the wall, his hands gripping her as he pounded into her with his thick cock, his mouth marking every inch of her skin, all as the steam encompassed them.

Her legs began to shake. Though her fingers were nothing like Tristan being inside her, it would be enough for the time being. She was close, so close.

The pounding on the entry door caused Piper's eyes to fly open and she yanked her hand away from the verge of a much needed orgasm.

"You have got to be kidding me," Piper huffed, quickly turning off the water and wrapping herself in a towel. The knocking ensued and she hurriedly tip-toed from the bathroom to the door. Fully expecting Lucy to be on the other side, she yanked it open.

Tristan's eyes widened in shock once the door flew open. The image before him was enough to get him rock hard in an instant. Though nicely covered in an oversized bath towel, Piper's hair and skin sparkled with the water still running over her. Tristan put the idea away, but the first thing he thought of was push-ing Piper farther in the room, tearing the towel from her body, and taking her on the nearest surface they could find.

"Yes," Piper asked, trying to gain her composure from the interruption.

Tristan picked up on it right away. Piper was flushed and breathless; there was something in her eyes as well, something he recognized from the night before.

He confidently leaned into the door jamb, a know-ing smirk creeping across his lips. "Did I interrupt you?"

Piper took a deep breath before responding, find-ing it difficult to meet the sparkling eyes staring through her. "I was just finishing my shower."

"Were you able to finish?"

Piper choked on her own spit at Tristan's choice of wording, which only elicited a deep and sexy laugh from Tristan. Piper tried to recover, tried to hide her embarrassment, though in the back of her mind she had to wonder if Tristan knew what she was really doing in the shower, and what had caused her to do it.

"Sorry, I just didn't expect you. I thought it was my sister at the door," Piper began, completely dis-missing Tristan's question.

He laughed and pointed to the peephole. "You know, that's what these things are for."

"I thought you had calls," she asked, quickly changing the subject. She thought about inviting him in, making their conversation more private, considering that she was standing in a towel, still dripping wet, in more places than one. She chose not to. If he were to cross that threshold and close them off from the rest of the world, it would be dangerous.

"Yeah. That's actually what I wanted to talk to you about." Tristan ran his hand through his hair feeling a little bad, but knowing it needed to be done. "I don't know if I'm going to make it tonight."

He watched as shock and disappointment crashed into Piper's face. In a sick way, he liked it. He allowed himself to assume that it had more to do with spending time with him and less to do with simply needing a date.

Before she could say anything, "I mean, I'm definitely going to try but I have...calls."

"Yeah, no, I get it," Piper managed. Her stomach felt like she had eaten something bad. She had to wonder if he was distancing himself. Earlier they had some honest and not so pleasant words, and now this.

Before either could say another word, a coughing from the hallway startled them.

"Okay, lover boy, we need to get ready," Lucy sang out.

Tristan stepped from the doorway allowing Lucy to pass by, all the while never taking his eyes from Piper. He hated how broken she looked, but everything was falling into place and one risk he wasn't ready to take would be doing something to mess that up.

"We'll talk later then," Piper told Tristan, pretending not to care that he would possibly be ditching her that evening.

She slowly started closing the door, but Tristan stopped her. "I'm going to try," he insisted. "Have fun getting ready."

"What? No goodbye kiss," Lucy hollered from inside the room, already splattering various pieces of makeup across the bed.

Piper whipped her head toward her sister and gave a menacing glare. Before she could turn back and conclude her conversation with Tristan, she felt a warm hand on her bare and damp shoulder, which quickly caused her heart to race.

When Piper turned, the knuckles of Tristan's hand glided upward along her neck until his palm rest gently along her cheek. He took a step forward and Piper had to tilt her head to look up at him. If she expected a raw, heated, and passionate kiss, she was sorely mistaken. Instead, Tristan dipped his head to the opposite cheek his hand rest on and gave her the sweetest and friendliest of pecks. When he pulled back he didn't even look her in the eyes, but only turned and said his goodbye.

"That was weak," Lucy screamed as the door closed.

Tristan rest his back against Piper's door, his heart pounding and his head a confused mess. Lucy's words echoed in his head, an unspoken challenge. Seconds passed as he debated. He could go back to his room and hope to have everything straightened out before dinner, or he could take just a minute more and surprise the hell out of Piper.

The knocking on the door startled both sisters. Piper looked at Lucy with confusion. She grabbed a robe this time and wrapped it around her before proceeding, this time taking Tristan's comment about the peephole into consideration.

"Who is it," Lucy whispered, as though an ax murderer was on the other side.

Piper was confused why he was back only a moment later. "It's Tristan."

She assumed there was something he had forgotten to tell her, perhaps something more about his sudden and mysterious calls. When she opened the door, Tristan made her very aware as to what he had forgotten.

Before a single word could escape her mouth, it was forcefully covered by Tristan's warm and pleading lips. Though completely shocked by the gesture, Piper didn't hesitate for one second and immediately allowed the kiss to deepen. His tongue was powerful against hers and her frustration from the shower soon returned when her mind began to wonder how well his tongue could work on other parts of her body.

It was just like their first kiss, and Tristan had to imagine that it would always be like that with her. Once he had her, it was difficult to let go. Her body melted into his so easily, with her giving him complete control over the situation, to take as much of her as he wanted, and lately he wanted a lot. The feeling of her nails digging into his chest through his t-shirt only caused the kiss to become that much more frantic.

He was just about to slam the door shut and tear her robe away when an unwelcoming voice brought them both back from the elated high the kiss had given them.

"Okay," Lucy screamed. "I get it! Geez, I won't ever pick on you about your game again."

They broke from their embrace, both finding breathing as well as standing to be quite difficult.

"What was that," Piper managed in a soft voice so that Lucy wouldn't hear.

"That," Tristan began, taking a step forward so that he could gently entangle his fingers with Piper's. "Was a kiss."

Piper couldn't hear anything after that. Her heart was beating so loudly and erratically, all from a kiss, a touch, a few words, but most of all, from Tristan, just Tristan.

\* \* \*

After drying her hair, Piper returned to the room where Lucy was already experimenting with makeup.

Lucy turned toward Piper and batted her eyes. "What do you think?"

"That's a lot of green and purple," Piper hesitated.

"Oh, come on. You're going to do your stupid neutrals again, aren't you," Lucy teased, although she knew the answer.

"It fits."

Lucy groaned and tossed a brush to the side. "Maybe that's your problem." Piper rose a brow to show that she wasn't following. "You need a little more color in your life."

"I have the strangest feeling that you're not talking about eyeshadow right now."

Lucy hated that Piper had to be so smart. The entire time she was playing in the mirror she came up with an excellent metaphor for men and makeup. Now it seemed ruined. "You two are good together," Lucy quietly admitted, taking Piper by surprise.

"It's nothing. It's just an arrangement for a week. He's doing me a huge favor." Even Piper didn't want to believe the repetitive words coming from her mouth.

Lucy doubled over laughing. "Shut up!" Suddenly she stopped as she recalled a tiny glimmer of useless information. She then turned rather serious as she thought through her next words. "This isn't just another set piece."

Now it was Piper's turn to laugh. "Where did you learn that from," she giggled, fully knowing that her sister knew the equivalent to Haven when it came to sports.

Lucy scoffed. "I needed to check my grades on your computer and I happened to read your article. I'll admit, I had to look a few things up, but damn was it good. Too good for Blythe's shit magazine."

"Thank you, I think, but you're getting off topic."

"Right, okay, so hear me out. So you said something about Tristan excelling in set pieces. I'm not going to lie, I was hoping that was sexual, unfortunately it's not," Lucy concluded with a sigh, faking disappointment in her usual silly way.

"Lucy!"

"Geez." She rolled her eyes. Even when she was trying to be serious, she couldn't help but try to add some humor to the situation. "Well, what I got is that those are like specialized maneuvers that are carefully planned. That's how all this started out right?"

In a way, Piper had to agree with Lucy. She didn't know which was worse, Lucy comparing her life to makeup or a sport that she had no knowledge of.

"It all turned to shit the first night, didn't it," Lucy asked rather boldly, finally getting to the point.

Piper still continued to play dumb. "What are you talking about?"

"Whatever perfect arrangement, foolproof plan, you two had. Somewhere between then and now you fucked up. You fell in love."

Piper turned from her sister. She couldn't let Lucy see her face right now. A small part of her felt foolish. What kind of person falls in love with someone after a kiss? After sex? After days? Stupidly she did. She had to go and fall for someone that she'd probably never see after the wedding was done.

She put on a brave face and pushed aside everything she was feeling. "It's not like that. We both know that this is over after Sunday."

# CHAPTER 22

Tristan quickly threw on a button up after turning his phone to speaker mode. He could have sworn that he heard Piper's door close not more than a few minutes ago. He had about ten minutes to wrap up his last call and he could still make the rehearsal dinner.

"I would never go out of my way like this, but when I saw your name," the voice on the other end continued as Tristan smoothed some product in his hair, ruffling it a bit. "I had no idea that you were cleared to play for this long. Even after that, I assumed you'd be headed back to play for Los Angeles."

"Things changed along the way. I take it that you've got all my medical reports then." Tristan tried to wrap the conversation up as quickly as possible.

"Absolutely. Our general manager will be up to talk to you tomorrow. Like I said, that's not something I'd do, but since you told me there's going to be a publication announcing your return, I want to jump on this immediately. He'll bring by some paperwork," he paused, realizing how unprofessional it all sounded. "Unless of course you'd rather have a meeting in the city with your agent and lawyers?"

Tristan laughed. "I can read. I think I can handle it."

"Well, I'm sure we've taken up enough of each other's evening. I can say, I'm looking forward to working with you."

Tristan concluded the conversation, stumbling to put on his shoes. He didn't think for one second that Maggie would hold the boat back for a minute past departure time. He grabbed his wallet from the nightstand and slipped his hotel card in it. Maybe it was his overconfidence, but rather than rushing straight to the door, he rummaged around in his suitcase for something else, and tucked it into the back of his wallet. He knew Piper wasn't the type of woman that would be game for anything, but that wasn't going to stop him from trying.

* * *

Piper didn't allow herself to get her hopes up. Tristan never did strike her as the type of person that adhered to a strict schedule outside of playing times. When he told her that he might not make it, she knew what that meant. That didn't stop her from looking her best.

After a great deal of arguing, Piper finally gave in to a little color by allowing Lucy to mix a subtle amount of green and gold on her eyelids. It actually looked great with her dress, but she neglected telling Lucy that. Lucy got a big head over the smallest compliments.

"I bet this dried up a couple oil wells," Nolan scoffed as they made their way into the elaborately decorated dining room.

Tan and pink hues were plastered throughout, from the table linens and chair sashes to the flowers.

"This is ridiculous," Lucy hissed. "It's like the wedding that never ends." Regardless, Piper watched as Lucy's eyes lit up when she saw the small bar that had been set up. "Sweet," she whispered so that only Piper could hear. "Open bar." She gave Piper a nudge and casually drifted from their parents.

Piper moseyed about on her own, heavily considering a drink as well to ease her nerves. She tried her best to avoid the small groups of people. Farther away she saw her aunt pointing into another room. Through the half open door there were chairs set up with an aisle running down the middle toward an altar.

"I take it this isn't what you would have done," an all too familiar voice spoke from behind.

Piper couldn't help but clench up as she turned to meet Jared. His face was strange, something between happy and somber, if there was such a thing.

"You are correct with that," Piper snorted.

She felt uncomfortable with their close proximity and took a noticeable step back. The situation only became odder when Jared's eyes slowly scanned over her body as though he was checking her out. Even when they were together he didn't look at her the way he was looking at her in that moment.

"You look beautiful." His voice was barely a whisper, and he looked around with uncertainty. Maybe he was making sure that Tristan wasn't around, or perhaps he was terrified that Samantha would hear those words.

Piper politely thanked him but crossed her arms, distancing herself even further. He began to say something else, but gasps and shrieks from nearby caught their attention. It was Margaret with the captain of the boat.

"It's 7:06," she insisted, tapping at her Rolex. "The boat was supposed to start moving exactly at 7:00. The rehearsal begins at 7:20."

"We will momentarily. I got a call about fifteen minutes ago from the resort insisting that I hold off," the captain calmly spoke.

Margaret had already garnered a great deal of attention, but she didn't bother letting up. "I paid for this and it was made clear that we leave at 7:00 and return at 10:00."

"Ma'am, it's only a few minutes."

"What is the purpose of this delay?" Her voice only continued to rise. From the other side of the dining room, Samantha started rushing over.

"One of your guests is running late."

Piper wasn't sure she heard those words correctly, but when she saw Margaret's head begin to spin demonically with flames bursting from her ears, she knew that she had.

"Excuse me," she screeched. "Who the hell thinks that they have the authority to do that?!"

Silence fell amongst everyone. The captain had no explanation for Margaret.

Honestly, he couldn't have planned it better. Everyone, except a few that were already seated in the makeshift chapel, turned when they heard heavy footsteps from the deck, growing louder the closer they got.

Piper had to bite her lip to keep from losing herself in laughter when she saw who stood at the entry.

Tristan gave a look of confusion with all eyes on him. At first he thought that maybe he should have worn his suit, but he nixed that idea when he saw Jared in a pair of khakis and Derek in what he could only assume were a dressy version of cargo shorts.

He hesitantly made his way in and the looks eventually began to fade. There were a couple whispers, but for the most part, everyone went back to whatever conversations they were having before he arrived. Almost everyone.

The first thing he noticed was Piper, her eyes locked on him, a playful glimmer in them. What he didn't like was how close Jared was standing next to her, void of any other guests. He fought to take his eyes from Piper, but the deathly glare from her aunt garnered his attention. Then he quickly noticed the man she was talking to and he quickened his pace toward them.

"Captain Patterson," he asked, extending his hand.

"I'm guessing you're the fellow this lady is all up in arms over." His words were a slow drawl that came from southern roots.

Tristan smiled proudly in Margaret's direction, which only further increased the combustion of her insides. "Sorry about that Maggie." He watched her face redden, but before she could unleash any venomous words on him, he turned back to the captain and withdrew his wallet. "Thank you so much for doing that...and dealing with this." Tristan didn't specify what *this* was, but Captain Patterson wasn't an idiot.

"It's not necessary," he replied, shaking his hand at the two hundred dollar bills Tristan produced.

"Please, I insist."

"Will you take the damn money and go do your job," Margaret quietly hissed, so that her guests wouldn't see her lose her cool any more than what she already had.

After he tucked the money away and thanked Tristan for the kind offer, he departed.

Tristan fully expected Margaret to let him have it, and if she did, he wasn't sure that he'd be able to keep a straight face. Fortunately for him, a frenzied middle aged woman with a clipboard pulled her aside and began insisting that all those not in the wedding party needed to take their places in the room beyond the dining area. She motioned for Jared to quickly take his place inside as well, which meant that Piper was now alone.

Tristan assumed he wouldn't have much time with her, but rather than listen to the orders being thrown out, he made his way to her.

"Hey." Gradually he was beginning to constantly feel more nervous around her with each meeting as their week drew closer to an end. He felt worse than when he asked his first girl to homecoming during freshman year. Piper often had a debilitating effect on him when it came to words.

"I cannot believe you," she playfully hissed.

"I knew how much you needed me as your date tonight. I didn't want to disappoint you." He didn't tell her the entire truth, the truth being that after that kiss it was a struggle to get through any of his calls. He had never looked forward to seeing someone so badly.

"If I were you, I'd watch your back tonight." Piper saw the look of uncertainty and elaborated. "Aunt Margaret looks like she is not above slitting your throat."

Piper melted when he gave a deep and genuine laugh and pulled her in for a kiss on the forehead. It only heightened her confliction. Every moment with Tristan, both in public and away from everyone, felt too real. Her head knew the difference but her heart had a more difficult time listening.

Tristan took a step back, sliding his hands down Piper's arms while his eyes drifted over her body. Her makeup was different. He didn't know how to compliment her on it without offending her, but it was something unique that he assumed she didn't do all that often. Her hair was a little wavier than he'd seen before and the blonde locks were delicately pinned to one side. He had a difficult time looking beyond her face. The dress fit her like it was made for her, but the animal inside of him could only think of ripping it apart. He knew the body it concealed and he also knew how badly he needed her again. Oddly, he had never felt that with any other woman, and he was beginning to think of the insane possibility that he never would.

Piper became slightly uncomfortable with Tristan quietly evaluating her. "Please say something," she managed.

Tristan gave a small chuckle, realizing the effect he was having on her. He moved forward on her and allowed his right hand to slip around her waist, while the other tipped her chin so that she could see the dark depths of his eyes.

"You look incredible," he breathed. Piper could smell a combination of his cologne as well as his fresh and minty breath. His hand on her waist slowly moved farther down until he was hungrily cupping the left side of her ass. Her entire body turned to flames from the small gesture. "With your presence, I don't know how the hell I'm going to make it tonight." Through all the lust, there was a painful look in Tristan's eyes.

Most of the guests were already in the next room, and the woman with the clipboard was attempting to pair the groomsmen and bridesmaids up with their respective partners.

"Care to elaborate," Piper pressed on, knowing their conversation would be cut short.

"Just know that if we weren't on a damn boat, we wouldn't still be standing here," he groaned, pulling Piper into him, slightly grinding into her so that she could feel how much he wanted and needed her.

"How does being on a boat make a difference?" She bit her bottom lip after saying those words. They were fairly bold for her and the flicker in Tristan's eyes as she said them instantly made her regret it. He was going to take it as a challenge.

"I'm missing a groomsman," the frazzled woman called out.

Tristan and Piper were immediately thrown back to reality. The reality was that nothing would be happening anytime soon.

"Reed! Dude! Stop flirting and get over here," Derek called out.

Tristan's heart was pounding from Piper's last comment. He didn't want to break away from her. The wedding may have brought them together, but the wedding could go to hell for him at this point.

"Go," Piper laughed, realizing that Tristan was a little speechless.

The sexual atmosphere that had fallen over them quickly washed away, but that didn't stop either from wondering where it could have gone with just a few more moments.

"What the hell was that," Lucy asked, standing at the entry waiting on Piper. When Piper didn't answer her, Lucy handed her one of the glasses of wine in her hands, and continued on while they made their way to a few seats closer to the back. "Seriously, that looked intense. Was he grabbing your ass?" Her words were a little louder than intended and brought about stares from some on Jared's side of the family.

Piper waved her sister off. Her insides were screaming for Tristan's touch, and talking about it absolutely wouldn't be doing her any favors.

"Okay, first set," the wedding planner announced as she entered backwards.

Brian and a nameless bridesmaid entered.

"Alright, now watch! When the pair before you gets right about here, you need to begin. And...next!"

Piper and Lucy both let out a small amount of laughter when Derek entered, Erin at one side and a beer on his other. Several more sets came through until the final pair. Piper couldn't help but take a deep breath and roll her eyes at the odds. Tristan and Bridget.

Bridget giggled and leaned in closer than needed, so much so that her head grazed Tristan's shoulder. She continued to whisper something which only made Piper bitter that she couldn't hear what it was that caused the small smile on Tristan's face. When they got to the end of the aisle to go their separate ways, Bridget leaned in and gave Tristan a hug. It lasted much longer than the typical hug between acquaintances.

Lucy nudged Piper and whispered, "I'm liking this side of you."

"What are you talking about," Piper whispered back through gritted teeth.

"Come on, you're seething. If looks could kill, Bridget would be as cold as ice right now."

"Alright, and now here comes the bride, everyone will now stand," the insanely loud woman announced.

Piper was surprised that Samantha's father made it; however, the expression on his face was easy to read. He would rather be anywhere else.

Thankfully everything following moved along a lot faster. For a minute, it looked like a full on wedding with commentary.

Just a little while after everyone had taken their seats and Samantha and Jared were being given instructions, Piper's phone began buzzing. Her mother shot her a look meaning that it should have been on silent. Piper quickly hit a side button to stop the humming, and watched as it sent a call from Blythe Carrington to voicemail.

She stared at the phone, waiting for a message to pop up. None came.

Piper's attention was diverted when Lucy's elbow prodded her in the side.

"What is wrong with you," Piper quietly yelled.

Lucy motioned with her head and eyes to the wedding party before whispering in Piper's ear. "He has not stopped staring at you."

Piper looked up to meet Tristan's intense gaze. She would have given anything to know what he was thinking. Warmth rushed down her body straight to her core. The butterflies that Tristan sent swarming through her were unlike any she had ever felt.

Piper was jolted from her daydream when her phone began to buzz yet again.

Blythe Carrington.

"I have to take this," she whispered to her mother and sister, as she slowly and discreetly rose from her seat.

Piper climbed over her mother, ignoring all the mumbo jumbo instructions from the front.

"Dad, move," she hissed to a very confused Nolan.

Her phone was still ringing. She didn't want to let it go to voicemail again, but aside from the woman speaking at the front, it was far too quiet for her to answer her phone.

"And after that we'll ask for any objections; however–"

Piper painfully stubbed her toe at that moment.

"Ouch! Shit," she screamed out of instinct, eliciting every set of eyes to come glaring in her direction.

Piper looked up, quite aware of the horrible timing. Off to the side she could hear a tipsy Lucy stifling a laugh. A woman a couple rows forward whispered, "She's the ex," more loudly than intended. While Jared and Samantha looked annoyed, Margaret was livid. There was no doubt that she'd be fuming all evening from Tristan, but now Piper just slathered another thick layer of icing on that cake.

"Is there something you'd like to add," the woman asked. She gripped her clipboard tightly in annoyance.

Piper suddenly realized that her phone was dangerously close to going to voicemail and Blythe Carrington was one woman she didn't want to send into a tailspin at the moment.

Piper hit answer on her phone. "One second," she said into the speaker. She held her phone up to the woman giving instructions. "I'm sorry. Important call. Continue." She then proceeded to trip over her father once again, barely catching her balance as she brought the phone back to her ear, rushing from the room.

"I'm sorry about that," she insisted once she was back in the dining area. Though it was chilly outside, she continued on to the deck so that hopefully there would be no distractions.

"Oh, did I interrupt you? What time is it anyway," Blythe mumbled.

Piper could hear the clicking of her keyboard and knew that she was on speaker. Blythe was no doubt still in her office. "It's fine. They're just doing the rehearsal stuff."

"Oh, good. I was hoping it was nothing important. I needed to talk to you about this article."

Piper took a deep breath and expected the worst. "Yes?"

There was a slight pause on Blythe's end before, "It's very good. I like it. I hate that I have to run it online and not in our monthly print edition."

"Oh?" Piper became confused in more ways than one.

"Yes. When Mr. Reed sent in his consent, he told me to run it immediately. He was quite vague about it, but got the impression that he's signing with a team. It was left out of your article, you know."

"That was one of his requests." Piper tried to hide her disappointment that Tristan hadn't told her, although now she could assume why he had so many calls throughout the day.

"You know those athletes. I'm sure he's wheeling and dealing for the biggest contract," Blythe disdainfully scoffed.

Piper didn't expect that from Tristan, but she couldn't imagine why he'd keep that from her. She hoped that he knew if he were to tell her something like that she wouldn't put it in her article.

"For procedure, I expect a résumé and at least five samples on my desk within the next week. I'll also need your help figuring out this assistant issue. Your temp is simply incompetent, and that's putting it nicely."

Though Piper's connection was a little sketchy, she caught every word of that, but she didn't understand it one bit. "I'm sorry?"

Unbeknownst to Piper, Blythe actually cracked a smile. "You are applying to write for the magazine, are you not?" When Piper fell speechless for a second too long, "I'll admit, our pieces on sports have been subpar. I'd like to branch into a well-rounded magazine, and we're severely lacking in a few areas. Do you know Haven actually walked out of a meeting again when basketball was brought up? Completely unprofessional, but she's too good to fire."

Piper held back a laugh, still trying to process what Blythe was telling her. Blythe continued to rattle on. "I'd like two pieces each month for print, as well as weekly ones for our online readers. We'll start with that."

Piper couldn't believe what she was hearing. Blythe was offering her a job as a writer. A moment of silence fell, the only sounds being the beating of the waves against the ship.

"I honestly don't know what to say," Piper stammered.

"Good. I'm guessing that means that you're interested?"

"Absolutely!"

Blythe sighed, contemplating her next words. "I do have to say, I am a bit disappointed."

Piper froze. Those weren't the words she expected to hear.

"I wish you would have expressed your interest with me," Blythe continued. "I didn't need to hear about it from some cocky show-off."

"I'm sorry, I don't understand." Piper knew the article she sent in was well-written. That was the only reason she imagined that Blythe was offering her the job.

"Your subject matter had a few words to say about your job as my assistant. From what I gathered, he thinks it's a waste of your skill and intellect. While I don't appreciate the way he spoke to me, it is something I've tossed around throughout the day. I have to say he's quite right. Now, I'm very busy and this conversation has taken longer than intended. Get me the paperwork I've asked for and I'll see you when you get back from whatever you call this little vacation."

Piper held on to the railing, peering into the water's depths, disbelief crashing through every thought. She couldn't quite comprehend any of it. Above everything, she couldn't believe how incredible Tristan was to her. She was woken from her daze with company.

"Is everything alright," her mother asked, her voice barely audible through the breeze.

Piper beamed. "Everything is perfect."

"You're all starry-eyed. Care to go into details," Emma pressed.

"I think Tristan helped me get a promotion." Piper shook her head. "No, not promotion, a new job."

"A new job," Emma repeated.

"I have to send in some paperwork, but I think I'm going to be a sports writer for *Rogue Times*," Piper laughed in disbelief.

"That's wonderful! But sports? Do you know anything about that?" Emma was beyond proud of her daughter, but she hoped that Piper wasn't getting herself into something she couldn't handle.

"Yes, mother. I don't have to know everything though. I didn't know shit about the oceans for that last freelance piece, but I researched and learned."

"This is what you want," Emma asked for certainty.

Piper nodded with a smile that could grow no more. It was. While there was a bit of hesitation with the subject matter, she'd rather spend grueling hours researching every aspect of every sport out there than have to plan another week of Blythe's breakfast orders.

Just as they were about to head back inside from the chill of the evening air, "Mom, do you think I'm insecure?"

Emma didn't understand where that was coming from.

A million thoughts had floated through Piper's mind after the conversation, and that was one of them. She should have told Blythe everything that Tristan said, albeit, in better terms.

"Honestly, I think at times you can be, but I wouldn't use that word. I think you're hesitant, afraid of making a mistake in every aspect of your life. Take Jared for instance. You would have married him because it was comfortable, you knew what to expect, you didn't have to worry about starting over. I know it hurt at the time, but I'm thankful that things played out as they did."

"I could never be the type of woman to stay after that," Piper sighed.

"Then you're not as insecure as you think. Just don't be afraid to take a risk. While I don't condone the things that your sister does and says, you could learn a little from her. Sometimes you need to say what you need to say. It's not always going to please everyone."

Piper was well aware as to her risk-taking, or lack thereof, over the years. While she didn't intend to go skydiving anytime soon, she could at least take her mother's advice and start speaking up. Starting with Tristan.

# CHAPTER 23

"Thank goodness they finally have some actual food," Lucy mumbled through a mouthful of crab cake. "I'm starving."

Piper tried not to focus all her attention on Tristan, but their brief contact earlier had left her wanting. Tristan actually followed along with what was planned out, eating at a table with other members of the wedding party.

"You know," Lucy began. She held off until she was able to swallow. "After you made a scene–"

"I did not make a scene! I had an important call," Piper insisted.

Lucy only laughed at that. "Whatever. First of all, I hate you for ditching me. I have to sit through that crap tomorrow too, only it'll be longer then."

"Where was this conversation going?"

Lucy had a difficult time staying on topic once she got going.

"Oh, right. It was hilarious! The wedding planner had everyone snickering at the end. She gave this big speech about how proper wedding etiquette would be to turn your phone off or leave it behind. I think you really pissed her off." Lucy thought for a minute.

"And Aunt Margaret, definitely Aunt Margaret." She paused for a moment. "I've been thinking about Tristan's nickname for that woman he mentioned. You know, the one he worked with or something?"

"Huh?"

"Yeah, the whole Elizabitch one. What would you think if I happened to call Margaret, wait for it...Maggot," Lucy giggled.

Piper shook her head. "I don't think you're ever going to grow up."

Focusing on Lucy became too difficult. On the other side of the room, Bridget had her arms around Tristan as she brought him a beer from the bar. He didn't ask for it. He decided he'd indulge in a couple drinks, but he didn't want them coming from Bridget.

"What are your plans after we get back," Bridget cooed.

"I think my girlfriend and I will settle in early." The word alone felt strange saying, but somewhere deep inside, he liked having that title reserved for Piper. An even deeper part wished that it was really true.

Thinking of Piper caused him to look up to find her once again. He had been watching her all evening, knowing that he'd rather be with her than some of the people he was surrounded with, especially a few of the touchy bridesmaids. This time, her eyes were glued to his from across the room. It didn't last long; she quickly looked away from him and went to her phone.

Tristan continued to watch Piper, wondering what she was reading or tending to. Her eyebrows clenched with uncertainty and her shoulders rose and sank with a deep breath or two. Once she put her phone down, her eyes quickly darted up to Tristan's. He narrowed his in skepticism when a second later he felt a buzzing from his jeans.

Piper's heart raced as she watched Tristan pull out his phone.

**Piper: Maybe I am a little jealous.**

Tristan knew how hard that must have been for her to admit. A small smirk crept to his face when he realized how long it took her to type that out.

Piper was soon alerted to an incoming text; however, with him watching her, she didn't want to be too eager.

"It's just this weird feeling I have," Lucy continued.

Piper had tuned out a good portion of her sister's ranting but now chose to give her attention, to distract her from rushing back to her phone.

"What do you mean," Piper asked. She hoped that Lucy didn't notice that she missed a good amount of the conversation.

"I'm just getting weird vibes. This whole week, it feels like a soda bottle."

Piper took a sip of her tea at the wrong time and nearly choked on it, fighting to keep from laughing. Her sister wasn't the best when it came to metaphors. Generally, Lucy's comparisons made sense only to Lucy.

"I'm serious," Lucy scoffed once her sister recovered. "It's like a soda bottle that's being shaken and shaken. I feel like someone is going to be brave enough or insane enough to twist the cap and then..." Lucy motioned with her hands so that it looked like she was describing a volcano or explosion.

"Where did that come from? Everything has been pretty dull and boring." Her time with Tristan most definitely wasn't, but she refrained from pointing that out.

"I just sense tension."

"I sense that you don't need another drink," Piper laughed as she finally reached for her phone.

**Tristan: It's understandable.**

Piper was livid. That was his response? She wrote only a single word, pressing for him to elaborate.

**Piper: Yeah?**

Tristan tried to contain his amusement as he watched Piper freeze upon reading his text. He hoped she realized that he was messing with her. Once he read her response that really wasn't anything, he was certain as to how to respond.

**Tristan: I'd be jealous too if I saw someone touching what was mine.**

The temperature in the room seemed to be rising. Just a few words on a screen sent waves of arousal through Piper. Rather than send something flirtatious back, she sent the serious truth of it and wondered how Tristan would handle it.

**Piper: That's funny, but you're not "mine".**

**Tristan: I could be.**

Piper read the words over and over, hating them more and more. She didn't like Tristan teasing in such a way. Things with them would never work out in the long run. As blurred as it was, it was all still pretend, just for a week. Though falling into bed with him hadn't been part of the plan; it was a nice bonus, one that couldn't happen again. She couldn't have meaningless sex just for the gratification, and in such a short amount of time, that's all that she would allow herself to call it. The truth was, if she allowed for things to continue, she'd end up heartbroken in a matter of days.

She stared at the screen, not sure how to reply. It was crushing that deep down those words probably weren't meant how she wished.

Instead of responding at all, Piper put her phone away. She looked up, knowing that Tristan would be watching her, only to be further disappointed.

She scanned the room but found him nowhere. He had vanished.

Moments later, "Hey!" Samantha appeared to be in a far better mood than they had seen all week "Okay, so...tomorrow night my bridesmaids and I are having a little private thing at a section in the resort bar, very nice, very classy."

Piper glanced toward a couple of the girls. Nice and classy weren't words that she would have used to describe them.

"Since you guys are family, I wanted to extend the invite. You too, Aunt Emma," she giggled.

Piper cringed at the statement. The whole messed up truth of it was that they were family; however, apparently that word meant more to some people than others.

Emma, Piper, and Lucy all exchanged rather uncomfortable glances.

It was Emma who spoke up. "Thank you, Samantha. We'll definitely try to make it."

"Oh, I really hope you will. It won't be anything big, but mother did have special wine brought in," she announced. She clapped her hands in a giddy way, but suddenly stopped as she looked up.

Piper felt a large hand give her shoulder a small squeeze.

"Excuse me, ladies. If I could borrow Piper for a few minutes," Tristan politely inquired.

Samantha nodded in awe, whereas Emma and Lucy exchanged rather confused glances with an even more confused Piper.

Piper quickly rose. "Yeah, sure."

Tristan's hand fell and entangled itself with Piper's, gradually leading her from the room and into the cold night air.

Piper refrained from saying anything. Half of her mind was wondering where the hell they were going, while half was still trying to figure out how that last message was supposed to come across.

Tristan led Piper up a spiral of stairs, down a smaller walkway, to a door that was unlocked.

"What is this," Piper asked as Tristan pulled her in, quickly closing the door from the wisps of cold air.

Her eyes widened when he gently placed her against a wall, his fingers twirling down the waves of her hair further down her body. With a deep and raspy voice, "It's the bridge."

"And where is the captain?"

The corners of Tristan's mouth rose just a bit, showing a sinister smirk. "He had to take a break for a minute, or ten to fifteen." He could see the skepticism on Piper's face. "It's fine. He said not to touch anything and we're all good."

Before Piper could ask another question, Tristan's lips were hungrily on hers. If she was surprised by the action, she didn't show it, only allowed him to set the pace for things to come.

That's when her thoughts got the best of her, and her head won over both her heart and any sexual desires rising to the surface.

"Tristan, stop." Her words surprising the both of them. "What are we doing?"

With a sexy grin, "I'm taking you up on the offer from earlier."

He stepped closer, sliding his hands to Piper's elbows and attempting to pull her into him so that he could continue what was just starting. Much to his dismay, she took a step back.

"That wasn't an offer," she sighed, partly lying. "We were just joking around."

"Oh, so you don't want to have sex on a boat...ship...whatever?"

Piper really wished he wouldn't have mentioned sex. Sure, she wanted it, but she wanted so much more. Just thinking that made her head feel like exploding. "That's the thing! We shouldn't be having sex at all. Everything is getting so complicated because of it. Last night was not part of the arrangement."

"Arrangement?" Tristan couldn't hide the defensive tone when he repeated the word.

Piper lowered her voice, truly not wanting to fight. "Yes, you helping me out this week."

"You can't be serious," he scoffed. When Piper said nothing, only looked at him with confusion, Tristan continued. "After last night, hell, even before that, you think that was all for show," he asked, not wanting her to answer, and his voice slightly rising.

Piper groaned, hating to see the frustration that flashed in the set of eyes that would not remove themselves from her. "You started it that first night when you kissed me in front of everyone."

"Maybe it started out that way, and then maybe I wanted to keep kissing you," Tristan admitted, beginning to close any distance with Piper.

Piper shook her head. She hated the way Tristan talked. No, that wasn't true. She loved the way he talked to her, but she hated what it did to her insides. "Look, the plan was simple, just pretend to be in a relationship with me."

"Then what was that text you just sent me, about being jealous?" His tone had changed. It was melting and seductive as his eyes raked over her body.

"That's my point," Piper began to ramble, needing to continue talking any nonsense to keep from throwing herself at Tristan. "I have no reason to be jealous! I shouldn't be, and I don't want to be."

In the smoothest and lowest voice, with barely a whisper, "I'm not pretending."

Piper was shocked. "So the arrangement is off?"

Tristan smiled and shook his head, not believing that someone who caught on to everything wasn't getting it. "For me, it has been since that first night."

Piper hesitated. "I don't understand." Although, the butterflies in her stomach told her that she might.

Tristan reached up, caressing Piper's cheek. He was thankful that she wasn't backing away or dismissing the gesture. Slowly he trailed his fingers down her neck and then her arms, knowing that even underneath the clothing she was getting goosebumps. "My words, my touches, my kisses, the incredible sex, that was all real. Jesus, Piper. I like you. I thought you knew that. Hell, I told you that."

"That was right before we were about to...you know," she managed.

"So because I was horny it didn't count," he laughed.

She couldn't help but smile. "Stop."

He pulled Piper into him, as he backed her into a control board, towering over her. He brought his thumb and forefinger to her chin, forcing her to look up at him.

"Tell me that you don't want me to kiss you right now." He was so close that she could feel the breath of every word on her lips.

Seconds passed and Piper could feel her throat closing up, unable to speak. Tristan's eyes, golden from the tiny glistening lights on the panels, sank into hers, begging for any response, all the while certain that he wouldn't hear those particular words come from her mouth. Her body was already giving away how badly she craved his touch.

When he finally kissed her, it was different than before. He was soft, cautious; it barely felt like he was touching her.

Even though there were so many thoughts and questions that Piper needed to get out, she put them aside. Whether it was just a fling, or something they'd work on in the future, suddenly didn't matter. They still had three days together to enjoy with as few complications as possible.

Piper tried with all her might to stop from falling any further for the man cradling her like glass in his arms. As much as she resigned herself to the idea that Tristan would only break her heart in the end, she was quickly welcoming that pain if it meant a few more moments in his arms.

Gradually, Tristan's kisses became harder, faster, frantic, until he was no longer holding back. He slipped his hands to the back of Piper's thighs and tossed her onto one of the lit up panels like a feather.

Piper inched forward, sliding her dress upward, so that she could easily wrap her legs around Tristan's waist. Her hands gripped at his crisp shirt, balling it in her fists while tugging him down.

"Damn, you're so fucking sexy right now," Tristan groaned.

Piper froze once his lips when to her neck, the side that was clean of their last encounter, and she pushed him back ever so slightly.

"No," she began with a smile. "I don't want you anywhere near my neck."

His seductive laugh, mixed with his warm breath and cologne, sent her head spinning.

"Sorry. It's a little difficult to restrain myself with you."

Before he could say anything that would continue to make her fall just a little more, Piper shut him up with her lips. Just as she desperately reached for his belt, Tristan steadied himself over her with his hand near her head, and everything came to a screeching halt.

The jolt of the vessel sent Tristan tumbling down, pressing a great deal of his weight onto Piper.

"Ouch! What the hell," she screamed.

"Oh, shit," Tristan breathed.

His line of vision was to the left of Piper's head, to some spot on the control board. In one swift move he had Piper on her feet next to him. It was only then that she saw several flashing lights that weren't there before.

"I think I hit something I wasn't supposed to," he sheepishly admitted.

Piper playfully swatted at his chest in annoyance; although, the next jerk of the ship sent a panic rushing through the both of them. Before either could react, a chilling gust of air engulfed them with the swinging open of the door.

"What in the hell," Captain Patterson roared. He made his way to the control panels, tapped on the screen and a few buttons and the lights on the board went dark. "Damnit. What part of don't touch a damn thing didn't you understand," he hollered, directing his words to Tristan. Though he tried to appear angry, he looked more annoyed by the inconvenience. He huffed and waved his hand around. "Just get out of here."

"I'm really sorry," Tristan began, reaching for his wallet.

"No, no. You paid enough," Piper heard as she stepped over the threshold, leaving the bridge. She watched as Tristan shook the captain's hand.

"Thank you," Tristan laughed, still a bit embarrassed by the situation.

Just as he left to follow Piper, Captain Patterson called out, not too loudly, but enough so that Piper heard. "Did she at least say yes," he asked.

It took Tristan a brief second to recall his lie. He glanced to Piper, who had stopped walking and stared at him questioningly. He looked back to the captain and gave a simple, "Yeah," before closing the door behind him.

Tristan found humor in the fact that Piper wanted to bring it up, but hoped he would mention it first. He had to stifle a laugh when she finally let her curiosity get the best of her.

"Did you pay the captain?"

"For some privacy, yes," Tristan admitted.

Piper's steps faltered and she came to a halt. Tristan turned around to see the shock and disgust on her face, clear as day in the darkened night.

"No, not like that," he quickly added.

"What did I say yes to," Piper asked. She folded her arms across her chest, leaving Tristan to wonder if she was annoyed or cold. In his eyes it looked to be a little of both.

Before continuing, he took Piper in his arms, so that he could rub over hers. He felt her shivering and knew they needed to get back inside.

"With all the technology, the captain could spare a few minutes away," he began, watching how Piper's lips twitched from side to side, probably anticipating where he was going. Rather than making a long story out of nothing, "I told him that my girlfriend was into ships and I wanted a private place to propose."

There were so many things wrong with what Piper had just heard. "But really, you just wanted to fool around?"

"And you deserved more than a bathroom," Tristan quickly interrupted.

Piper dismissed the comment. She wanted to point out that he had used the word girlfriend, but there was no sense in beating a dead horse. "That isn't exactly the best place to propose on a ship," she laughed, finding humor in how ridiculous Tristan could be. They continued down the deck toward the dining room, Tristan's arms lingering around her, their warmth setting her on fire.

"Oh, really. Then where?"

Without having to think, "The bow."

"No way," Tristan countered. "One of them gets nervous, the ring is dropped, gone forever in the icy depths of the sea."

Piper turned her attention to Tristan's face, finding comfort in his playful expression.

In that moment, they both saw something in the eyes of the other. Hope.

# CHAPTER 24

Just as they entered the dining room and Tristan was about to escort Piper back to her seat, he changed his mind, holding her back, away from the crowd for just a moment more.

There were a few times in the last few days where he had been nervous around her. He'd never tell her, but that night when he arrived in New York, he couldn't sleep. He spent the entire night a wreck at the idea of finally meeting her in person again, this time knowing that it would be more than the casual pleasantries they had exchanged during her time with Jared.

Her brows had clenched, waiting for whatever it was he felt compelled to say. She wanted to ask him if everything was alright, but stopped herself once his lips parted and he drew in a shaky breath.

"Spend the night with me."

It wasn't a question, at least that's not how he phrased it. It was his desire, his want, his wish. Piper could feel and hear her heart beating so hard that she thought her head might explode.

Ever since she left the previous night, she had hoped that it had been more than just sex for Tristan. The look on his face said it all. More.

When she didn't respond, he placed his hands around her waist. There was nothing sexual about it at all, rather, it was romantic. Piper was left feeling safe and adored.

"I want you to be there when I wake up," Tristan continued, with words that were foreign to his own self.

Piper nodded and quietly whispered, "Of course."

* * *

"I was worried," Lucy huffed as soon as Piper took her seat.

"About what?"

"Seriously? You didn't feel that out there. I wonder if we hit something," Lucy went on.

Piper was curious what drink Lucy was on by this point as she seemed even more loose and erratic than her sober self.

"I don't even want to know what the two of you were up to if you didn't feel that," Lucy said as she made gagging noises.

Tristan watched Piper blush from across the room. Her sister didn't hold anything back and he was fairly certain that they were talking about him.

"Dude," Brian whispered with a nudge. "Your fly is down."

Tristan's hand quickly went for his lap. It wasn't extremely noticeable, but indeed it was down. He remembered Piper fumbling with his belt, but he didn't know she had gotten that far.

"Come on, we saw the two of you leave and come back all touchy feely, we're not idiots," Derek chimed in as he brought more beers to the table.

"We just went for a walk," Tristan lied, hoping to end any talk of Piper.

"I have to say, I didn't expect this from you," Brian went on. The few men around him paused their conversations to listen in, Jared included.

Curious, Tristan took the bait as he reached for one of the beers. "What are you talking about?" He couldn't help but look up to see Piper laughing with her sister. Her face was as red as could be from embarrassment. When she glanced across the room in his direction, she nervously bit her lip and quickly looked away, a small gesture that sent Tristan's insides on fire.

Brian laughed as he watched Tristan. "That! That right there. You look like you're two seconds away from getting down on one knee."

Tristan shook his head. "Not even close, and maybe you should lay off after that one," he said as he clinked his bottle to Brian's.

"Yeah, they've only been dating for a month or two," Derek felt the need to point out.

Tristan clenched at the comment. Dating. If he didn't scare Piper off in a couple days, he hoped that would be the case.

He briefly met Jared's eyes from across the table. Something was different. He didn't look agitated or looking for a fight. He looked genuinely distraught and concerned.

* * *

Once everyone made the brief walk from the docked ship to the resort, groups began dispersing. Almost everyone over the age of forty went back to their respective rooms, as did Lucy. She claimed the boat had screwed up her stomach, not once admitting to how much she drank. Most of the groomsmen and bridesmaids continued to the resort bar.

Piper headed in to the lobby while Tristan and Brian concluded their conversation outside. Though she was exhausted, her mind was racing at the thought of spending the night with Tristan.

Just as she closed her eyes, took in a deep breath, and allowed her head to fall back, she felt the sofa move from someone else taking the other half. To say that she was shocked when she opened her eyes and looked over was putting it mildly.

"Hey," Jared quietly announced.

"What are you doing here?" Piper didn't mean for her words to come out as coldly as they did. While she still thought Jared was scum, she was over their whole situation. "Sorry. I mean, I thought you'd be at the bar with Samantha."

"She and some of her friends went to change out of all their frilly dresses first."

"Okay," was all Piper replied, turning her attention away.

Jared took a deep breath and began interlacing his fingers together, never finding a comfortable position for them. It was a nervous habit that Piper remembered.

"Look, I was hoping we could talk," he said with an uneasy tone.

Piper had no clue what he could possibly want to talk about, but she really didn't care either.

"I'm actually waiting on Tristan. He should be coming in soon," Piper said with little emotion.

"Maybe tomorrow? I'll text you? Unless you blocked my number a long time ago." He tried to make the statement light by laughing it off, but something about it came across as strange, as though he was anxious and on edge.

"I'm not that hateful, although I'd be lying if I said that I didn't change your name to something uncouth," Piper sighed, desperately wanting the conversation to come to an end.

Jared gave a small grin and shook his head. "It's well-deserved." He glanced back upon hearing familiar voices entering in the distance. "I better catch up with Samantha. I'll talk to you later," he concluded with rushed words.

Moments later, Piper felt Tristan's hands cup her shoulders from behind. It was only then that she wondered how much of Jared's departure had to do with Samantha as opposed to Tristan.

"What did he want," Tristan asked, attempting to mask any skepticism and jealousy.

"I really have no idea," Piper groaned.

✳ ✳ ✳

Piper eyed Tristan with confusion when he pressed his back into her door and waited for her to withdraw her key card from her purse.

"At least this way you don't have anywhere to run to, and I don't plan on leaving until morning." His voice was low and seductive, already heating Piper's skin.

Piper sighed and shook her head as she rummaged through the small clutch. "I told you that I'd stay the night."

"Why did you leave," he asked, as she handed over the card.

Piper didn't answer until they were in the confines of her suite, needing time to figure out an appropriate answer. She decided to go with pure honesty. "There were several reasons," she began, although she didn't plan on telling them all. "I guess...Well, I've never done the whole one-night stand thing. I didn't know what the protocol was."

Tristan didn't mean to laugh, but he couldn't contain himself. Piper didn't see what was so humorous in the statement and became slightly defensive.

"Sorry I'm not like all those girls that just line up for you."

Tristan's laugher faded and his expression turned serious as he slowly began closing the distance between them. It was a hit he didn't expect, but he didn't mind it. He only wished Piper would give a little bit of that to her aunt.

"I know," he whispered, gazing down at Piper. He brushed a few strands of hair from her face, unable to contain his racing pulse from their closeness. "I wasn't laughing about that."

Piper's eyes narrowed and her lips tilted to one side, not understanding where Tristan was going.

"Just so you know," he continued, snaking one arm around her waist and pulling her into him. "You still haven't done that. A one-night stand. One night. Sex. No emotions. The end. You walk away."

Piper wasn't able to let out a breath until Tristan released her. "Are you always so intense," she mumbled.

"It's something you love about me." He quickly turned from Piper and made his way farther into the room. He was certain the she caught the word. He meant to say 'like' instead, but why that other word slipped out was beyond him.

Piper busied herself with removing her jewelry and shoes. She didn't have a smartass or sarcastic response for Tristan's comment, and when she thought about it, she didn't want to. His intensity was something that she *liked* about him.

"So, what now," Piper hesitated. She fully expected it to be similar to the night prior, where Tristan barely let her breathe, much less say a word.

A silent awkwardness ensued.

Then a melting chuckle came from Tristan as he turned to face Piper. "Go take you a shower, or bath, or whatever. From what I do know about you, I know that you have no intention sleeping with all that," he said, motioning his finger up and down her face.

Piper shifted from one foot to the next. "Just so I'm clear–"

Tristan interrupted, shaking his head. "Yes, alone. I might go back to my room and do the same. I have your key," he said, twirling the card in his fingers.

"I'm sorry about that comment from before. If I said or–"

"Stop." He crossed the room until he stood a breath away from Piper. He placed his hands softly on her shoulders. "You did absolutely nothing wrong. I know you've had a long day and you'll feel better after a hot," he paused, wondering for a brief second.

"Bath. I prefer baths, but usually I only have time for a shower." The smile on her face and pink tint to her cheeks made Tristan really not want to be an affectionate gentleman.

"Alright," he continued. "I know you'll feel better after a hot bath. While that dress is sexy as hell on you, I also know you'd feel a lot more comfortable in your pajamas."

"I just thought," Piper sighed.

"You thought wrong. I don't just want to screw you and fall asleep." With that, Tristan gave Piper a sweet kiss on her forehead and turned to leave.

# CHAPTER 25

The first rays of morning light began to enter the darkened room, gradually waking Piper. A flurry of butterflies rushed through her once she became aware of the situation she was in.

A muscled and artistically painted arm wrapped around her stomach while warm breaths tickled at her neck. Memories of last night flashed through her mind as she turned slightly to face a sound asleep Tristan.

Whatever she had expected and assumed to happen, absolutely didn't, and yet, she still had the most remarkable night with him. She couldn't remember the last time she had stayed up until after two in the morning talking to a guy. Actually, she probably could. Never. There was something about doing that with Tristan that made it so intimate.

"Good morning," Tristan groaned into Piper's neck, pulling her closer to him. "You look so hot in that shirt." As he said that a fire flashed across his eyes. Seeing Piper cuddled next to him was more awakening than any dose of caffeine.

Piper tried to contain the heat creeping to her cheeks, although the devilish smirk on Tristan's face gave her the indication that he noticed what his words did to her. She had intentionally worn the black t-shirt he had given her days prior, remembering how he looked at her when she came out of the bathroom with it on.

"Want to go get breakfast," Piper asked, trying to ignore the fact that Tristan held her impossibly close to his naked torso.

The sheets were pushed low enough so that she could see that he only wore a pair of solid navy boxers. She tried to hide any expression on her face as she slowly brought her eyes back up to Tristan's, but the grin on his face meant that he most definitely noticed that she could see how much he wanted her.

Before another word could come from Piper, Tristan closed the distance, hungrily bringing his lips to hers, her soft moan from the initial contact echoing through him. He wanted to take things slower, to be more passionate. Part of the reason he didn't make any major moves when they got back the night prior was because he wanted to squash any doubts Piper might have that it was only about sex.

Now wasn't the time to tell her, but staying up and talking to her, getting to know her, made him feel as though they'd done that a thousand times. However, upon waking, seeing her in his shirt, pressed up next to him, only led to one thing on his mind.

Tristan rolled from his side onto his back, pulling Piper so that she crashed on his chest, never allowing the kiss to break. Her soft golden waves fell all around him creating a coconut scented veil. It tickled his skin and sent a chill down his spine. Every little thing about her had an effect on him.

Piper's nails dug into Tristan's shoulder when his tongue began exploring her mouth. His kisses were incredible, deep and demanding; they alone caused reactions that Piper never imagined.

Tristan tried to calm down. If he had done what his dick wanted, her clothes would already be torn to shreds. Slowly he slid his hands down her back stopping just barely above her ass. In one sharp movement he pressed her roughly into him, grinding into her so that she could feel him through the thin pieces of fabric. It was only then that Piper came up for air.

Breathlessly, "You have no idea how much I need you right now."

Tristan gave a slight chuckle and stilled their movements. He could feel it. Her arousal was already soaking through from her panties into his boxers.

Piper rose, pulling her hair back, as she straddled Tristan. He knew she could feel him pulsing beneath her. She was one of the only women he had really taken his time with. Though he had been told he was a great kisser, most of the time there was little of it. He never needed all the small touches and prolonged make-out sessions just to have sex. With Piper though, he wanted everything. He wanted to savor every moment.

Slowly he brought his hands from her lower back to her stomach, slipping them beneath her shirt. Piper inhaled sharply from the touch. Tristan's hands crept higher, at a pace he wasn't accustomed to. As he neared farther up, he could feel Piper's breathing become slow and heavy. Once he held a breast in each hand and used the pads of his thumbs to massage her hardened nipples, Piper's eyes closed and she bit down on her bottom lip. Her body took over and began rocking against the bulge beneath her. She needed a hell of a lot more, but Tristan's teasing only made her desire that much greater.

Eventually it became too much for Piper. Tristan was far beyond addicting, and she needed every part of him. He was only further frustrating her by how slow he was taking their morning session.

With Tristan still massaging her breasts, gradually becoming rougher, Piper slid down his body, clasping a few fingers into the waistband of Tristan's boxers and working them down as well. As soon as his cock sprang free, the temptation to climb back on top of him and continue was pushed aside.

Tristan's brows furrowed in confusion as Piper slipped from his grasp, wiggling farther down the bed. The playful and daring look in her eyes turned him on more than he'd like to admit. Before he could say anything, before he could pull her back to him, which he was seconds away from doing, the warm wetness of her mouth closed itself on an erection he didn't think could get any harder.

He sucked in a breath, surprised by Piper's boldness and the fact that she was taking control. She was in control, and it felt amazing. Her tongue swirled and danced around the tip as one of her hands slowly and softly stroked his shaft. She was giving him a tease, just barely enough. Tristan bit his lip and took the sheets into his fists, attempting not to lose control. His head became clouded of all normal and rational thoughts. There was only one thing running through his mind. More.

Piper took her time, taking him deeper, picking up the pace. Every time she gave him a little bit more, his breathing and groaning intensified. There were a few times he thrust into her mouth unexpectedly, but he quickly calmed himself, making Piper question how long he could continue to hold back. It didn't take long for that answer.

Piper yelped when she felt herself being pulled away and flung upward onto Tristan. Half lying and half sitting, Piper brought her eyes to the fiery set fixed on her.

"If...if you would have kept going, you would have been sorely disappointed in the long run."

Piper took pleasure in knowing how close she had gotten Tristan.

A strange madness flickered in his dark eyes, as his hands fell to her waist, gripping it so tightly that Piper squirmed, a delightful moan escaping her swollen lips.

"As much as I love seeing you in this shirt," Tristan began, playfully tugging at the edges that covered way too much of Piper's body. "It has got to go." Before he finished the sentence, the shirt was already falling to the floor.

He sensed a slight level of discomfort and uncertainty from Piper. After all, she was nearly naked, on display, on top of him. He raked his hands over every inch he could, enjoying watching her skin heat in the process.

"That feels really good," Piper managed, when Tristan's fingers roughly and aggressively slid down her back. "You don't know what you're doing to me," she admitted.

Tristan gave a small chuckle. "If it's the same as what you do to me, then I have a pretty good idea."

His fingers twirled along the lacy fabric of her panties, the only thing left separating them. Piper's jaw dropped when she heard the first rip. It was soon followed by another and the little fabric that once covered her melted away.

Feigning disapproval, "Was that necessary?"

"Absolutely."

Tristan wrapped her hair around his fist and pulled her in for a kiss. The foreplay was over.

Frantically, he kicked off the boxers that had only made it down to his knees. He grabbed his cock and massaged the tip along Piper's entrance, coating himself in every drop of her.

Piper tried progressing things at a faster rate, needing Tristan to fill an empty void that continued to grow with each passing second. He persisted in toying with her, only barely pressing into her. When he finally pushed in all the way, Piper couldn't help but let out a painful and pleasurable gasp. This was only their second time together, and prior to that it had been a pretty dry spell for her. Getting accustomed to Tristan's size was new.

Not even seconds after he finally slipped inside her, he partially rose, attempting to push Piper off. "Shit. Condom."

Piper wasn't ready for the emptiness and brought herself down, her lips leaving wet marks along Tristan's neck. "Pill. Clean," was all she managed as she started to roll her hips into Tristan.

He completely froze and Piper sat up, uncertain about what was happening. Their eyes met; however, while Piper looked into his with a mix of anticipation and confusion, he appeared skeptical, eyes narrowed and carefully watching her.

"Same," he responded dragging the word out, making it sound more like a question than a statement. He quickly corrected himself. "I mean about being clean, not the pill, obviously." If Piper expected a laugh to follow, none did.

She became nervous. "I mean, if you want to use one I understand. I just meant that we didn't need to stop, that–"

Tristan cut her off, before she could continue rambling. "If you're okay, I'm okay." His words were far from the truth, but it was difficult to say much else while he was still buried between Piper's legs.

Piper sensed something, but she wasn't sure what. Her hands were placed on Tristan's chest as she sat on top of him. Her right one now vibrating from the pounding coming from within him. He was nervous, and Piper couldn't begin to answer why.

Piper opened her mouth to continue whatever ramblings she had left, but Tristan stopped her, attempting to come back from the strange moment that had just taken place. "I swear," he said with the cutest boyish grin. "Unless the next words out of your mouth are going to tell me how you want it and what you want me to do to your body, you should probably stop talking." His comment caused her to do nothing more than give him the biggest and most radiant smile.

Tristan cautiously pulled Piper down until their lips met. He started over, slow at first, fully knowing that he had put some concern in Piper. Thankfully that faded as soon as their tongues intertwined, engaging in a dance that they were beginning to know quite well.

Tristan let his doubts slip away. He hated that he ever had any to begin with. He should have known that Piper was different.

Piper gave Tristan full control of her body. At first he was slow and tender, with thrusts doing just enough to relax her, but she needed more. With Tristan, she was quickly seeing that she always needed more, in many ways.

Tristan tightened his grip on Piper's hips once she began rocking into him, silently begging for him to go faster and harder. It drove him insane at the effect she was having; it had never felt so good. She had nearly finished him off with her mouth. Embarrassingly, once inside her, he knew he didn't stand a chance at lasting long. The fact that he could feel her, void of any latex, only heightened the sensations pulsing through him and into her.

"Oh, god, Tristan," Piper moaned, her eyes rolling from the sensations pulsing throughout her body. She threw her head back and embraced what was building inside. "Please...Don't stop."

Tristan groaned at how incredibly sexy she looked, her perfectly natural breasts bouncing up and down as he pounded into her. Her words only drawing him further to the brink of explosion, knowing that he was doing it for her.

"Yes...that..." she barely managed to breathe before the tingling bursts of euphoria began shooting through her. "Oh, god," she cried out. "Tristan!"

Watching her embrace her orgasm, his name coming from her lips in screams of ecstasy did absolutely nothing in postponing his own release. Rarely, if ever, had he been able to finish with a partner, but with Piper, he could barely hold on long enough. Halfway through her orgasm, he had to give in. A groan of explicit language, half of what he would never remember, tore from deep within as he allowed himself to fall along with her, Piper still shaking uncontrollably against him.

Piper felt Tristan pulsing inside her, sending an unfamiliar warmth shooting through her as well. When she could take no more, she collapsed on his chest, their naked bodies still very much connected.

Slowly, Tristan pulled out, creating a cold and hollow emptiness felt by the both of them.

"Wow," Piper sighed. That was about all she could say. She needed water, lots of water. Her mouth was dry from screaming.

They rolled from each other so that they were on their sides facing one another. Tristan gently brushed a few locks of Piper's hair, tucking them behind her ear.

"You look so beautiful," he sighed.

Piper couldn't help but ruin the moment. "Why did you get nervous about the condom?"

Tristan chuckled. His hand fell to Piper's bare shoulder and began soothing her with little circles from his warm finger tips.

"It's just a thing," he said with a smile.

"A thing?"

It wasn't a conversation he wanted to dive into after some of the best sex he had ever had, but it was a piece of honesty that decided to share with Piper.

"I've always been careful. There's some crazy people out there. The last thing I'd want is to knock up some random one-night stand." He clenched his eyes close as soon as he said those words, terrified to open them. He could already feel Piper's body tighten in his grasp. "Piper," he whispered. After a deep breath, "That came out wrong."

"You don't have to. It's fine."

"No," he insisted. He pulled her in, wrapping her in all his warmth. "I had a lapse of judgement when you said that. You're not crazy, and you sure as hell aren't a one-night stand."

It was perfect way in, Piper could finally get some sort of answer without having to bring up an awkward conversation at a random moment. "Then what am I?"

Without even thinking about it, Tristan only gave one word. "Different."

That didn't help. Different. What the hell did different mean?

Piper decided not to press on. In a few days it wouldn't matter anyway. At least that's what she kept repeating over and over every time she fell just a little more.

"So, this was a rare experience for you," Piper laughed, rising to find her discarded shirt.

Tristan sat up, propping himself against the headboard, watching Piper's every movement.

"Very," was his only response. He didn't need to go into further detail.

Piper headed for the bathroom, mumbling something about meeting Lucy and her plans for the day. Tristan paid little attention, his thoughts were still on what had just taken place, which only caused his body to become fired up for another round.

He was jolted by a ding from his phone on the nightstand, although when he grabbed it, he realized it was Piper's; however, that didn't stop him from reading the message alert quickly fading from the screen.

**Dipshit: Can you meet me out on the beach in an hour? We need to talk.**

Tristan felt knots tighten in his stomach. He knew the text was from Jared; although, Piper could have found a more vulgar nickname after everything she had gone through with the jerk. What was beyond him was why the hell Jared needed to talk to Piper the day before his wedding.

Tristan put the phone back on the nightstand and decided not to bring it up. It was Piper's business. After giving her a kiss goodbye, he headed back to his room.

His chest tightened when nearly an hour later, as he was getting ready to head to the gym, he heard Piper's door open and close. Some jealous and over-protective part of him wanted to storm after her, to find out what Jared thought he was doing. Instead, he took a deep breath and threw his water bottle into a small gym bag.

# CHAPTER 26

Piper sat down on the bench, as far to the end as possible, and let out a sigh. "What do you want?"

The sun that had poured through the windows illuminating Tristan in his sleep was now hidden behind never-ending clouds, making the beach colder and darker than Piper expected.

"How are you?"

Piper was more skeptical than usual. When she thought about the possibilities of what would happen this week, sitting at the beach, having a general conversation with Jared, did not flash through her mind in the realm of possibilities. Then again, neither did Tristan.

"I'm great, Jared. Why did you need to talk to me?"

Jared fumbled with his hands a bit before shifting, turning his body toward Piper, and in doing so, also closing some of the distance.

"I think I'm making a mistake," he quickly blurted out.

Piper really hoped the conversation wasn't going where she thought it might. She tried to give Jared as little as possible, already feeling the air between them growing heavy.

"That's something you need to think about and–"

"I have. The biggest mistake was leaving you."

There it was.

Bile rose in Piper's throat. They were words that she no longer wanted to hear. Rather than backing away, telling him that she couldn't have this conversation, running away like a distraught little child, Piper corrected him.

"You didn't leave me. I left you, after I came home to you screwing my cousin." She stood now, a growing rage to her voice. "You do remember her, right? You know, the woman you're marrying tomorrow?"

A couple walking along the beach slowed, intrigued by the conversation.

"And I'm saying I fucked up. Big time." He now rose as well, though tried to keep his voice a little lower than Piper.

Piper glared at him. "Why now?"

Jared fumbled for words. "I just...I saw you again and–"

"You saw me happy and with a great guy and it pissed you off that I could do better." Saying those words fueled Piper's adrenaline. She had never felt better. It was like every weight every placed on her had been lifted.

Jared's jaw ticked at the comment. "You don't know him like I do. He's only going to break your heart."

With a maniacal laugh, "That's so rich coming from you."

Jared shocked Piper by reaching out and grabbing her hand. She tried to pull away but he tightened his grip.

"I mean it Piper. He's my friend and all, but he's a dog when it comes to women. Don't set yourself up by thinking that you're different."

*Different.*

The word echoed in her head.

Jared sensed a crack in the tough act that she was putting on and took a step closer.

"I know I can't take back the past, but I can change everything from here on," he continued.

Jared took his free hand and brushed a strand of hair behind Piper's ear. It didn't feel the same. It didn't feel like when Tristan did it earlier. Jared's fingers lingered a second longer at Piper's neck.

Before she processed what was happening, his lips tore at hers with such ferocity. His hand that still clasped hers yanked her into him, while the one on her neck made it difficult to pull away.

The kiss was sloppy, cold, and forced. Piper hated everything about it. Most of all, it wasn't Tristan.

While trying to tug her right hand from Jared's grasp, she pushed at his chest with her left. It was enough to break the unwanted contact; however, once Piper caught her breath and composed herself, she took it one step further.

Her hand across his cheek was long overdue.

"What the hell was that for," Jared spat, covering the stinging on the left side of his face.

Piper raised her index finger, screaming, "Don't you ever touch me again!"

She didn't give Jared a chance for one more word. She turned and stormed off, fuming.

He could be an asshole, she knew that. Never did she imagine the scene that she had just left. Tears burned in the far corners of her eyes. She wiped her mouth with the back of her hand. Disgust radiated from every ounce of her body.

*  *  *

"You sound like you're out of breath," the voice replied once Tristan answered the phone. He immediately knew who it was. Earl Gander. All recruiting and purchasing of players went through him.

"Sorry, sir. Just finishing a workout," Tristan managed as he chugged his second water.

"I hope you're not exerting yourself. Your doctor sent in all your records. It would be a shame if–"

"Absolutely not," Tristan interrupted, before he even thought about who he was interrupting. "I just know I need to stay in my best shape if I'm going to be competing alongside some teenagers."

Earl chuckled at the comment. "Sadly, though you're a decade older than we'd like, I know if you're on your game, you can do circles around some of the new ones."

Tristan would be lying if he said that comment didn't make his ego soar.

"My wife and I just landed. While this could have waited until next week, I thought we'd take a weekend. She heard the resort you're at has a nice spa."

The mentioning of that sent Tristan's mind to one thing, one person, one brief moment.

"Yeah," he quietly admitted. "There's a great massage parlor here."

"Wonderful, wonderful," Earl began. Tristan could hear some clanging in the background and knew that Earl was attempting to cut the call short. "Anyway, tonight? Say around 7? I'll look up a few places in the area for us to meet. Or perhaps there's something at the resort. Yes, dear! I've got it! It's two nights, two nights," his voice blared through the phone. "I do apologize Mr. Reed. I'll be in touch."

Tristan didn't get the opportunity for a response. Silence ensued.

＊ ＊ ＊

"Okay, what's the deal," Lucy asked through a mouthful of food. She slung her fork around, still with a piece of salmon on it as she spoke. "You've barely touched anything and you look like you just flushed your goldfish."

Both Nolan and Emma stopped eating and three sets of eyes watched Piper carefully. She should never have gone out to lunch with them, but that was one of those hindsight things.

"I'm just not feeling well," Piper admitted, although that was putting it mildly. She was a complete mess after this morning.

Things with Tristan were perfect, though very murky in terms of the near future. Then there was Jared. Not only did he try to get in her head and fill it with doubt, but he had the nerve to kiss her.

"You're not–"

Piper interrupted her mother before she could say something ridiculous. "Please don't finish that." She took a deep breath. "I'm tired. I'm exhausted. This whole...whatever this is, has been the biggest waste of time. And all for shit family that I won't see for who knows how long." She tossed her napkin down and walked out of the restaurant.

Only a few steps outside, she could feel her arm being tugged back. Lucy.

"Stop. I have never seen you look so conflicted. I'm not letting up until you tell me what the hell is going on." Lucy's arms were crossed in defiance.

Piper closed her eyes, wondering where to begin. "So much."

"Is it Tristan?"

Piper nodded. He was easily a good portion of her turmoil. "I fell for him, so hard. I know it was fast, but...I love him. He makes me feel at ease and...happy."

Lucy gave a small chuckle as she shook her head. "And your face never lit up like that when you talked about Jared."

Piper felt her cheeks reddening, not believing that she just admitted that aloud.

"I get your concerns. He's...well...he's Tristan Reed, but he doesn't seem to care about that when he's around you. Just have faith that things can work out, even despite a little distance."

"I can't believe my little sister is trying to give me relationship advice," Piper laughed, blinking away tears that were so close to falling.

"Eh, you should hear the advice I give when I'm drunk," Lucy said with a wink, but quickly turned serious. "That's not all though, is it?"

Piper knew if there was one person she could talk to, it would be Lucy, or perhaps Haven. She shifted on her feet and attempted to avoid eye contact. This was a conversation she did not want to have. If she could have erased her entire day from when she got out of bed, she would.

"Jared kissed me," she blurted out, unsure how to begin.

Lucy pursed her lips and waved her hands in short and robotic motions as if to tell Piper her confusion or for a pause while she attempted to process.

"What do you mean he kissed you? How?"

Piper arched a brow, unsure of what her sister was asking. She began from the beginning, starting with the text message.

"I would have done more than slap him," Lucy scoffed. She did a quick evaluation of Piper, hesitant of her next words. "Wait. You're not actually thinking of getting back–"

"God, no," Piper screamed. "Never."

"Thank goodness."

Piper nervously bit her lip. "I don't know what to do. Do I tell Samantha?"

"Honestly, I know you're always the good guy. You have a conscience and all," Lucy groaned, throwing in an eye-roll as well.

"But you don't think I should."

"I mean. It was just a kiss, even though he did basically tell you that if you were willing he'd drop her for you..." Lucy fell silent and thought for a moment. "No, I still wouldn't. Samantha knew what kind of guy he was when she got involved with him, and I promise you, the maggot will find a way to make is appear as though you're the aggressor. Just leave it."

Though a part of Piper felt guilty, that was probably for the best. Once a cheater always a cheater. Samantha and Jared started their relationship with Jared being unfaithful. Why would he change now?

# CHAPTER 27

Piper reluctantly agreed to go and make appearances at Samantha's little gathering that evening. She desperately wanted to spend her last bit of freedom from the city with Tristan, but unfortunately he had plans. He didn't specify, but the night before a wedding, she could only imagine what the guys would be doing.

She could hear Lucy and her mother in her bathroom getting ready. They had fallen in love with her suite, so of course they insisted on bringing all their things to get ready there. Every moment or two, Lucy would poke her head out only to roll her eyes or take a very unnecessary deep breath of disapproval at the fact that Piper was still in a pair of sweatpants.

With everything that was going on, she needed to clear her mind, to focus on something else, anything other than love and the wedding. Sadly, when she became overwhelmed in her personal life, work was her escape. She was quickly compiling an amazing portfolio that was sure to blow Blythe away.

Her laptop slammed shut, her fingers barely making it out unharmed.

"Stop working," Lucy squealed. Her voice was like nails on a chalkboard when she did that.

"Wait until you're out of college and have to deal with all this." Piper had to blink her eyes a few times. She had been looking at nothing but a white screen and text for hours.

Lucy snorted at the comment; however, knew that she was incredibly lucky for only having to work a few hours every other day at the university bookstore.

When Piper finally looked up, she saw that her mother and sister were completely dressed, with their hair and makeup done as well. She patted around for her phone.

As if Emma could read minds, "Yes, it's late. Margaret told us to be down by 7 and it's already after 6:30."

"Shit," Piper hissed, stumbling off the bed.

She yelped in pain. For hours she had been sitting on the bed, legs crossed, fully engulfed in work. Only now did she realize how stiff she was.

Like a madman she rummaged through her things, attempting to put together a look that made it appear as if she put some effort, and not one that screamed that she could barely tear herself away from the television and a tub of ice cream.

After finding a pair of skinny jeans and an elegant and whimsy blouse, Piper brushed on the faintest amount of makeup. A little blush and some subtle eyeliner was all she needed. A high ponytail with some loose pieces around her face and she was good to go.

"It'll do," Lucy said. It definitely wasn't a compliment.

Piper didn't see the point in making too much of an effort. It was just a bunch of girls meeting at the bar for some snooty imported wine as an early send-off for Samantha's nuptials the next day.

Of course it wasn't as simple as that. Aunt Margaret had rented out the resort bar's private party room.

"Who knew there was a room back here," Lucy whispered as they walked through the dark glass.

"It's mirrored," a familiar voice came from off to the side.

"Spencer," Piper gasped. "Good to see you again."

"I see your family is going all out tonight," he said, pushing a cart of several bottles of wine and trays of hors d'oeuvres.

"Please use that word loosely," Lucy scoffed, though quickly became enamored by the room. "Wait, so if I flash all the people in the bar right now, they can't see me?"

Spencer directed his words to Piper. "Sadly, I've heard worse." He shook his head as a server began dispersing food and drinks.

* * *

Just as Tristan looked at himself in the mirror, debating on whether or not to add a tie, leaning more in the direction of not, he heard his phone go off in the other room. He rushed to it, expecting Earl Gan-der, but cringed when he saw the name. *Dad.*

He hadn't spoken to either of his parents in weeks. It wasn't that they had any problems between them, Tristan simply wasn't big on communication and going into details about every aspect of his life, which his parents were sure to inquire about. Reluctantly, he picked up the phone.

"Hey."

"Hey," his father scoffed. His mother's gasp in the background meant he was on speaker. "That's how you answer after three weeks of silence?"

Tristan smiled and shook his head. "I've been busy."

"Oh, you're going to have to do better than that. Be grateful I'm the one calling you and not your mother, although she is listening in. She promised to control her temper," his father admitted.

Aside from three weeks of silence, he couldn't imagine what his mother would be upset about. Attempting to tread lightly, "I've been staying out of the tabloids."

His mother shouted from far away. "Oh, for the love of–"

"Honey," his father warned, interrupting her. "Yes, son. We're thankful for that. Your mother has a fit every time she goes into the grocery store and sees some trash with your picture on it."

"Not to be rude, but I really have to be going. I have a meeting soon," Tristan said, beginning to search for his dress shoes.

"With a team."

The comment stopped him dead in his tracks. Now he knew why his parents might be a little more than irritated. "I forgot to mention that..."

"Imagine our surprise when someone at the firm casually mentions it, as though the whole world knew. I suppose they do now. Shortly after some article it was vaguely mentioned on a couple sports shows, although everyone appears to know nothing more than what was in *Rogue Times*."

"Yeah, aside from that, I haven't given any statements on the matter," Tristan sighed, not seeing the big deal.

"Sweetheart," his mother's voice came through. "We thought you might be thinking of settling down. Playing again means more traveling and, not to be one of those mothers," she felt the need to begin. "But I'd like to have grandchildren in my future."

Tristan laughed. "I'm working on that too."

As soon as the words came out and silence fell, Tristan would have given anything to take them back. "Sorry, I didn't mean it like–"

His mother screaming on the other end meant that his words were too late.

"Grant! Grant, did you hear that! Oh, I'm over the moon!" She then directed her words back to Tristan. "Who is she? How long have you been together? When can the two of you visit?"

"One moment, son," his father spoke. An uncomfortable silence from a muted phone followed.

Tristan checked his phone for the time. He really couldn't afford to continue the call for much longer. He found his shoes and began finishing up with dressing.

"Sorry about that," came his father's voice. "I insisted that I needed to speak to you privately."

"Hey, I really am sorry that I didn't mention playing again. I guess I didn't see it as a big deal."

"I knew the day would come. You've been putting every drop of effort into making a recovery," his father chuckled now, seeming a lot calmer than when Tristan first picked up the phone. "I also noticed that you didn't correct me when I assumed you were meeting with a team. I'm going out on a limb but I take it that you're not going back to Los Angeles?"

Tristan sighed. "It's complicated."

"The girl?"

Tristan couldn't help but smile as his thoughts drifted to Piper. "Something like that, but that's complicated too."

"You sure know how to make a mess of things. How long have the two of you been together? This is the first I've heard about a girlfriend."

"She's not exactly my girlfriend, or at least, she probably has reservations about that," Tristan grumbled.

"Shit, boy. Is she married?"

A deep laughter filled Tristan's room. "No. Definitely not married."

"Then what's your problem," Grant huffed.

"I was just supposed to be her date for this wedding, someone to fill in for the fact that she isn't seeing anyone. Dad, she's Jared's ex," Tristan finally admitted.

"Damn, when you screw shit up you sure go all the way." There was a pause and when Tristan didn't respond, his father continued. "So things didn't go according to plan? You fucked up the play and fell in love with her?"

"You don't have to put it so eloquently."

"How does she feel about your career decision?"

Tristan rolled his eyes. Of course his father would ask that. For a second, Tristan thought that Grant would ask how Piper felt toward him, but he found a way to swing it back to the game.

"I don't know honestly, but that's why I don't want to go back to Los Angeles. I can't do a long distance thing and I don't get the impression that she could either."

"Where then?"

"New York."

Through the phone, Tristan heard his father suck in a breath. He knew exactly what he was thinking before he said it. His mother broke down when he went to California. New York was even farther from the family home in Colorado.

"We'll wait to tell your mother about that piece of information," his dad laughed. Grant heard Tristan take a breath or two on the other end as if he was about to say something but stopped himself. "There's more?"

Tristan groaned. He didn't like beating around the bush, and a quick check of the time told him he needed to head down to meet Earl Gander. "She doesn't know."

The light conversation took a turn at that point. "You're prepared to move across the country for a woman you're not even dating and you haven't told her," Grant hissed. "What the hell has gotten into you?"

Tristan would be lying if he said those exact words didn't cross his mind a time or two over the last few days.

"Dad," he sighed. "How long did it take you to fall in love with mom?"

His father didn't answer at first. Tristan knew why. If his father spoke the truth, it would be a confirmation that everything he was doing, despite how ridiculous it sounded, was right.

✻ ✻ ✻

"Not enjoying yourself in there," Spencer asked when Piper came up to the bar and simply asked for a beer.

"There was a twenty minute conversation about nail art. Nail. Art." She tossed her head from side to side, completely flabbergasted that she wasted time of her life listening to that. "I just don't fit in with them, you know?"

Spencer laughed. From what he gathered, just looking at Piper's wardrobe, he knew she didn't fit in.

"You do know that you're trading that imported Italian wine for a domestic beer?"

She leaned in over the counter. "Oh my god," she whispered in a hushed tone. "Have you tried it?" When Spencer shook his head that he had not, "It's disgusting. It tastes like piss and Sweet'N Low."

A woman on a stool snickered at the comment.

"No, please, be more specific," he said sarcastically. He handed Piper her beer, but refused payment. "I'll add it to their tab at the end of the night," he told her, motioning toward the reserved room.

"Sorry about that," Piper mumbled under her breath.

"Don't apologize," the woman began with a hint of a French accent. "I've had my fair share of wine and trust me when I say, just because it's expensive does not mean it's good," she laughed.

Piper got a good glimpse of her. No doubt she was probably accustomed to the finer things in life. She looked to be in her forties, although it was hard to tell with the contoured makeup and perfectly dyed chestnut hair pinned on the top of her head. She wore a designer red dress, plastered perfectly to her slim body, although she had several assets that protruded out, both top and bottom. Then there were the shoes. Shoes that Piper would never spend that much money on, those heels with the red-lacquered outsole.

Piper smiled sweetly to the woman and headed back. It was no surprise that she was met with Margaret's scowl as soon as she entered with her pint of beer.

# CHAPTER 28

Tristan looked around the bar, but saw no one even close in resemblance to *the* Earl Gander. He glanced down at his phone. Oddly, he was still a few minutes early. Thinking of how the evening might go, he fired off a quick text to Piper.

*  *  *

"Ooooh, that sounds ominous," Lucy giggled over Piper's shoulder while balancing three plates of food.

**Tristan: I need to talk to you. Can I come by your room later tonight?**

Piper didn't hesitate, only quickly responded and fell back in conversation with her mother.

**Piper: Absolutely.**

Something along the lines of excitement and a nervous fear ran through Tristan's veins upon reading the message. Who knew that one word from a girl could do so much?

"I must say, you clean up well," a foreign voice next to him spoke.

Leaning on the bar, Tristan turned his head, then his whole body, toward the woman that spoke to him. He didn't recognize her at all. She was at least a decade older than him, although her body appeared to be that of a woman in her early twenties.

"I'm sorry, I don't–"

"Of course you don't know me," she laughed. She touched his forearm in the process which only caused greater hesitation on his part. "I'm Juliette Gander, Earl's wife."

Tristan let out a sigh of relief. For a split second he thought she was hitting on him. He attempted to shake her hand although she came in for a hug, while also giving those pretentious kisses on the cheek.

"It's wonderful to meet you. My husband hasn't stopped talking about you," she admitted. Tristan noticed that she looked a bit annoyed when she divulged that.

"I'm a little confused." Tristan slowly drew his words out as he glanced about his surroundings. "Where exactly is Earl?"

Juliette huffed in aggravation. "I knew it! I knew he would do this shit." She caught herself. "Excuse my French," she giggled. Tristan couldn't help but find humor in it due to the fact that she was French. "Anyway," she continued. "He told me to come fetch you. He also told me he'd give you a call in advance about the changes, but I see how well that went." She tossed back a sip of wine.

"Changes?" Tristan desperately wanted a firm answer. He needed to talk to Piper. The last thing he wanted was to mention anything only for it to fall through.

Juliette seemed to sense Tristan's doubts. "Oh, everything is still good. Earl is just an idiot sometimes. He's been on calls trying to get everyone in order. He was waiting on a small conference room from the resort, but he didn't know which one to tell you, so he told me to meet you here."

Tristan wasn't following at all. Last he heard, he expected to meet for a drink and discuss his playing for New York over a dinner nearby. He knew nothing of a conference room.

"I'm really not following," he admitted. "Who's everyone?"

* * *

Piper's insides clenched up the minute Tristan walked into the main room. He didn't look dressed as though he was going out with the guys. Then again, he had never told her what his plans were for the evening. Like a fool, she had assumed.

She nearly lost it when the woman in red from the bar placed her hand on Tristan's wrist. He didn't seem bothered by it, never even flinched.

Lucy noticed how quickly Piper grew quiet and followed her gaze through the dark glass.

"What the hell," she whispered in Piper's ear so that no one would take notice.

Piper only shook her head, she didn't know what to say. For a split second she thought that it might be an innocent meeting, but once the woman drew herself in for a hug and kissed Tristan on the cheeks, she knew differently. She felt like some sick voyeur watching beyond the coated glass, but on the other hand, like a masochist, she couldn't tear herself away, despite what looking on did to her.

Somewhere deep inside, she felt the heavy blow. Her blood boiled in a jealous rage. Her insides flipped more than being on the most insane rollercoaster known to man. She dug her nails into her palms to keep from shaking. Tears stung at the back of her eyes, but she wouldn't allow them to make themselves known, at least not now.

Then, the coup de grâce. Tristan took out his wallet, paid for the woman's drink, and left the bar with her.

The only thing that could make the moment worse for Piper was that she wasn't the only one who watched that lovely scene play out.

The room that moments before was filled with boisterous voices and girly laughter seemed to die down a notch or two as conversations began to turn to whispers. Piper was able to compose herself quickly, although she knew the second she was alone she'd crumble.

"Well, that's a bit unfortunate," Samantha spoke from a nearby table toward Piper.

Piper met her gaze as well as several others. Nothing in Samantha's eyes spoke sincerity, and why should it? Next to her was none other than Aunt Margaret, a sneer on her face as if she had concocted the whole scene herself.

"Jared told me that Tristan was always a player. Don't feel bad," Samantha went on.

Piper wanted to scream at her. While, after what everyone had just seen, that was the truth, Samantha had no right, not when hours earlier her fiancé would have walked had Piper given him the answer he wanted.

"Well, I guess I know why he brushed us off," Bridget whispered to Erin. "He's into older women."

Piper wasn't stupid. Bridget's whisper could not have been any louder. The look she was giving Piper meant that she knew her words were heard and all because she just wanted to be a bitch. That was the only way to put it.

She couldn't even begin to allow their words to bother her, not when all she could think about were the images of Tristan and that beautiful woman.

Eventually everyone went back to the disgusting wine and talking about how gorgeous Samantha was going to look in her dress. Piper was unable to focus on a single conversation, even when her mother or Lucy spoke to her; the words were muffled and distant.

It took longer than she wanted to finish her beer. She was sure that as soon as she left, her aunt would have some unkind words, but at this point she didn't care. She was over everything. The wedding. Aunt Margaret. Samantha. Jared. Even Tristan.

For once, all she wanted was to be back in New York, back where she could focus on herself and her career. That was one good to come out of the week. If it weren't for Tristan, she might never have gotten the opportunity that Blythe was handing her. Apparently, that was all he was good for.

Piper made her way through the main bar, attempting to look as though she wasn't falling apart. Unfortunately a vaguely familiar voice called out to her.

Spencer stepped away from his post, and rushed to her like a concerned friend.

"You saw that, didn't you?"

"I had fucking front row seats," Piper scoffed, swallowing the sadness about to spew.

"I'm so sorry. I didn't hear what they were talking about, and then she asked him to pay for her drink and he did, and…" His words drifted off for a second, realizing he wasn't doing Piper any favors. "If it helps, I overcharged him, like a lot."

Piper tried to give a friendly smile. "Doesn't help, but thanks."

"Are you going to be okay? Do you want a drink? On the house."

For once, Piper would have loved to have erased everything with alcohol, but the last thing she wanted was to be hungover for the wedding. "I'll have to pass, but thank you for everything. You're a great listener and just a great person." She gave him a friendly pat on the shoulder and left before he could continue. If he said just the right thing, she was certain she would no longer be able to hold in the waterworks.

It was only when she reached her room that she allowed herself to truly process. The anger quickly turned to betrayal, anguish, and inevitably, heartbreak. Her entire chest felt as though it was glass, being hit with an onslaught of stones, shattering to tiny bits, never to be replaced. It was only then that she realized how fast and hard she had fallen for Tristan. No other guy had ever made her feel so alone, miserable, and defeated, and despite hating him, hating that he was with another woman while she was sprawled on the bed drowning in the salty river of agony, he still held a place in her heart that would take a long time to forget.

# CHAPTER 29

After the projection screen faded from the conference call, Tristan sat back in awe, fully not expecting what had just taken place.

He let out a deep breath, trying to calm himself from the high he was on. "You didn't have to call all of my people in," he admitted.

"Well, when I'm assigned to get things done, rest assured that I do them. No point in wasting time beating around the bush," Earl Gander admitted. His wife placed a glass of scotch in front of him now. She raised her eyes toward Tristan, but he shook his head, declining. "I know this is a bit unconventional, but the higher-ups insisted that I get you to sign at any cost, although there are limits to that cost, if you know what I mean. As they see it, even if you suck, your name will look good for the team," he laughed jokingly. Everyone fully expected Tristan to come back to the field with a vengeance. "We figured that you'd have a lot to clear up in Los Angeles, so we wanted to make this as quick and easy as possible."

Earl continued to ramble on as Tristan looked over the stack of papers in front of him. He was informed earlier that the pay would be a bit of a cut. He didn't care about that, not when he was still in the top ten percent of highest paid players in America.

With each page, each signature, each initial, his heart pounded. Excitement and nervousness took over as he thought about seeing Piper once the meeting was over.

"I'll meet you shortly. I need to go freshen up before dinner," Juliette whispered in Earl's ear.

Once she left, "Sorry about that," Earl coughed. "I didn't expect the call to run that long. I know we were supposed to–"

Tristan smiled and shook his head. "It's fine. I have somewhere I need to be as well."

"Women," he scoffed. "She found some snooty place off the water, said I owe her a romantic dinner." He rubbed his temples in annoyance, but it was all for show. Tristan saw the way the two looked at each other.

\* \* \*

Lucy watched Piper feverishly bang on the keyboard. For a split second she thought to ask about the work that Piper was engrossing herself in, but she didn't know if Piper even knew. She had learned long ago that it was a survival mechanism for her sister.

She gave Piper a little over an hour to herself before joining. By the time she had reached Piper's room, Piper was already in her pajamas and hard at work. Though she had taken a shower, stains of what she saw earlier in the evening had left their mark. Her eyes were red and swollen. Some of her eyeliner had not come off in the shower, only making her look like a raccoon. Her nose and effortlessly rosy cheeks looked cracked and scarred as though from wind-burn, only that wasn't the case.

"If you want to talk," Lucy began. Only then did the tapping on the keys stop.

Piper looked up at her sister with squinted eyes. They burned so much, partially from the computer screen, but mostly from all the tears that she quickly turned off upon her sister's arrival.

"I don't have anything to talk about," Piper insisted. It was difficult to talk. Her throat was dry. It felt like she was swallowing sandpaper.

Lucy rose from her chair near the window and stomped over to her sister. She yanked the laptop away and slammed it shut.

"Hey! What was–"

"Stop it," Lucy screamed back. "Stop bottling everything inside."

Piper scooted upward on the bed until she was upright but resting against an enormous amount of pillows. "I cried. I'm done. I'm fine. I need to get back to work."

"I get it, okay. I know this hurts worse than Jared."

"I told you, I don't want to talk about it. If you're going to keep harping on it, maybe you should leave," Piper spat.

"Maybe if you had that fire in you with a few other people..." Lucy began, allowing her words to drift off before changing the subject. "I don't know how you feel, but I can see it on your face. You've never been in this much pain, this hurt over a guy."

Piper opened her mouth to object, but her sister wouldn't allow it.

"I don't care how long you two have known each other. I know you love him more than you ever did–"

A ding from Piper's phone caused Lucy to stop. Piper groaned upon reading it and tossed it to her sister.

**Dipshit: I just want you to know, I'm really sorry about earlier. I was out of line.**

"What an asshole. Just be glad that you're done with him," Lucy scoffed. She was about to hand the phone back to Piper when another text came in.

**Dipshit: I care about you. I always have. If you ever need to talk, I'm here for you.**

"Oh, shit," Lucy hissed under her breath, which piqued Piper's curiosity.

"What? What is it," she insisted.

Lucy sighed and sat on the bed near Piper. Piper grabbed the phone and tossed it aside once she read the next message.

"Great. Samantha already told him," she scoffed. "You know," she began as she flailed her arms around. "This is just perfect! I thought he was trying to get in my head, but look! He told me Tristan was like this. I just thought that he could have at least faked it one more day."

"Jared is the horrible one. You know he's sitting there just waiting for you to tell him how much you need him right now," Lucy growled. She never did like Jared; his actions in the last twelve hours only reinforced that.

Piper didn't want to argue with her sister. She was beyond exhausted. Jared didn't want her, he never did, and she couldn't be happier about that. All he wanted was a toy that someone else had. Now that the toy was chewed up and discarded, he had no interest. His messages right now only rubbed salt in the wound. If she acknowledged them, he would only point out that he was right.

They sat in silence. Lucy had turned on the television, but kept the volume incredibly low, should Piper want to talk.

Their eyes shot to each other in confusion when a rhythmic knock came from the door.

"Mom," Piper asked her sister.

"No. I told her I'd come spend the night with you. I knew you didn't need all the motherly advice about how you'll find someone who will treat you blah-blah, whatever. She went back to her room with dad, planned on turning in early."

The knocking proceeded, which only caused Piper's insides to twist. Aside from Lucy and her mother, there was only one other person who knew that this was her room. She really didn't want it to be that person.

Sensing her sister's uncertainty, "Want me to see who it is?" Although the look on Piper's face told Lucy that she already knew who it was without moving.

Every part of Piper wanted to cower down, let her sister do her dirty work. She hated confrontation, which is probably why she never said anything to people like Blythe or Aunt Margaret.

She took a deep breath and shook her head. "No, I need to do this," she softly spoke as she scooted to the edge of the bed and slipped her bare feet into a pair of flip-flops.

She composed herself, and wiped around her eyes, fully aware that she had done a poor job of washing her makeup from her face. With each step her feet felt heavy, like she was dragging a weight, and the closer she got to the door, the more the weight pulled her back.

She placed her hand softly on the cold handle and debated putting the chain in place so that the person on the other end most definitely would not try to take a step over the threshold. She shook the idea and, like ripping off a bandage, pulled the door open.

Her suspicions as to who stood on the other side were correct. Though she had a difficult time meeting his eyes, she did.

Tristan was beautiful and put together, just like he was when she had seen him leave with the woman in red with a French accent. His suit clung to his body like a second skin, tailored perfectly for him and him alone. If the evening had gone in a different direction, Piper would no doubt have pulled him in and have had him halfway undressed by now; however, that ship had sailed, or sunk. It didn't matter. They were done.

As soon as Tristan saw Piper, butterflies ran through more than just his stomach. His heart raced, eager for a discussion he had been anticipating since he first made contact with New York. The sensation faded once their eyes met.

He wouldn't say it to her face, but for the most part, she looked like hell. Her eyes were puffy and bloodshot. Her cheeks and lips were dry and chapped. A wet and matted mess of hair was clipped up with several strands falling around her face that he desperately wanted to push back. Something inside told him that wasn't a good idea.

He was surprised to find that she was also in her pajamas. He had told her only a couple hours ago that he wanted to see her tonight. It wasn't that late. She also didn't wear pajamas for anyone other than herself. If she had been in his shirt and a pair of panties, he knew it would have been for him, but this was entirely different.

Not wanting to leave her eyes for too long, he glanced briefly behind her, only to see Lucy sitting on the bed with her arms tightly crossed, giving him a death stare.

"What's going on? What's wrong," Tristan quickly asked.

He attempted to take a step into the room, and that's when he felt as though a ton of bricks had landed on him. Before his foot even hit the carpet,

Piper brought the door forward, narrowing the entry space.

Tristan couldn't read her face; it looked exhausted and expressionless, but something was seriously wrong.

"Piper..."

It was difficult to find words with him standing right in front of her, his eyes begging her for whatever she could give. "I think you need to leave," Piper managed.

Tristan blinked rapidly and fought to regain his breath from that blow. He didn't understand what she was saying. He was the problem. He was the reason for her state of being right now.

"I'm confused. What happened?" He tried to step forward once more, but to no avail.

Piper took a deep breath. It had to start somewhere.

"I need you to leave. Whatever we had this week is over," she announced quickly and coldly. If she gave too much thought to her words, she wouldn't be able to get anything out. She had to be firm and direct.

Tristan couldn't refrain from the growing agitation. "What the hell is wrong with you? What happened since this morning?" He wouldn't say it, not yet. It looked like she had done her fair share of crying and he didn't want to cause more trouble, but if she thought that it would be so easy to send him away, she had another thing coming.

His rising anger only rubbed off on Piper.

"You tell me," she spat.

"I have no idea! I told you I wanted to meet tonight. I had something important that–"

"Oh," Piper's voice boomed. Her words dripped with a venomous hatred. "I bet you had plenty of important shit today."

Tristan's eyes narrowed; his lips formed a tight line. She was dangerously close to bringing out the worst in him. He placed his hand on the doorjamb and watched as Piper's attention went straight to it. The calculated look on her face told him that she was seconds away from slamming the door on it.

She sighed, her expression barely softening, mostly from tiredness. "I know this wasn't real, but you could have had a little more decency. We get it! Hot soccer star! You can have any woman you want. You don't have to flaunt it."

Just briefly he saw tears reach the corners of her eyes, but she was too strong. She wouldn't break down in front of him.

"So what was this? What was this morning? You screw around with me like some groupie but as soon as Jared texts you, you run to him lapping up whatever he'll give," he roared.

Piper faltered. She couldn't breathe. She couldn't believe he said that.

"I saw the text come in. I thought it was my phone. I heard you leave too. I know you went to see him. I just don't get why," he snapped. "Is that what's happening here, you're still so hung up on him that you can't even begin to let another guy–"

Lucy couldn't take it anymore. "This conversation is over," she screamed from across the room.

Her movements were as fast as a cheetah upon its prey. As soon as she reached the door, she pushed Piper aside and closed the door behind her, shoving Tristan into the hall and following him.

She poked her finger into his chest several times. "How dare you say that to her," she hissed.

"I just came to talk and she went all–" He stopped what he was about to say as soon as Lucy crossed her arms and huffed. This was going nowhere fast. He took a deep breath and tried to reason with Lucy. "I really need to talk to your sister. I don't know why she's so upset with me."

"Are you being for real right now?!"

"Yes! Sometime between getting out of bed this morning and now, she's completely lost it."

"Oh! So now my sister is crazy," Lucy proceeded to shout back, now drawing attention from people at the end of the hall.

Tristan groaned. He regretted not taking Juliette up on a drink with Earl. "We're not accomplishing anything like this."

"She said what she wanted. She doesn't want anything to do with you. You're just like him," Lucy screeched.

*Jared.*

"I'm nothing like Jared. If she would talk with me, she'd know that. I'm trying everything to make this work," Tristan insisted.

"Bullshit. You're all the same. Why don't you just go fuck Bridget while you're at it!"

Tristan couldn't believe what he was hearing. Just as he tried to interject, "And that comment. That was pretty fucking low. You want to know something," she began, her voice slightly lower but still as angry as ever. "She is over Jared. She was over him before they even broke up. Not that you even deserve to hear this, but she cried more tears tonight over you than she ever did for him." Lucy huffed and ran her hands through her hair. Tristan was unsure if he was supposed to say something, so he waited for her to continue or conclude. "Just leave her alone. After this, just go back to California and lose her number."

Tristan was just about to speak when a man in a polo bearing the resort logo approached.

"I'm sorry," he hesitated. If he were to be honest, he was relatively new and had never dealt with a public lovers' quarrel. "We've received some complaints and I'm going to have to ask you two—"

"Forget it," Tristan interrupted him. "We're done." Rather than return to his room, he headed for the elevator.

# CHAPTER 30

It was something he never did. Alcohol was never an escape, but right now, he needed to forget, even if only for a minute.

He couldn't get Piper's face out of his mind. She looked so broken. Worst of all was knowing that somehow he had been the one to do that to her. He still didn't understand what had happened. The yelling with her and her sister went nowhere. All he could do was wait for everything to calm down. There was still tomorrow. Saturday. The wedding.

"Hey," he called out to the bartender once he took a seat on one of the stools. "Can I get a beer? You pick. I don't care."

The man gave him a nasty glare. Tristan rolled his eyes and thought nothing of it. Ever since leaving the conference room with Earl, his night had turned upside down. What of it if the bartender was going to be a jerk?

The man slapped a coaster down in front of Tristan and not so delicately placed the glass on top of it, sloshing beer all over and onto Tristan's cuffs, as his arms had been folded along the bar.

"What the hell, man?"

"That'll be $10," the bartender announced.

Tristan reached for some napkins farther down the bar. "Jesus! You spilled half of it."

"My bad," was all the bartender said. He held out his hand waiting for payment.

With everything that was running through Tristan right now, he had half the mind to tell the man which way to go; however, he had already been mildly involved with security once that night. The last thing he needed to do was cause a scene that would get him in the press, especially after signing. Although, as it stood right now with Piper, soccer had to take a backseat.

He reached in his wallet and withdrew a ten dollar bill. He knew damn well that's not how much a beer cost, but he was drained from arguing. Right now he just needed to take the edge off, regardless of the cost.

When he handed the money over, that's when something hit him.

"I know you," he quickly stated, apparently taking the bartender off-guard.

"Spencer," he responded, though not sure why. He followed with, "You were in here earlier." He left it at that.

Suddenly the name rang a bell.

"No. Well, yeah, but I remember you from earlier in the week."

"Sorry. I don't have time for a reunion. I have a job." He began to walk off.

"Dude, what the hell is your problem? Shouldn't you be a little more hospitable to be working at a place that's all about hospitality?"

Spencer stopped and spun around in dramatic fashion. "Excuse me?"

"I didn't do anything to you, so I don't know why you're being like this to a paying customer," Tristan announced.

Spencer came back and leaned on the bar, inches away from Tristan. "You're right. You didn't do anything to *me*."

He downed half of whatever amount of beer didn't spill out of his glass. "Obviously I did something."

"Piper is pretty awesome."

That is where he remembered Spencer from. Piper was chatting with him when he came to meet her at the bar that first day.

"I'm guessing by the look on your face there's some clarity," Spencer continued. "She told me the story, at least the basics. I thought when you two came in here a couple nights ago, it was a date."

"It was," Tristan stressed. He held out his empty glass.

Spencer looked down at it and debated, but ultimately yanked it away and refilled it with something on tap. Tristan couldn't tell what he was drinking anyway. Beer was beer. He reached in his wallet but Spencer let his conscience take over and he waved at Tristan to put it away.

"Beer on tap is only $5," he admitted.

Tristan couldn't even pretend to be annoyed. If this guy knew something about Piper that he didn't, he'd gladly pay double for a beer.

"I'm going to keep this short and sweet, because I really don't like you right now," Spencer began, shaking his finger from side to side.

"Take a number," Tristan muttered under his breath.

"Why you would cheat on that girl is beyond me. I thought it was adorable, in a weird way, how you'd come to your friend's wedding with her. I mean, that had to be something for her, to show up with not only one of soccer's hottest stars, but a friend of the groom. I mean, what a slap in the face that must have been to those idiots. Was it a little shallow–"

"Wait. Wait," Tristan interrupted Spencer's useless rant. He had heard nothing past the first sentence. "You think I cheated on her?"

"Well, okay, technically I guess not, not if you weren't really together." Tristan growled at the wording. He had heard it enough from Piper. "Okay, let me rephrase. Everyone at least thought you two were together, meaning that seeing you hugged up on someone else counts as cheating."

Tristan took another sip, trying to process. "What the hell are you talking about?!"

"The woman from earlier."

Tristan still wasn't following. "Yeah? Juliette Gander. What about her?"

"She hugged and kissed you and you bought her a drink," Spencer quickly pointed out.

"She's French and a little touchy, and I guess you could say the wife of my boss. I was being nice," Tristan groaned.

"Oh…"

"How does that have anything to do with cheating on Piper?"

Spencer bit his lip. Although still a little skeptical, he was beginning to believe Tristan. "There was a little gathering here tonight," he quietly admitted. Tristan hung on to his every word. Maybe he'd finally help clear up whatever the hell had happened in the last few hours. "You see those windows?"

Tristan followed to where Spencer was pointing. Black glass ran halfway along one of the far walls.

"That's one of our private party rooms. The bride's mother rented it out tonight for a little gathering with all the bridesmaids and female family members." His voice grew quiet.

Tristan didn't need him to continue.

"Shit. She saw me meeting with Juliette and got the wrong idea." His stomach rolled over and over. From the outside looking in, he couldn't even begin to imagine what Piper would think. He left the bar with a very attractive, although much older, woman. It didn't take rocket science to assume what any other woman would think.

"Not just her. Like everyone. She didn't say much, but you know how snarky and catty women can be, especially when they're jealous to begin with."

"I have to fix this," Tristan quickly responded. He finished the rest of his second beer and put a twenty down on the bar. He then rose from his seat.

"Hey," Spencer gasped, genuinely shocked. "I've overcharged you enough."

Tristan was able to manage just the faintest of grins, even though all happiness in him was squashed. "That's not for the beer."

Spencer watched as he hurriedly left the bar. He gave a shrug and tucked the bill into the pocket of his slacks.

✳ ✳ ✳

Tristan stood at Piper's door, for how long, he didn't know. He desperately wanted to knock, to force her to talk to him, but the events from an hour prior continued to flash through his mind. If her sister was still with her, there would be no discussion. As much as it pained him to do, he swiped his key card to his door, feeling like a coward.

He paced the room, flipping and twirling his phone in one hand. He couldn't leave things the way they were. He'd never be able to sleep unless he said something. Without a doubt, he didn't expect her to answer his call, but he was pretty sure that she'd at least be curious enough to read a message; however, trying to clear up the entire misunderstanding needed to be done in person, face to face. She had to see how serious and sincere he was.

Not thinking, just going for it, he sent her a text.

**Tristan: Can we talk?**

Minutes went by and there was no response. He could have sworn that he heard the television on in Piper's room, but maybe that was his mind playing tricks on him. He wanted so badly to believe that she was awake and would message back soon.

**Tristan: I'm sorry for earlier. I hate fighting with you. I have so much to say, but this isn't the way.**

"Just turn your phone off," Lucy grumbled with a mouthful of popcorn. "Between him and Jared, you'll never get to sleep."

"You do realize that you're the one keeping me awake," Piper sighed, still clutching the phone.

She wanted to text him back, but she simply couldn't. She was too torn. It was easier to just ignore it, to push the events of the evening to the back of her mind, to focus on anything else.

**Tristan: Tomorrow then. Goodnight.**

Piper's insides felt like they were being shredded apart. Did Tristan even realize that she knew? How could he be so cool and sweet, as if he hadn't just spent the evening with another woman? She'd have to talk to him eventually, but for now she didn't want to think about that conversation. Hopefully it would be short and to the point, then they could both go their separate ways.

Ultimately, Piper muted her phone and flipped it face down on the nightstand. She then buried her head in her pillow, Lucy having now turned off the television, and allowed sleep to take her away.

# CHAPTER 31

Piper awoke to a bright burst of blinding sun and smells she couldn't place. She glanced across the room, squinting her sore eyes from the light.

"What the hell did you do," she grumbled once she saw her sister.

It looked as though Lucy had ordered every breakfast item available on the room service menu.

Lucy swallowed before answering. "I let you sleep in, but I got hungry."

"You do know that I'm not the one being charged for all this," Piper pointed out.

"Oh, I know." The devilish gleam in Lucy's eyes told Piper that her sister was well aware that Tristan was paying for the room and everything that went with it.

Lucy let out a burp and rubbed her stomach. "I think I ate too much," she admitted. She took a sip of what appeared to be orange juice, although the glass it was presented in suggested that it wasn't just juice. "Since the wedding doesn't start until 5, I thought we could go walk around some of the shops in downtown. The brochures in the lobby made it seem cute and quaint."

As soon as Lucy mentioned the shops, Piper's mind drifted to Tristan and their time exploring the streets. Piper grabbed her phone, expecting many more messages. Lucy continued on, despite being ignored. Piper was a little stunned to see that all she had was an email from Blythe acknowledging that she had received Piper's files. There was a single text from Haven, but that was about it.

**Haven: Yay! It's almost over! This week has sucked without you.**

"Mom will be here around 2 to start getting ready, so that leaves us with about four hours," Lucy concluded.

"I'd rather stay here."

Lucy's face scrunched up. "No. You're not sitting here moping all day."

"Please don't start. I don't want to talk about it. I don't want to talk about him. I'm fine. Just don't bring it up." Piper quickly rose and made her way to the bathroom. "I'd rather not run into any more family or wedding guests until I have to," she called from the mirror.

She really did look like hell. She was surprised Lucy didn't point that out. Her hair was a tangled mess and she didn't know what she was going to do about her swollen eyes and nose as red as Rudolph. She splashed her face with cold water, only to see Lucy standing in the bathroom's doorway from the mirror.

As if she knew exactly what Piper was thinking, "I'll fix you up later. For now, throw some clothes on and let's go."

Piper thought about objecting, but spending time with Lucy would definitely brighten her mood. Also, with the wedding hours away, she assumed that none of the party would be meandering around town.

* * *

The resort's shuttle service dropped them in the heart of downtown shortly after 10:30. Lucy was in awe with the place and wanted to go into every shop she saw. Within an hour she had two bags of clothing, a vintage lamp, and several boxes of handmade confections. Piper was grateful that of the few shops Lucy passed on, one was the very boutique she had gone to with Tristan. She didn't want the memory of that day when she walked in the doors; she also couldn't bear the upbeat and flirtatious sales clerk.

They now sat in a tiny café, Piper picking at a turkey sandwich while Lucy dunked her grilled cheese into a bowl of tomato soup.

"I really don't know about the whole master's thing. I mean, it feels like a lot of time and money for very little reward, you know," Lucy rambled. "I know you did, and I think that's why they're pushing me, but–"

"Decide for yourself. Yeah, I went a little further, but that degree had shit to do with where I'm at now."

"Look at you, you're killing it." Piper scoffed at her sister's praise. Some days she felt like she was working a step closer to her death. "Okay, so it hasn't been ideal, but you're going to be writing! Your name will be in print in *Rogue Times.*"

Before Lucy could go on, Piper quickly pointed out, once again, that her master's had little to do with her new promotion.

Just as they were about to finish and wrap up a couple last minute stops, something through the café window caught Lucy's attention. Piper followed the gaze of disgust on her sister's face, and she really wished that she wouldn't have.

She'd recognize that woman anywhere. Her image was etched in Piper's mind after last night. Piper didn't know her name and she had no desire to. Instead she watched the woman and an older gentleman hold hands, leisurely strolling along the sidewalk across the street.

"What a skank," Lucy huffed.

Piper had to look away. Of all the miserable odds, it had to be that she would see that woman again.

"I bet she's an escort," Lucy speculated.

Piper glared at her sister. Regardless of her feelings toward Tristan right now, she could never imagine that he'd need to hire an escort. Lucy must have read her mind.

"Maybe he has some weird fetishes..."

"What are you talking about," Piper gasped.

"Tristan. He's hot. Half the women Samantha invited want to sleep with him. I bet he's into some freaky stuff. That's why he'd hook up with a stranger."

Piper groaned. She didn't want to think of Tristan hooking up with anyone. She didn't tell Lucy, but her idea sounded preposterous; however, that didn't stop her from overthinking it. They had relatively normal encounters. She didn't get any strange sexual vibes from Tristan, and he didn't seem to act like the sex was boring in the least.

It all came down to a couple annoying questions. Who was the woman, and why did Tristan meet up with her?

Sadly, there was only one person that Piper could get some answers from, if she so chose, and she fully intended to avoid him for as long as possible.

✳ ✳ ✳

"Thanks for going out with me," Lucy told her as they made their way through the resort.

Piper grunted. Her arms were draped with bags of many unnecessary items that Lucy insisted she needed. They continued through the resort, in the direction of Lucy's room so they could drop off the bags.

Large double doors were propped open in one of the main hallways, and Piper allowed her curiosity to take a peek inside. It was the ballroom where Samantha's reception would be held later that evening.

Bright pink and champagne hues of lace, streamers, balloons, linens, flowers, and many other

321

decorations littered the room. It was over the top in every way. It screamed Aunt Margaret.

"You're not going to cry, are you," Lucy whispered in Piper's ear, bringing her out of whatever daze she had fallen into.

"Huh?"

Lucy playfully nudged her sister. "Seeing what should have been your day."

"Ouch. That's a little screwed up, don't you think?"

Lucy giggled. "I'm only messing with you. I can see it on your face. You look like you're about to vomit."

Piper shook her head and let out a huge sigh of relief. "I honestly thought this would be harder. I thought I'd feel worthless and devastated. After all, she's marrying the guy I was supposed to." Piper thought for a moment, before she continued. It was something she never wanted to admit to. "I'm happy. I'm so happy that we didn't." The faint smile on her face showed that she meant it. "I was comfortable with Jared, but that's it. I think I was so consumed with work that I didn't want to have to go through the effort of dating someone new, that we'd just keep going through the motions and make it somehow work. Looking back now, we should have broken up before he cheated on me. Does that sound weird?"

"No," Lucy squealed. "God, I'm so glad that you realize that. I never wanted to bring it up, but not once did you ever talk about your thoughts on it. I never knew how you felt and after a while, I was afraid of opening old wounds."

Piper leaned into the opposite wall, still watching the last minute decorations going up. A huge feeling of relief washed over her. As much as she thought she'd be depressed about seeing the marriage between Jared and Samantha unfold, she was ecstatic that it wasn't her. Despite how big of a jerk Tristan ended up being in the end, he made her see that she would never have been happy with Jared.

"I didn't think I'd see that today," Lucy admitted, carefully watching Piper.

"What?"

"That smile."

It was only then that Piper realized that she was indeed smiling so much that it hurt. That's when a little part of her knew that everything would be okay.

She nodded her head down the spacious hall. "Come on. Let's get this crap to your room so you can help me with this rat's nest on my head."

* * *

"Shit," Derek huffed, throwing the piece of fabric down. "I don't get why we couldn't just use clip-ons.

Tristan rose from the couch and tucked his phone into his jacket. He checked it religiously, but there was nothing from Piper from the night prior or even now. The wedding was due to start in a little less than two hours. He needed to remain patient.

Tristan picked up the tie and walked up to a moody Derek. "Here," he said as he popped up

Derek's collar and pulled the silky fabric around his neck.

Derek tried to look down so that he could see what he had been doing wrong, but Tristan was too quick about it.

"There. You're good to go," Tristan informed Derek as he pulled the collar down over the now tied bowtie.

"Dude," Derek gasped. He looked into the mirror and was obviously pleased with what he saw. "Damn. I look like James Bond."

Tristan rolled his eyes and sluggishly made his way back to one of the couches. He had been trying to keep occupied, but in doing so, had obviously gotten dressed well before the rest of the groomsmen.

Brian walked over and sat on the other end of the couch next to Tristan. He had a drink in one hand and his phone in the other. Obviously something on his phone had him smiling from ear to ear. Tristan gave a brief glance but waited for Brian to share if he saw fit.

No sooner than he thought that, "Look at this." Brian held his phone up to Tristan.

It was a picture of two children and a dog playing in the mud. Even the dog had a smile.

"Cute."

"They're adorable. I don't know what I'd do without them. I can't wait to get back," he sighed.

Tristan didn't know what else to say. It wasn't a common subject that he could relate to. Although for a split second, he wondered if Piper wanted kids. He clenched up and pushed the idea away. It was insane enough that he was moving across the country for her. They were leaps and bounds away from starting a family. The strangest part of it, he had never in his life thought about that with any other woman. There was just something special about Piper.

"That's sweet and all, but not for me," Jared laughed, taking a seat on an adjacent couch.

"Seriously," Brian gasped as if shocked.

"Yeah, Samantha and I talked about it. When we first got together we wanted the family thing, but we'd like to travel and have fun, just the two of us."

Tristan thought it was the most selfish thing he had heard.

"What about you," Brian asked, nudging Tristan.

He desperately wanted the subject to change. "I don't know. We're not that far into the relationship for that discussion." It was an honest answer.

When neither responded he glanced back and forth between the two. They gave each other ominous and skeptical looks. Tristan took in a deep breath and exhaled louder than needed, knowing exactly what the unspoken topic was.

"It was a misunderstanding," he growled. "I'll fix it."

Jared held a sinister smirk. Never in Tristan's life did he want to punch someone so badly, and especially someone who was supposed to be a friend.

"I know Piper," Jared began. "From what Samantha told me, trust me, there's no fixing it."

It was at this point that Brian decided to take a bathroom break, leaving Tristan and Jared alone.

"We all get it, you know her. Like I said though, I get what they saw last night, it was a misunderstanding."

"I know you can charm the panties off some women, but if Piper thinks you've cheated, you'll be lucky if you get two words in," Jared scoffed.

"Well, I guess you would know," Tristan hissed, keeping his voice low so that the rest of the men didn't hear the increasing tension.

Jared clenched and unclenched his fists. His lips were a tight flat line.

"Tell me this," Tristan continued. The curiosity had gotten the best of him, although he didn't expect an honest answer from Jared. "Why did you text Piper yesterday morning? Why did you need to meet with her?"

Jared's eyes widened and his face went white. He shifted uncomfortably in his seat and refused to meet Tristan's eyes.

"You check her phone now?"

"It happened to be on my side of the bed when it went off." Tristan was well aware that he was pushing Jared's buttons. "I was curious why you'd need to see your ex the day before your wedding." He made certain that when he said the word ex, it stood out. He saw the way Jared had looked at Piper on the boat that night, and something seemed off. He didn't know what game Jared was playing.

"Whatever. I just wanted to make sure everything was cool." He rose and started to make his way as far away from Tristan as possible.

Tristan noted how Jared's demeanor had changed. Without a doubt Jared had lied to him. Perhaps it took Piper to make him see that their competitive high school friendship was nearing its end.

# CHAPTER 32

Piper had to give Lucy credit. For the canvas she handed over to her sister, she never expected the result to be the *Mona Lisa*. Perhaps that wasn't the best comparison.

After washing and drying her hair, Lucy put elegant waves and pinned them halfway back, allowing some to drape over the shoulders. Lucy also insisted that darker shades of browns would help conceal her red and puffy eyes. By the time she was done, Piper hardly recognized herself from the hours prior.

The grey dress she had saved for the wedding was elegant and tasteful. It covered all the right spots and cut off just above the knee. It was a subtle sexy with a great deal of sophistication, something that would be noticed but didn't scream for attention.

So that the wedding could start on time, all guests were asked to be in their seats at least fifteen minutes prior to 5. As Piper made her way the chapel with her parents and sister, she became very aware that standing feet away from the entry doors were the bridesmaids and groomsmen, arranging themselves to begin their walk down the aisle.

Tristan's eyes locked on hers immediately and she had to force herself to look away. Just that moment, it was enough to create a storm inside her, a flurry of butterflies. Lucy must have noticed.

"Are you okay," she asked as soon as they took their seats.

Piper could feel that her throat had turned dry and only nodded in response.

Lucy poked Piper in the side, causing her to inhale sharply, which only made Lucy laugh. "Don't forget to turn off your phone," she teased.

Although her sister was being playful, she remembered that her phone was indeed on ring. Upon reaching in her clutch to silence it, she felt a sickening feeling from the empty screen. Tristan hadn't text her all day. A part of her wanted to scream but another part knew that it was for the best. If he realized it was over and gave up, it would make whatever arrangement they had that much easier. It would make going back to reality a bit more bearable if they both accepted that they had allowed things to get out of hand and something real was not going to work out between them.

\* \* \*

After seeing Piper, Tristan thought about giving up on the whole wedding thing. All he wanted was to pull her aside, to make that empty look of disappointment in her face go away. Instead, he buried his impulses, for now.

"How do I look," Bridget cooed next to Tristan.

Tristan gave her a brief glance. What was she expecting? She was wearing the same hideous neon pink dress as every other bridesmaid. He wasn't that brutal though. "Fine."

His comment didn't seem to please Bridget and she let out an exasperated huff. It had never been in her nature to give up so easily and now that Tristan and Piper appeared to be over, she was going all in.

"So, tonight is our last night," she began.

Tristan had a million things running through his mind at the moment, but entertaining Bridget in conversation was sure as hell not one of them. "Yeah," he acknowledge with more than a hint of agitation.

From the corner of his eye, he saw Bridget tinkering with her bouquet until she pulled something out of it. He narrowed his eyes when she tried handing the object to him. He wasn't an idiot, but he was really hoping that she wasn't that brazen, or stupid.

He stared at the key card in her hand for a moment before bringing his eyes to meet hers. She must have noticed the annoyance on his face, and rather than letting him have a chance to say anything, she hoped that she could change his mind before he dismissed the idea.

"Why don't we make the most of it," she suggested.

Tristan opened his mouth to speak but was too shocked to form a sentence that wouldn't leave this woman in tears moments before walking down the aisle.

"I promise, you won't regret it. It'll be fun," she said in a low and seductive voice.

Bridget then attempted to slip the card in Tristan's outer jacket pocket. Before she succeeded, he brought his hand up and lightly brushed hers away, leaving her in disbelief.

"You've got to be joking right now," Tristan growled.

"No?" Bridget pouted, not understanding. "Do I need to spell it out for you? You're single. I'm single. You're hot. I'm hot. Why not have one hell of a night?"

"Are you drunk or that damn stupid," Tristan spat. He realized it was a little harsh, but a part of him knew that it was the only way to deal with someone like Bridget.

"If you're worried that it'll be anything more than a one-night stand, don't," Bridget continued to press, hoping that he might still change his mind.

Tristan wanted to set her straight with how he felt, but he couldn't say those words to her without telling Piper first. "I have a girlfriend that I care about very much. I don't know what the hell possessed you to pull this shit in the first place."

Bridget let out a mocking laugh. "It didn't look like you had a girlfriend last night."

Tristan was nearing his end. He wanted to explode. Everyone had the same assumption.

"You and all your gossipy entourage need to mind your fucking business," he hissed, growing more irate by the second. "Here's what's going to happen.

I'm going walk you down the aisle, because somewhere someone hates me and wanted me to suffer having to spend another second around you. Then I'm going to drop your ass off and it's done. Whatever you're trying to do here, it's not happening. It will never happen."

His words cut her deep. Her face turned a bright red but it wasn't from embarrassment. She was outraged at being so cruelly rejected. She spun on her heels and darted off to a few other bridesmaids.

Tristan took a much needed deep breath and tried to calm himself. Between Jared and the crazy nymphomaniac, his patience was deteriorating.

From down the hall, the frazzled wedding planner was briskly marching toward them, barking orders before anyone could hear her. Oddly, the only reason Tristan was grateful to see her was because that meant this fiasco was one step closer to being over.

"I swear, if any of you have phones," she began.

Tristan tuned her out, but quickly pulled his from his jacket pocket. There was still nothing from Piper. Even though it tore him up, he respected her for it. She wasn't the type of girl who should let any man treat her poorly. He just needed to prove to her that he wasn't the type of man to do so.

He noticed that he did have texts from Elijah.

**Elijah: I think you're insane as hell!**

**Elijah: Nonetheless, good luck! I hope it works out.**

Those few words were enough to put a faint smile on his face and ease his nerves.

"No," the wedding planner hissed at Derek. "Your arm here, and her arm..." Her words drifted off as she placed Derek and his partner in the correct position to walk down the aisle. "I swear, did anyone pay attention at the rehearsal?"

It was a rhetorical question, everyone knew that. Everyone except Derek, who felt the need to point out that he was drunk at the rehearsal. It elicited a few giggles from the girls, but only sent the wedding planner into a fit.

When she got to Tristan and Bridget, she rolled her eyes. "Well, you two certainly look happy to be here," she pointed out, more sarcastically than needed.

Soon enough, the music started and pair by pair they filed in like cattle.

Tristan got a glimpse of Piper, but she didn't allow her eyes to meet his. He had lost hours of sleep thinking about how to make things right, how to make her listen, how to clear things up. Halfway through the night, he realized it wasn't only Piper who needed to hear it. Bridget had only further proved that earlier.

Lucy nudged Piper once Tristan and Bridget passed by their row of seats.

"I wonder what's going on with them," she whispered.

Only then did Piper let her eyes drift to Tristan. He looked edgier than she had ever seen. Needless to say, Bridget looked no better. There was an obvious tension between the two that created an air of animosity around them.

The signal was given and everyone stood for the bride's entrance. Piper could admit it. Samantha looked incredible. While the top part of her gown was bordering on a piece of expensive lingerie, she looked good. She looked happy. Despite everything, Piper couldn't find fault with that. Once her father dropped her off in Jared's waiting hands, everyone took their seats.

The preacher began, talking about what a glorious day, what a joyous occasion. Piper had been to weddings before, but she never paid attention to the time, mostly because she never had the desire for them to hurry up and end more than she did right now. Shortly before she left her room, she did google *how long do wedding ceremonies last*, so that she knew how long she'd have to put on a fake smile and be attentive. Google suggested between twenty and thirty minutes.

Lucy interrupted her thoughts when she leaned in to whisper. "Are you paying attention?" Her voice was teasing, hinting at something.

"I'm trying to," Piper whispered back.

"I'm not talking about the ceremony. I'm talking about him." Lucy discreetly gestured with her finger in the direction of Tristan.

Piper really wished that she wouldn't have followed once their eyes met.

"His eyes have been on you the entire time. It's like you're the last drop of water in a desert," Lucy pointed out, giving Piper a strange sense of déjà vu, as she remembered two nights ago and the rehearsal ceremony. She was nearly certain that Lucy used the same words.

It was enough to make Piper melt, to make her forget how upset she was. His dark eyes spoke to her without saying a word. She was thankful that he couldn't say anything to her right now. Something in her told her that regardless how angry and upset she was the previous night, she'd listen to him. She'd give him the chance to feed her whatever bullshit lies he'd come up with.

His eyes on her could not make her more uncomfortable. He made her feel naked and exposed, as if it were only the two of them in the room. He might as well have been touching her. That's how much she felt him.

The moment her eyes stayed for a second longer, it gave Tristan hope. Hope that the argument last night didn't mean anything and that he could indeed make things right with Piper. It was difficult to look anywhere else.

Suddenly, Piper felt more than Tristan's eyes on her. The preacher had paused and looked through the crowd, before continuing. She glanced back up to Tristan, who was smirking and shaking his head.

"What did I miss," Piper shyly asked her sister.

Lucy shook her head. "You two have it bad." When Piper didn't answer, Lucy went on. "It was the part about any objections. Boy was Aunt Margaret giving you the stink eye," she giggled.

Piper groaned and allowed her perfect posture to slip out the window as she sank back in her seat.

Moments later, the kiss, clapping, and the end. The guests waited patiently in their seats as the wedding party followed Jared and Samantha down the aisle. Piper and Lucy shot each other skeptical looks when Tristan and Bridget met up. He didn't bother extending his arm for her and it appeared that she honestly had no desire for it either.

"Oh, yeah. Something happened with those two. My guess is Bridget had your name all in her mouth and Tristan–"

"Get up," Piper insisted. It was now their row's turn to exit.

The guests began to make their way to the reception for drinks, dinner, and dancing; however, the wedding party wouldn't be in for another half hour or better, as they still had pictures.

Piper desperately wanted to skip out on the reception. Maybe she should have. There was a storm brewing inside her that she couldn't control. Tristan was going to talk to her at some point and she wasn't prepared for that conversation. Thankfully all else was calm and content. The wedding went smoothly with no hiccups along the way. Only a few more hours and it would be over. Tomorrow this time she'd be back in New York, back to the insanity that was her sanity.

# CHAPTER 33

The pictures took longer than expected, although if Aunt Margaret had anything to say in the matter, it was surprising that they finished in under an hour.

"I don't get why we couldn't just go ahead and eat," Lucy scoffed. She ran her finger around her second glass of wine.

"Don't be a brat," Emma teased.

"After that breakfast and lunch I can't imagine you'd still be hungry," Piper added.

The wedding party entered, followed by Jared and Samantha and roaring cheers as they all made their way up to the head table.

Piper would at least be able to get through the meal with Tristan up there and not next to her. She only glanced at him briefly but noticed that something had changed. That confidence that usually seeped from every pore in him had faded. He looked nervous and distressed. Not once when Piper looked up at him would he allow his eyes to meet hers.

A handful of waiters began bringing out plates.

"Really," Nolan spat. "I like weddings where there's a caterer but we can make our own plates."

"That's only because you take twice as much meat as you're supposed to," Lucy pointed out.

After the head table was served, plates started making their way to the round tables in the crowd. Piper was shocked to see a familiar face.

"What are you doing here," she gasped.

"We're short on staff and the bar was running slow tonight," Spencer grumbled as he placed a plate in front of Piper and another one in front of Emma, much to Nolan and Lucy's disappointment. "Hey," he continued. "I hope I'm not overstepping here, but did everything get sorted out last night."

"Not even a little, but it's okay. I'm okay."

Spencer narrowed his eyes. "Did you talk to him?"

"No, not really. I'm not sure I have any intention to," Piper finally admitted, both to Spencer and her inner self.

"I think you should," he started once again. He would have said more but the frizzy haired wedding planner in the distance began snapping her fingers at him. "Damn, I have to go. I'll catch up with you before I head back to the bar."

Piper was in awe. Spencer was supposed to be on her side, at least that's what she thought when she left the bar last night. Why would he suddenly insist for her to talk to Tristan?

Only now did she look down at her plate. She was shocked to find a hearty meal. A beautifully seared filet mignon and a buttery lobster tail begged her to be devoured. It was quite different after seeing the food that was served on the first night, but no one was complaining.

"Someone please tell me that I'm not the only one who secretly wanted Samantha to trip," Lucy mumbled through a large bite of lobster, oily residue of butter glistening across her painted lips.

Emma and Nolan appeared to have tuned her out. Very rarely was Lucy serious. It was even rarer that her comments contained anything of substantial value. Though she was quite smart, she liked to keep that side of her hidden. In doing so, it allowed her to get by with a lot.

Piper took it upon herself to engage Lucy. "Apparently, you're the only one."

Lucy raised a brow. "Seriously. Even after everything–"

"Yes," Piper interrupted. She pursed her lips and discreetly shook her head, not wanting Lucy to bring up anything about the incident with Jared.

"Since when did you become such a saint," her sister scoffed back, though barely, as her mouth was still stuffed with food.

"I'm by no means a saint." Sadly, she could feel her cheeks redden at the statement. For some reason Tristan drifted into her thoughts. She quickly shook the image forming; however, in the back of her mind, she was well aware how difficult it would be to erase her memories over the last week. "Just let them have their day, their few hours in the spotlight. *After everything*," she enunciated, using her sister's choice of words that she had interrupted earlier. "They need this. I have a feeling this will be as good as it gets for them."

Lucy sighed, not liking her sister's very grown-up answer. "It still would have been funny if she would have fallen in those spikes she called heels.

Piper chuckled but gave her sister nothing back. All she could think about was this being over. Dessert and a few speeches, that's all that was left. Thankfully it had been decided that speeches would be held after the meal. Piper intended to slip out right after the speeches, before the first dance began. Once the dancing started and everyone began moving about, certainly Tristan would take the opportunity to talk to her.

Piper preferred to get a good night's rest, get on a plane the next morning back to New York, and deal with Tristan from nearly 2,700 miles away.

No sooner than she began thinking of Tristan and what was left of the reception, particularly the dancing, another memory bombarded her. Even though she tried to push it away, to think about anything else, even work, the vision of dancing with Tristan that first night flashed in her head. She had to give it to him, he was an incredible dancer, and the way he held her body against his before kissing her...

With that, Piper gulped down the rest of her champagne.

Tristan poked around at his food. Despite having a minimal breakfast and lunch, he wasn't hungry. The only reason he ate was to counter the small amount of alcohol in his beer, as well as knowing there would be champagne in the foreseeable future.

"No comment on that?"

Tristan broke from whatever trance he was in to respond to the person nudging him on his left. He was flanked by both Derek and Brian, though it was Brian that addressed him.

"I don't mind telling you, you've been miserable conversation since the whole ceremony started," Brian said quietly enough, although Derek overheard.

"Is this about Bridget," Derek chimed in.

The question caused Tristan to neglect chewing the piece of steak in his mouth and swallow it the wrong way. Quickly he grabbed for his beer and chugged.

When he was finally able to allow words to come, "What the hell are you talking about?"

Derek shrugged, as if it was common knowledge. "I saw the two of you having a little spat before the ceremony." He eyed Tristan before continuing, but the lack of emotion on Tristan's face gave Derek no sign as far as how to continue. "It looked like a lovers' quarrel."

Brian shook his head at Derek just as the words began to flow out. Though Derek playfully bumped Tristan with his elbow, the look Tristan now gave suggested that the comment was not taken lightly.

"There's no incentive in the world that would make me touch that," Tristan growled back.

"Damn, dude. I was just messing around."

"Don't. You know I'm with Piper and that shit isn't funny," Tristan snapped, far from the playful direction Derek tried to take the conversation in.

He watched as Derek and Brian gave each other rather confused looks and fell quiet, too quiet. Both of them turned their attention away from Tristan and back to their almost finished plates.

Tristan dropped his fork and pushed his plate away in annoyance. "What?"

Derek had no intention of taking the conversation where he and Brian were thinking. Thankfully, Brian knew that Derek didn't have a way with words. If something was going to be said on the matter, it was best that he brought it up.

Brian hesitated. "We don't want to put you in a mood, but we just heard a few things about last night."

Tristan sat back and crossed his arms, knowing exactly what Brian was referring to. "Oh yeah?"

"Yeah," Brian carefully treaded. "They said that you left the bar with some woman."

Tristan's teeth nearly cracked with the infuriation running through his veins. "They?" He then tossed his head to his left and nodded in the direction of a flock of giggling women at the other end of the table. "You mean the gossiping sorority from hell?"

"Look, he didn't mean to rile you up," Derek interjected. "We can see what a fucked up mood you're in. It obviously has to do with your breakup..."

Tristan tuned him out after the word, and tried to rise from the table as gracefully and respectfully as possible, when in reality he wanted to bolt up like he'd been stung by a deadly creature and let his chair ram into the stage behind him.

He placed both hands on the table and bent his elbows slightly. Rage flashed across his face as he shifted his head between Brian and Derek, directing his words to both. "You know what I think? I think everyone here needs to mind their fucking business and focus on their own pathetic, delusional, lives."

Tristan didn't realize how his words had carried, though he could feel the eyes of several others at the table burning into him, curiosity scampering through their bones. Before another word, another look, another breath, could come, Tristan left.

Once the air hit his face, he realized just how cold it was. Back inside it felt like an inferno. He felt confined, unable to breathe, exhausted from people. Now all of that could escape him, even if only for a little while.

\* \* \*

Breaking away from the traditional cake and cutting of the cake, Samantha had opted for a cupcake bar. It was unveiled shortly after removal of the dinner plates began. It also received a ten minute presentation and before anyone could make their way to the monstrosity of sugar overload, a photoshoot ensued.

"Ugh," Lucy groaned. "Why didn't they say something before I ate all that?" She took a sip of champagne and twisted from side to side."

"What in the hell are you trying to do," Nolan asked with a great deal of confusion.

Lucy's movements stopped. She rolled her eyes as though her behavior was completely normal. "The fizz from the champagne and the act of shaking it in my stomach will help me burp faster, in turn, making more room so that I can try every flavor up there."

"That's gross," Piper teased, which only got her a glare from Lucy.

"Honestly," Emma huffed. "If you weren't wearing a dress, I suppose you'd be unbuttoning your pants as well."

Lucy responded with an arched brow and a smirk that rose more to one side than the other. It said it all without saying a word.

Piper allowed the conversation around her to fade into obscurity. The light music that had been playing from the stage stopped, though with the chatter bouncing throughout the room, it appeared that no one noticed.

The frazzled woman that had been presented as the wedding coordinator bolted about with cords. At one point Piper saw a microphone in her hand. The woman tinkered with a board of switches off to the side of the stage. She appeared to need technical assistance, and despite feeling slightly bad for her, a darker side of Piper found humor in it, with the anticipation of the narcissistic speeches soon to come.

Nolan rose from the table. "I think I'll head out for a quick smoke," he announced.

Emma narrowed her eyes. "You don't smoke."

"Damnit, woman. It means I'm going out to get some air," he joked.

No sooner than he made his departure, the dessert bar opened up and a line was quick to form, with Lucy attempting to nudge and cut her way ahead in whatever way possible.

\* \* \*

Tristan tensed when he noticed the other presence farther down the railing. While they weren't extremely close, they were still within speaking distance. He wasn't sure what the protocol was after the last twenty-four hours.

As though Nolan could hear Tristan's inner thoughts, "Don't worry, I intend to mind my own business."

Tristan let out a sigh of relief which Nolan was quick to catch.

"Oh, I still have my opinions. I just think whatever is going on between you two needs to be worked out between the two of you."

Tristan groaned and crossed his arms over the railing with most of his weight bearing down on them.

After the passing of a few more seconds, "It was all a misunderstanding."

"Again, not my business."

Nolan tried to hide his smirk, fully knowing that Tristan was at the point that he was about to unload everything without Nolan saying a word.

Tristan turned to face in the direction of Nolan. "I know you don't know me, and whatever you've seen in the tabloids–"

"I don't read that crap," Nolan interrupted.

"Well, after what you probably heard today, I know your opinion of me isn't too high."

Nolan turned to Tristan and took a few steps toward him so their voices could remain at a comfortable level through the wind.

"Those three women in there mean the world to me, and you hurt one of them pretty bad."

Nolan immediately saw the effect his words had on Tristan. In that moment he was easily willing to listen to the boy. Something about Tristan's face told him that all was not what it appeared, all was not what he had heard through the never-ending grapevine.

"I'd never do anything to hurt Piper. Whatever they all saw last night is so far from the truth," Tristan insisted, growing angrier with each passing second. Angry that Piper saw that play out without any context. Angry that people couldn't mind their own business and had to spread rumors like wildfire. Angry that what was supposed to be a surprise, a real start for a real relationship with Piper got all fucked to hell. "That woman," he continued, but forced himself to stop when Nolan raised his hand.

"I'm not the one you need to be having this conversation with. From what I can tell, you really need to sort things out with Piper. She's the one who needs to hear whatever it is you have to say on the matter."

Tristan hesitated. "You don't seem as mad as I expected."

Nolan laughed. "I like to tease my girls, and I can get a little overprotective, but at the end of the day, they're adults. If I'm being honest, looking at you right now, I can see you're a little anxious, a little torn up, maybe a little regretful."

Tristan shook his head, but agreed.

"You look like you've either done something stupid or you're about to do something stupid," Nolan admitted.

"Maybe a little bit of both."

The conversation slowed and both stood a little while longer in the chilly evening, taking in the silence that existed beyond the party.

"I swear," Lucy managed as she started on her third cupcake. "When I get back to school I'm only eating ramen for like a month.

"Isn't your apartment directly above a twenty-four hour pizza parlor," Piper teased.

"On weekdays," Lucy corrected. "Nothing but ramen on weekdays, for about a month."

"Did you want to get any dessert," Emma asked.

"I'm good. I was even thinking about slipping out of here before the speeches start," Piper admitted.

"Oh, don't do that. I'm sure they'll be interesting," her father announced from behind her, returning to the table.

"Enjoy your smoke," Emma snorted sarcastically, to which Nolan gave no response.

Piper was stunned. "I did not expect that comment from you."

"Eh, you know your aunt. She's got to keep this three-ring circus going for as long as she can. I'm sure something..." He paused and hesitated before, "*Stupid* will happen before the night is over, and I use that word to be left to interpretation."

"Whatever," Piper sighed. She'd go back to her original plan and stay until the dancing took place.

A sharp and piercing technical shriek rang out, drawing everyone's attention to where the band once stood. There on the stage was the nameless coordinator.

"Excuse me," her demanding voice rang out, although through the microphone it came across as far more squeaky. "The speeches will take place in ten minutes. We're just working out some technical difficulties."

Piper couldn't help but laugh to herself. There was no one aiding the woman and she appeared fairly clueless when it came to anything with a cord. She stumbled from the stage in her heels and rushed out a side door, no doubt to find assistance.

"Sweetie," Emma directed to Piper. "I'm going to the restroom, care to join me."

Piper glanced to Lucy and back to her mother who only sighed. It appeared that Lucy wouldn't be rising from the table anytime soon.

Piper scooted back her chair in acknowledgement and zigzagged through the tables with her mother to the direction of the ladies' room.

Just as they approached the doors, a handful of giggly and inebriated bridesmaids and other friends of the bride stumbled out, nearly stampeding over Piper and Emma as they swayed about, deep in shallow conversation.

Upon slipping into the restroom, it appeared empty, but then there was a faint squeak of a stall door. On the inside Piper groaned, careful not to vocally express her frustration. So far she had managed to avoid Aunt Margaret and all her critical and snobby comments. As rotten luck would have it, here they stood, just the three of them.

Aunt Margaret skipped any pleasantries and went right into it. "Oh, it's just you." Neither were sure to which of them the comment was directed toward. "The wedding planner is supposed to help me with this thing," she said. She held up the most complex little clip-on microphone Piper had ever seen.

Thankfully Emma spoke up. "She said something about technical issues. She seemed to have a problem working the controls."

"I swear," Margaret huffed. "It's so hard to hire good help."

Piper cringed at the statement and made her way to a distant stall, but before she could reach it, Margaret's words made her stop abruptly.

"Then I suppose it's good that you're here. I'm sure as an assistant you have to deal with trivial matters like this all the time."

If Piper clenched her teeth any harder, they would most definitely shatter. Upon glancing behind Aunt Margaret, she watched her mother let out a silent sigh and give her pleading eyes.

Suddenly, Piper didn't feel the need to pee anymore.

# CHAPTER 34

Piper tinkered with the awkward device. It was no doubt state-of-the-art as far as high tech microphones were concerned. Had Aunt Margaret been giving a State of the Union address, maybe the ridiculous thing would be warranted. After thinking a moment more, even the president used a regular microphone.

"Margaret," Emma sighed after seeing Piper struggling to figure the thing out. "They had a handheld microphone, you could just use–"

"Absolutely not! First of all, my speech is roughly ten minutes."

Piper nearly dropped the gadget in the sink when she heard that. That was practically a third as long as the ceremony itself.

"Also, I don't want that monstrosity in the pictures with me. This is much more refined and elegant." Directing her words toward Piper, "Have you figured it out yet?"

She wasn't entirely sure, but at this point she didn't care. She'd pin the damn thing on Aunt Margaret's dress and be done with it. If she went on to screw up her speech, so be it at this point. After this,

351

she was headed out and hopefully wouldn't have to deal with any part of that family until another wedding or funeral.

"I think so," Piper lied.

Margaret placed herself in front of Piper and raised her head, standing proudly like a queen about to receive her crown. Piper reached for the dress's jacket lapel and began fiddling with the microphone and tucking the delicate cords inside with one of the clasps when all of a sudden a piercing sound rang out.

"Jesus, girl!" Margaret took a step back and rubbed her ear like she had just been near the front speakers at a rock concert. "What the hell did you do," she hissed, her lady-like manner quickly fading.

"It's fine," Piper insisted. "I think it just did that from the proximity to your necklace."

"It's gold, you idiot!"

Piper let it go. It seemed like a plausible explanation, but she wasn't a scientist or a tech expert. She didn't know what would have caused the unexpected noise, but it was gone.

Though the idiot comment mildly annoyed her, "Regardless, you should be fine now."

Margaret huffed and looked into the mirror. She smoothed around the wrinkles near her eyes, making sure the makeup hadn't clotted in the crevices. She then turned the sink on to just a faint drizzle and moistened her fingers so that she could fix a few loose hairs that no one would have noticed.

When she was done, she glanced back into the mirror, only this time, instead of looking at her own reflection, she watched Piper, who stood behind her, no doubt waiting for her to leave. Margaret turned around and took two steps forward so that she was less than an arm's length from her niece. They stared at each other, neither saying a word. From their peripheral vision, Emma stepped out from a stall, but Piper nor Margaret withdrew their line of sight.

"What is your problem?"

Piper tried not to act shocked by her aunt's words, but the comment itself shook her. There was so much disdain and animosity behind it.

"I don't know what you mean."

When in doubt, play dumb. It was the best advice Lucy had ever given her.

"Oh, get off your high horse," Margaret spat.

Piper quickly glanced to her mother who stood in confusion.

"You've tried everything you could to ruin this for my Samantha."

Piper needed Aunt Margaret to stop talking. She could remain calm in most instances. Working for Blythe had quickly taught her to do so. However, she was starting to lose it. Some ridiculous analogy of Lucy's briefly flitted through her mind, but she couldn't grasp it enough to remember it.

"Why are you so jealous of my daughter?"

A mild silence filled the room and only faint whispers amongst the intimacy of one's own table could be heard.

"You need to stop. I've never been jealous of any of my family."

Lucy and Nolan shot each other panicked glances and looked around the room for the all too familiar voice.

"Yes, we all get it. You want to act like you're someone special living in New York. That ridiculous job cost you a good husband and you can't stand it that he found a much more suitable partner in Samantha."

"Shut up!" Piper's voice had increased in volume and vibrated from the speakers. "Just shut up! You delusional bitch!"

The coordinator fumbled with a few switches which only ended up dimming some corner lights.

"Where are they," Lucy hissed at her father, her hands shaking after hearing how riled Piper was.

"I thought they were going for dessert," Nolan began. "Or maybe the restroom?"

✳ ✳ ✳

Margaret gasped and clutched her chest as if Piper had slammed her fist into it. Emma stepped forward to ease the situation but Piper shook her head and held up her hand.

"No, mom," she managed in a much quieter and calmer voice. "Maybe no one else will say anything.

Maybe you're all afraid of her, but I need to say a few words."

She turned back to Margaret. If her irises could have turned to flames and steam could have come from her ears, that's about what her appearance suggested to Piper.

"My job had nothing to do with Jared. Things with us were dead and miserable, so I poured my heart into work. The only reason I never left him was because I was comfortable enough. I didn't feel like having to go through the dating process in my late twenties." Piper had to almost laugh at finally admitting that, but the conversation was about to get serious. "Samantha changed all that."

"You've never had any respect for my Samantha. Don't blame your inability to keep a–"

"I walked in on the two of them in my bed screwing each other's brains out," Piper screamed at the top of her lungs. "While we were still together," she felt the need to point out.

Margaret snapped her mouth closed, unable to make a quick comment as the information sank in.

"Yeah. Exactly. I was nice to her. You could have paid for her to live in the damn St. Regis for a couple months while her apartment was prepared, but no, being the fucking doormat of the family I agreed to help, and that's the thanks I get! Her in bed with my fiancé! So, no. No, Aunt Margaret, I have no respect for a slut like that."

Piper couldn't believe the words that were coming from her mouth. She never talked like that. If she did, it was only if she and Haven were a little drunk and talking about some reality television show.

Emotionally Margaret dusted herself off from the near fatal blow and returned the hit.

"I see where all this anger is coming from," she laughed in a sickeningly sinister way, giving Piper pause. "You're taking all your frustration out right now and directing it toward my family because you will never have that, especially after bringing that trash with you. Come to think of it…" Margaret's eyes rolled up to the ceiling and she tapped at her bottom lip with her forefinger as though she was really giving thought to her next words. "I recall him being the one to leave with another woman last night."

Without hesitation, "Tristan is not trash."

"Oh, dear," Margaret groaned. "Just look at him. He looks like some gangster and he doesn't even have a job. Then to top it off, he cheats on you."

"Okay," Emma interrupted again. "I think we should–"

"No!"

Piper's eyes said it all, and as much as Emma didn't want to helplessly stand there and watch her sister and daughter battle it out with some question-able words, Piper wasn't giving her much of a choice.

"First of all, you're crazy. Tristan is a retired soccer player." Piper quickly caught herself and changed her phrasing. "Was. He was a retired soccer player. He was in the top ten percent of highest paid American players. So, I have no idea what you're talking about."

Now came the hard part. It was an admission Piper dreaded, but it was necessary.

"He never cheated on me."

Aunt Margaret let out a boisterous laugh. "And you call me delusional when you saw it with your own eyes!"

"We were never together!"

Piper paced back and forth amongst the stalls. One of the last people she wanted to share this with was standing right in front of her and it was one of the most difficult things to do.

"Some part of me was so insecure about showing up alone to this shit that my friend and I picked a random guy on social media to ask to be my date. Actually, not even that random. We intentionally asked a friend of Jared's." She didn't intend to go into further details on the matter. That was sufficient and she felt a weight lifted off her when she admitted it. "Because Tristan is so laidback and easygoing, he went with it. I'm not going to say that I didn't enjoy getting a rise out of you and Jared."

Margaret tsked and shook her head, causing Piper to stop speaking. "That is quite pathetic. Which just goes to show that you are jealous of Samantha and intended to ruin this for her."

"The only thing you're right about is it being pathetic. Yeah, I guess I was desperate to have someone. I don't even know why. Maybe to show all of you that I was over Jared, that I wasn't *poor, lonely Piper*. In the end, it was one of the most ridiculous things I've done, and in the end, Tristan didn't cheat on me, so you can choke on that comment."

Apparently, Margaret had very little to say after that. Piper found it hard to believe that she could be out of insults so quickly. Either way, she took the silence as a quick means for escape, but stopped herself just shy of the doors leading back to the main room. She debated heavily if she should try for one last shot. It would definitely be a play to end the game, but was it worth it? For once, she went with her impulses.

She turned back to face her aunt. Oddly, Margaret held a satisfied look on her face, as though she had won some imaginary war with Piper, solely on the fact that Piper appeared to have had enough and was the one to take leave.

Piper looked to her mother, who had prepared to leave as well, but was partially blocked by Margaret. She was well aware that her outburst would have an impact and lasting effect on her mother's relationship with Margaret. It was already a bit shaky at times, but this had only worsened it.

She tried to control her trembling hands and muster up the little bit of fight she had left in her before she tore from the room.

Finally, the words came. This time they were toned down, but still firm and direct.

"I had no intention of bringing this up," she began. "I knew this would hurt Samantha's relationship with Jared, but after all that you've accused me of and thrown in my face, I see no reason not to."

Margaret's lips were pursed so tightly that the wrinkles were like little faults and fractures that would impress any geologist. She crossed her arms and arched a perfectly threaded brow for Piper to continue.

"Yesterday, that wonderful husband of Samantha's, that perfect placeholder in her life, with the perfect job, would have left her in a heartbeat."

Margaret's expression changed drastically and Piper sensed the confusion. She could see that her mother was equally confused.

"Thankfully, I don't have the low self-esteem that you may think, the kind that your daughter possesses, and I stopped him as soon as he shoved his tongue down my throat."

Both Margaret and Emma gasped in disbelief. With a quick glance to her mother, Piper saw that she was less upset about what happened and more annoyed that Piper had not said anything to her. A brief silence followed.

* * *

Jared could feel the many eyes upon him. Inches away he caught the chill of Samantha. It felt like her body had turned into an iceberg, and that side of his body was dropping in temperature by the second, while his face grew in degrees equivalent to the heat of Venus.

There was one pair of eyes standing across the room near the doors to the veranda that Jared could not ignore. Once he met them, he knew without a doubt that the friendship was over. He had seen Tristan angry before, but masking his anger now was something far worse. There was a look of pure hatred that told him there was nothing he could ever do to make up for what he had done. Tristan couldn't give two shits if he existed or not.

The only thing Jared could be thankful for was that on this occasion, Tristan didn't lose his mind and charge at him like a bull on steroids. Without a doubt, the heat in Tristan's eyes said differently. If no one else was around and he could have had Jared outside, Jared would be in an ambulance in a matter of moments.

Jared tore his gaze from Tristan and reached for Samantha's hand. He was quite surprised when she didn't rip it away.

"Samantha," he whispered softly in shame.

She didn't allow him to say a word after her name. "Is what she said true," she asked coldly.

"It's not what you think," he began in the most basic way that any amateur liar would do. The only difference was that he was far from amateur.

"Stop. We'll get through this evening, act as if nothing is wrong, and fix this later," she insisted with a forced smile.

* * *

"You're just a little liar," Margaret hissed.

Exhaustion washed over Piper. It didn't matter what she said, and at this point, she didn't care. "You can believe who and what you want. But all this," she said, waving her hands back and forth around the empty restroom, the intent clearly not there. "I get why you had to do it. All you and Samantha have is your money. You think I'm the jealous one? I think you are. I can't believe it took so long for that to click, but I get it."

"What are you rambling about," Margaret asked with a nervous stutter.

Piper shook her head with a small smile. "I went to college, I have a career with, by the way, the promotion of my dreams. I struggled, and I worked hard, and I have something to show for it. You have nothing but money. Most of all though, unlike your daughter, I don't need a man or a husband to ensure my survival. She does. You and I know that's all she'll ever be, a pretty little wife."

"You insolent–"

Before Margaret could finish the sentence, the bathroom door ominously creaked open and coolly resting against the door jamb stood Lucy with a smug look on her face slowly clapping.

The three women in the room looked at her like she was crazy. Lucy then made a shaking motion with one hand, as if she was holding a bottle and flailed her arms around as she made a little explosion sound.

"You know, she began, I thought about interrupting when Tristan's name was mentioned, but damn am I glad I didn't," she laughed.

"Wait, what? How did..."

When Piper paused for words, Lucy took a quick look over to Aunt Margaret and made little jabs in the direction of her blazer.

"Apparently her speaker was on and the coordinator couldn't figure out how to shut down the controls."

A sick dizziness fell over Piper. Her tongue felt as though it had become paralyzed. Somehow she managed to ask, "Everyone heard that?"

Lucy spread her arms wide. "Everyone. I must say," she began, but stopped and finished her sentence by resuming her slow clap.

"Shit," Piper hissed under her breath. As much as she wanted to get her shots in with Aunt Margaret, she had no intention of letting the entire party hear everything, especially the parts about Tristan and Jared. She couldn't even imagine what people were saying and thinking right now. "I have to go."

With that, she pushed past her sister and headed in the direction of the lion's den. It seemed the only way out was through hell.

# CHAPTER 35

Once the hallway opened into the dining space and ballroom, Piper came face to face with what seemed like a stadium full of stares, full of surprise, disbelief, a few even held looks of humor.

She glanced around to the exit doors on the far side of the room. Before anyone could stop her, she darted in between the tables toward them.

Somewhere above, the god of sky and thunder must have taken notice to the scene unfolding, as the sensation that washed over Tristan was nothing short of a bolt of lightning through his veins. Without thinking too much, he hoisted himself on the stage and grabbed for the microphone in place for what should have been the upcoming speeches.

The familiar voice ringing out across every speaker in the room caused Piper to come to an abrupt halt just a few yards shy of the doors leading out into the rest of the resort.

Though she was far away, when she turned, Tristan could see her face clear as day. It held a mixture of hurt, sadness, anger, embarrassment. Deep down he was hit with the knowledge that he had done that, which only made what he was about to do that much more important and so very much needed.

The room had grown quiet after Piper's outburst, but now it was in complete silence. Not even the noise of a fork scraping the last bite could be heard, as all eyes and attention were directed on Tristan and Piper.

The invisible spotlight cut through Piper and a cold bead of sweat ran down her back. Before Tristan could say more than her name, she turned and took a quick and giant step in the direction of the exit. That's when she nearly slammed into an unexpected acquaintance.

"What are you doing," Piper hissed in a hush tone, although she was quite sure that the tables around her would hear every word.

"You need to listen to him," Spencer insisted, not bothering with whispering.

Piper wanted to explode at the sighs of affection from a nearby table. It reminded her of the women in the theater when the couple finally kissed after the most overdramatic script ever.

Piper became annoyed. "I thought you were my friend, on my side."

Spencer rolled his eyes. "One thing I know, not everything is what it seems. Listen to him."

Piper opened her mouth to say something, but was silenced with the speakers.

"Piper, I'm not good at this, but I need to talk to you."

She turned to face Tristan. From across the room, sincerity and uncertainty brightly lit his face. Her feet were frozen. She couldn't leave, but staying felt like standing on hot coals.

"I don't know where to start..."

Tristan paused when Piper shook her head, silently pleading for him to stop, not wanting her business to be aired for her whole family, and then some. Had it not been for the gossip in the last twenty-four hours he would have. He hesitantly took a few steps from the stage, realizing that Piper would not be making any effort.

He couldn't think of the words. The silence around him was deafening, making it impossible to think. For once, the attention was too much for his nerves. The only thing keeping him grounded was the woman across the room.

When he saw her take a step back and begin to turn toward the exit once again, he couldn't stop the words that fell from his lips.

"Piper, I love you."

Her wide eyes that searched his from afar made Tristan's insides twist. Those words had never been said between them. Any person with a sane mind would know it was too early for that, but despite the way she was looking at him, and whether or not she felt the same way, when he said those words, a weight lifted off of him and relief soared through his bones.

Any doubt was gone. Time had no effect on how he felt. He had fallen for Piper, hard and fast. In the end, he was completely in love with her.

No words followed the horrified and ghastly look that Piper still had plastered across her face, forcing Tristan to speak. He had to say something after that bomb.

"I know that's probably not what you were expecting, or even what you wanted to hear," he nervously began. After pausing for a moment and taking a deep breath in hopes of calming the overactive heart that was thundering throughout his entire body, he started over. "This last week has been something that I never would have thought possible. I enjoyed getting to know you before this and I never expected what I'd start to feel when our conversations went beyond a screen. That first night, that kiss, it changed everything for me. Your plan, this arrangement, your rules, they didn't matter because I thought we were really going somewhere."

Piper appeared shocked at what Tristan might be saying. Her heart pounded wildly until the drumming rang out in her ears. Piper shook the thoughts. Regardless what she felt, a real relationship with Tristan seemed complicated, if that's even what he was suggesting. She still didn't know the full purpose of his speech. She had a hard time getting past those few words he had blurted out, obviously without intending to.

Hoping to end the very public conversation that should have been kept private, "Stop. You don't have to do whatever this is. You did exactly what we agreed to." Piper felt her cheeks reddening with a mixture of anger, embarrassment, and devastatingly enough, memories of the week with Tristan. She cleared her throat, and continued, loud enough so that Tristan could hear, also loud enough that most everyone else had a front row seat. "Thank you, but you don't have to do this. This is done."

"I don't want it to be done," he quickly spoke before she could end the conversation.

Tristan could see something more in Piper's face. She didn't want what was happening between them to be over. She was simply hurt, and he needed to fix that.

"I did something to make sure that we'd have a chance, a real chance, for this to play out."

Piper swallowed heavily. Her knees felt weak and she needed to move before she passed out; however, her feet were still unwilling to cooperate as Tristan now stood in the center of the room.

"You have to know that I care about you, and what you saw last night...Piper, I'd never cheat on you," he stressed.

"It's fine!" Piper's voice was nearing a scream. "Everyone knows, so just stop it. We're not in a relationship and we never were. It was all for show. Nothing was real." The words sounded cold and bitter even as they repeated themselves in Piper's head. She felt the heat of tears beginning to surface and she tried her best to blink them away.

Tristan didn't allow her words to affect him negatively, instead, they fueled him to continue. "It was for me."

Piper's lips tightly closed at the comment, not knowing how to respond. He wasn't giving up.

Without leading in whatsoever, "That woman was Earl Gander's wife."

The name was one Piper knew well in the world of soccer. Her eyes darted to Tristan's immediately, and a sense of relief appeared in the glowing darkness of his irises at the idea that he could fix the misunderstanding. However, clearing up the matter brought about the rash and impulsive revelation of switching teams and moving across the country for a girl he had only spent a week with. In his heart and his mind it was an easy decision, but he was well aware as to how the blow would be to someone with Piper's tendencies and way of life.

It was at that moment that Piper took slow steps in Tristan's direction and he couldn't hide the smile making its way to the surface.

"What are you saying?"

From the distance he could barely hear her voice that had softened since her earlier yelling.

He decided to let it all out. The sooner he did, the sooner he'd know her answer and keep his chest from exploding.

"I'm saying that I've fallen in love with you. I know this is real because it's never been like this. I also know that you feel something too, and I don't want that to end for either of us."

Tears started to form in the corners of Piper's eyes as their distance apart slowly decreased. Her mind ran in all directions with everything he was telling her. Not ready to deal with what he just said, she took a step back, needing to clarify something that she wasn't following.

"Why would you be seeing Earl Gander's wife?"

"I told you I had calls and meetings. He was the last one that night and he was running late," Tristan revealed, tiptoeing around a direct answer.

Piper wasn't stupid and pressed on. "Why?"

Tristan sighed. In a few more seconds they would be close enough to touch. He craved her touch and could only hope that his next words wouldn't scare her more than anything else he had already told her.

"We had a conference call with some people involved in the decision making process for his team."

He left it at that and waited, fully knowing that when it came to soccer, Piper was very well aware as to who Earl Gander was.

"And?" She drew out the one word into a question, but when Tristan didn't answer within a second of silence, she felt the need to point out the obvious. "His team is based in New York."

Tristan said nothing. A smirk of satisfaction slowly made its way to his face, though he wouldn't allow himself to get too carried away. Piper's expressions and words were still very difficult to read. He still had no idea how she might feel about it.

With shaky feet, Piper allowed herself to move forward just a little more. Her thoughts were racing. Deep down she always knew Tristan would try to attempt to return to the field for just a little longer, but the ugly truth that she wouldn't point out was the fact that he was thirty. Most soccer players at that age were thinking about retirement. Then there was Earl Gander. He couldn't seriously be thinking about signing Tristan just like that.

Tristan must have sensed all the confusion and mix of questions tumbling around in Piper's head. Finally she was right there, right in front of him so that they could have a normal conversation that didn't involve raising their voices to be heard from across the room, albeit still in the middle of a crowded ballroom.

"They signed you, just like that," she whispered.

He watched intently as her eyes nervously flitted from his to the floor. It was only then that he dared to touch her, hoping to ease any discomfort she may be feeling. Each of his hands enveloped one of hers, and immediately she brought her eyes to meet his, now unwavering.

"I have to go through a few physical tryouts, but for the most part, it seems so." He smiled when her lips parted to ask another question, already knowing what it would be. He cut her off with, "If all goes well, it's for three years."

Piper didn't move; she couldn't. Even swallowing was more difficult than she expected.

"Why," she managed.

Tristan shook his head and softly laughed. "I didn't plan on doing a long distance relationship."

Piper felt as though she needed to tap her chest with her fist to make sure it was still working. Relationship. He wanted a relationship, a real lasting relationship.

Tristan clenched Piper's hands a few times to the point that it felt like the steady beat of his heart coming through to her.

"Please say something," he quietly begged. Her silence was nothing short of torture.

"Me too."

Tristan tried his best not to laugh. She was more nervous than he had seen her all week. "You too?"

Piper shut her eyes and shook her head. If she had the time perhaps she could have written and revised everything that was spinning in her mind into something coherent and fluent, but that wouldn't be happening.

She sucked in a breath and held it until she allowed the words to tumble out. "I can't do long distance either."

Tristan bit his lip, a giant smile already spreading widely across his face. "So, you're saying you want to date me? For real?"

Piper shifted slightly on her feet, the heels and locked knees ruining her blood flow. "No...I mean, yes," she fumbled. "I do...but...that's not it."

Tristan felt the discomfort and nervousness pouring from her skin through him, her hands in his turning cool and clammy. "I'm really confused here," he finally sighed, fearing indecision on Piper's part coming to the surface.

"I love you too," she managed in a trembling voice. At first she wasn't sure Tristan heard her, but his eyes, like always, said it all.

His mouth, however, made not a sound, which only caused a nervous Piper to begin to ramble, in turn, revealing more than she intended.

"I felt so stupid and naïve all week. I even felt like such an idiot whenever you messaged me and I caught myself smiling and blushing. I couldn't believe that I was feeling something so easily. I was...I am...terrified."

When Tristan didn't stop her, she took a deep breath and continued, unable to withstand any awkward silence at this point. "Just now, if you didn't mean that, if–"

Tristan cut her off, suddenly not liking the direction she was headed. She had no reason to even think of giving him an out.

"Piper, I haven't lied to you. I didn't tell you about New York because I knew it was fast and I didn't know what was going on between us. When I said I loved you, I meant it. That was both the hardest and easiest thing to admit. I can't even explain what it feels like to hear you say that back."

They had grown impossibly close, so close that each could feel the heat radiating from the body of the other.

Tristan pulled Piper in so that he could whisper into her ear, privately, away from the crowd that for a moment seemed to disappear when he looked into her eyes.

"How about we forget about this and get out of here?"

His breath on her skin was teasing, full of both lust and love, but even more so, full of hope.

Piper only managed a quick nod when she felt soft and tender lips press to hers. Despite their familiarity, something about them felt new. The kiss held a promise, a new beginning, and an unspoken arrangement that she was ready to play all the way through.

# THE END